Carolina Isle

BOOKS BY JUDE DEVERAUX

The Velvet Promise

Highland Velvet

Velvet Song

Velvet Angel

Sweetbriar

Counterfeit Lady

Lost Lady

River Lady

Twin of Fire

Twin of Ice

The Temptress

The Raider

The Princess

The Awakening

The Maiden

The Taming

The Conquest

A Knight in Shining Armor

Holly

Wishes

Mountain Laurel

The Duchess

Eternity

Sweet Liar

The Invitation

Remembrance

The Heiress

Legend

An Angel for Emily

The Blessing

High Tide

Temptation

The Summerhouse

The Mulberry Tree

Forever . . .

Wild Orchids

Forever and Always

First Impressions

Jude Deveraux

Carolina Isle

DOUBLEDAY LARGE PRINT HOME LIBRARY EDITION

POCKET BOOKS

New York   London   Toronto   Sydney

This Large Print Edition, prepared especially for Doubleday Large Print Home Library, contains the complete, unabridged text of the original Publisher's Edition.

An *Original* Publication of POCKET BOOKS

 POCKET BOOKS, a division of Simon & Schuster, Inc.
1230 Avenue of the Americas, New York, NY 10020

ISBN-10: 0-7394-6288-1

Cover design by Lisa Litwack
Cover photograph © Gen Nishino/Getty Images

Manufactured in the United States of America

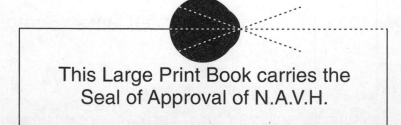

This Large Print Book carries the Seal of Approval of N.A.V.H.

Carolina Isle

Chapter One

"I will *never* marry David Tredwell!"

Ariel Weatherly looked in the mirror and rehearsed her speech to her mother. "I am twenty-four years old and I will choose my own husband." No, she thought. That's not right. "I have chosen the man I want to marry and I will do so." Yes, better. Much better.

There was a soft knock on the door.

On impulse, Ariel messed up her hair. She liked what she saw.

"Come in," Ariel said, and a maid opened the door.

"Your mother would like to see you downstairs."

"Yes, of course," Ariel replied with a sigh.

The maid looked behind her to make sure Mrs. Weatherly wasn't nearby. "I like your hair," she said, then closed the door.

Ariel grabbed her brush and smoothed her hair, then she smiled. She wasn't sure yet, but she may have come up with a way to get out of marrying David, to marry the man she truly loved, and to keep from being disinherited. Still smiling, she left her room and started down the stairs. If only Sara would agree. She must! Ariel thought. If she doesn't . . .

But Ariel couldn't think of that now. She only knew that she'd use whatever means she had at her disposal to get her cousin to agree to her plan.

Chapter Two

Sara read Ariel's letter, then read it again. She couldn't believe her eyes. As always, the letter was written with a fountain pen on thick paper that Sara was sure cost half her year's salary. But it wasn't the extravagance that shocked her; she was used to that.

Ariel wanted to trade places with Sara. She wanted to be Sara, and Sara to be her.

"She wants to be *me?*" Sara whispered in wonder as she put the letter on her lap. Wouldn't it be wonderful to have the leisure to sit around all day and plan adventurous schemes? she thought. Or time to plan anything, for that matter. Time to do anything other than whatever your egomaniac boss could think up for you to do? Sara had come to care about her cousin a great deal over the years, but that didn't keep her from being jealous.

Sitting in her tiny New York apartment, her feet up, exhausted from yet another day running around doing her boss's bidding, Sara gazed out the window to the brick wall across the alley. She could afford a better apartment, but after a lifetime of struggling to make ends meet, she'd rather have money in the bank than spend it. And then there was the fact that she was constantly telling her boss that she was quitting. If she quit, how long would it be before she got another job? But choosing to live as though it might all be gone tomorrow didn't make her feel any less jealous about her cousin's big house with the servants, and about the two trips a year that Ariel and her mother took to New York to buy clothes. What would it be like to have a dress made just for you? Sara wondered.

She looked down at the letter. "Just for a while," Ariel had written. "Temporarily." Sara smiled at that. Poor Ariel, so spoiled, everything given to her. She wouldn't have a clue how to work for somebody like R. J. Brompton.

The whole idea was absurd, of course, but it was nice to daydream. In fact, Ariel's letter opened Sara's eyes to a secret she'd kept even from herself: She wanted to see Arundel, North Carolina. Not just see it as a tourist would, but see it from the inside. She wanted to make her own judgment about the place. Her father had told her Arundel was "the center of hell," yet Ariel wrote of the glories of her hometown.

Sara knew she had relatives in Arundel, but she'd never met them. Because of old wounds, she was sure that if she showed up there as Sara Jane Johnson she wouldn't be welcome. But what if she got to know them as Ariel and showed them she wasn't like her father's side of the family? What would happen when she finally told them who she was? Would they welcome her—or hate her?

Getting to know the people of Arundel sounded good in theory, but the truth was, she was afraid of the place.

For seventeen years, what had been "done to them" was Sara's father's favorite topic of conversation—if you can call monologues that never ended conversation. She'd heard in detail how her mother grew up as part of "the family" in Arundel, a place that, according to her father, was the center of all snobbery on earth. "It begins there and radiates outward," he said. "Like the rays of the sun?" she asked when she was a child and still thought her father was actually talking to her. "No, more like a spreading disease," he said. He told Sara that her mother had been one of the bluebloods, one of the elite, the four hundred, whatever he could think of to call them, but she had fallen in love with him—and that had been the end of her. Sara's father's family was dirt poor, like the sharecroppers of the olden days, he told her, making his family sound noble. "But your mother's family couldn't stand people who worked for a living," he said. "Honest workers, that's all we were, but they *hated* us."

Sara's grandfather had disowned his daughter after she eloped. She died in a car wreck when Sara was three, and her father finally drank enough to kill his body when she was seventeen.

Sara looked back down at the letter.

She was just finishing her freshman year of college when she met Ariel for the first time. Sara had been in the study room of her coed dorm, up all night cramming for finals. She hadn't showered in three days and her hair was hanging in greasy strings around her face. She was in her usual uniform of sweatpants and a stained sweatshirt, and her feet were encased in worn-out running shoes. Not that Sara ever ran. Or did any exercise. Like most college students, she lived on pizza and Coke.

At first Sara felt, rather than saw, Ariel. It was like when people say they feel a ghost. When Sara looked up from her book, the room was silent, and everyone was staring at a young woman standing in the doorway. She was pretty in her simple dress, a dress Sara was willing to bet cost more than she'd spent on all the clothes in her closet. To Sara's astonishment, the young woman walked straight toward her. "Could we talk?" she asked.

Feeling clumsy and dirty, Sara mumbled, "Yeah, sure," and followed the elegant young woman outside. Sara wondered if she wanted her to cut her lawn. Growing up, Sara had been the kid who cut the lawns and pruned the boxwoods. She was the kid who baby-sat.

The perfect young woman sat down carefully on a stone bench under a flowering dogwood. She stared at Sara for a few moments, then told her they were cousins. "I was told we looked alike," Ariel said.

Sara smiled at that. *Never* had she looked like this woman did.

"I didn't call first because I didn't know your number. I hope it was all right to just show up. I really wanted to meet you."

"Yes, it's okay," Sara said, her eyes wide from looking at her cousin so hard. Could she really be related to this beautiful creature with her perfect hair, perfect clothes, perfect everything?

"Do you think we could correspond?" Ariel asked.

"Write letters?" Sara asked. "Sure, why not?" She was thinking that she'd have nothing to say to a woman whose life was so obviously different from her own. Ariel reeked of money, education, and manners. Sara had a flash of memory of her own father sprawled on the couch, snoring in a drunken stupor.

For a moment the two young women sat in silence, then Ariel looked at her watch—a tiny thing of gold and diamonds. "I wish I could have gone to college," she said, sighing.

Something about the way she sighed made Sara decide that there was more to Ariel than she saw on the surface. Yes, she sat perfectly straight, and yes, she wore clothes that had probably been on a runway, but maybe, just maybe, there was a person inside. "College isn't that great," Sara said.

Smiling, Ariel said, "I have thirty minutes before I have to leave. Tell me everything about your life. Please."

"Only if you tell me about your . . . I mean, our relatives."

"I'd love to," Ariel said, then they started talking in a surprisingly easy way, almost comfortable with each other. Ariel was a good listener and a good storyteller.

While they talked, Sara studied Ariel as though she were a specimen under a microscope. Sara wasn't sure Ariel knew it or not, but she was as regal as a princess. Her gestures—the way she sat on the bench with her back straight and her ankles crossed—was something out of a 1950s charm school.

Sara, her legs folded on the concrete seat, often pushed the hair out of her eyes, but Ariel sat straight and still, and her perfect pageboy haircut never so much as moved in the breeze.

Sara looked at the way people on campus stopped and stared at Ariel. A group of rowdy boys, obviously laughing over something dirty, saw Ariel and instantly became young gentlemen.

Suddenly, Ariel got up. "I have to go. You won't lose my address, will you? Actually, it's the address of a friend of mine. Just whatever you do, don't call my house or send anything there."

Sara stood up too and they were eye-to-eye, both five feet three. "I understand," Sara said, her teeth clamped together. "You don't want people to know that you're related to someone of my class."

Ariel looked at her blankly, obviously not understanding. "You're my first cousin. How can you be a different class than I am? No, it's my mother. She'd be quite unpleasant if she knew I had any outside contact with the world. She'd make me marry David tomorrow."

Inside, Sara was smiling. Me the same class as this perfectly dressed young woman? What a ridiculous concept; what a divine thought. "Who is David?"

Reaching into her exquisite little handbag, Ariel pulled out a photo of a young man in a football uniform. She handed it to Sara, who looked in astonishment at a truly gorgeous man. In college she was surrounded by masses of good-looking people, but this man was in a class all his own. "You do *not* want to marry this guy?"

Ariel looked at her watch again, and said, "I'd explain, but I *must* go." The next second she was hurrying down the sidewalk. To her waiting limo? Sara wondered. Ariel waved her hand over her shoulder, then was out of sight.

Sara stood there for a while, staring into space. Her cynicism made her wonder what it was that Ariel *really* wanted. But as hard as Sara tried, she couldn't come up with anything she had that Ariel might want. The photo of the unwanted David was still in her hand. He really was the best-looking male she'd ever seen. She slipped the picture into her pocket, then headed back toward the dorm, but when she got to the door, she stopped.

Her state university didn't have a good football team. Actually, it wasn't all that good in any sport, but what it did have was a great drama department. In fact, there were several well-known actors who'd started at her university. Sara had toyed with trying her hand at acting—after all, hadn't she been acting when she'd smiled and told people that things were great at home? But the head of the drama department was known as a real bastard. To get into his department you had to prove to him that you were worthy. He didn't let you read a part that someone else had written, but made you perform a character of your own creation. You had to do this in front of him and all his students, and Sara was told that his criticism was brutal, meant to humiliate. More than one student had left the university after just five minutes with him.

Sara had thought about performing a character like her father, but that would have been telling too much about herself, so she didn't try out. But as she had her hand on the door into the dorm, on impulse, she turned away and started toward the drama department. Sara knew that at the moment she looked her worse, but that was good. If she could imitate Ariel while looking as bad as she did, then she knew she could get into that department.

She kept Ariel in her head as she walked into Dr. Peterson's classroom. And because she was Princess Ariel, she didn't knock. Sara gave a wildly exaggerated performance, a caricature actually, of Ariel. The truth was that Sara created a character who looked like Ariel but who acted like the people her father had described. She felt a little bad doing it, but when she saw the eyes of her audience, she knew she had them. At one point, Sara haughtily asked Dr. Peterson if he was gay since everyone knew that only gay men were on the stage. Dr. Peterson was a notorious womanizer, so that got a lot of repressed snickers from the class. Sara kept it up for about ten minutes, then pretended that she was in the wrong classroom and had actually wanted fourth-year calculus. Once outside, she leaned back against the cool concrete-block walls and breathed again. Her heart was pounding. All her life she'd tried to take the attention away from herself; she'd never wanted anyone to know how bad it was at home for fear that she'd be put somewhere worse. But today Sara'd made a true spectacle of herself—and found that she'd enjoyed herself.

When Dr. Peterson opened the classroom

door, Sara stood upright. He looked her up and down and she could tell that he didn't like what he saw. Now that Sara was herself again, she felt overweight and timid. "You're in," he said, but he was shaking his head as though he couldn't figure out how she'd been able to transform her dirty self into a princess for even ten minutes.

So it turned out that meeting Ariel changed Sara's life. That summer she started in the drama department, and since she was a whole year behind the other kids, she had to take more hours. She never got a summer vacation, but Sara loved every minute of it. When she graduated, she went to New York with a nearly empty bank account, but with the conviction that she was going to set Broadway on fire.

Two years later, she was broke and had to get a job as an undersecretary in a big office. Sara could act, but she couldn't sing or dance, and in New York she was competing against people who were great at all three. She would have gone to L.A. to try her luck, but she'd been brainwashed that the only real theater was in New York. And she always felt that she was right on the edge of making it big.

Through all those years, Sara exchanged letters with Ariel. No e-mail, no faxes, nothing new or modern, just old-fashioned letters. Ariel wrote three or more letters to each of Sara's because Ariel had more time. With each of the letters Sara came to enjoy them more. I can't wait to tell Ariel! became a constant thought. When Sara went to New York, where she knew no one, and where she failed at one audition after another, it was Ariel's ever-cheerful letters that kept her going. Ariel was Sara's anchor, the one who was always there, the one person in the world who knew where Sara was and what she was doing.

Then, when Sara turned twenty-three and was beginning to realize that she just might never make it on the New York stage, she had another one of those life-changing events. The CEO of the company Sara worked for, R. J. Brompton, pointed at her and said, "That one. I want *her.*" That's all he had to say. He was so revered, and his word was such law, that Sara could believe that she'd been chosen to test out a new guillotine.

It was worse. He'd chosen her to be his personal assistant. Not his secretary—he had two of those. His PA. Sara soon learned what the duties of a personal assistant were. She did anything her boss asked of her. She was a wife without the sex—not that Sara wanted the sex or that R. J. Brompton had a wife. No, she thought, humans have wives and families. And after eighteen months of working for R. J., Sara was sure he wasn't human. No human could work as much as he did. He was a robot who gave her more money every time she told him she wanted a life and that she was leaving his employment.

By the time Ariel's letter saying she wanted to exchange lives reached her, Sara knew exactly how she felt. She hated herself for having no spine and not being able to tell R. J. what he could do with his job. She hated herself for not having enough talent to make it on Broadway. She had come to hate everything about her life, and more than anything, Sara wanted to do something besides work for R. J. Brompton.

It was because Sara was so tired and so fed up with R. J.'s 3:00 A.M. phone calls that she was going to agree to try Ariel's impossible scheme.

The idea of having Ariel's life of leisure,

with nothing to deal with but a mother who sounded rather lonely, was the best idea she'd heard in years. Of course the idea of exchanging lives would never work, but it sounded nice. Three sirens went by and Sara thought of the quiet of a small Southern town. She had to haul a big basket of laundry down to the basement tonight and she dreamed of dropping her dirties in a hamper and having them reappear, clean and pressed.

She grabbed a Post-it note, wrote "Love to!," then put it in an envelope and addressed it. She'd mail it on the way to the laundry.

"Leave everything to me," Ariel wrote back, and Sara did. But then, she was too tired to do anything else.

Chapter Three

Ariel felt bad that she'd lied to her cousin, but she knew it was necessary. If she'd told Sara the truth, she would never have considered exchanging places. And wasn't it true that all was fair in love and war? Ariel just hoped that her cousin would forgive her when she found out that she had done everything for love.

It had started over a year ago when Ariel was in New York with her mother on one of their twice-yearly clothes-buying trips. Ariel had to attend some boring fund-raiser with her mother and a lot of other old people who wanted to show off how much money they had.

For the first hour Ariel made small talk and

listened to people tell her how quaint they found Arundel. Their tone said that they couldn't imagine living in a place that had no food delivery, but still, it was an adorable little town. "So clean," they said.

When her mother's eagle eye was turned away, Ariel tipped a waiter a twenty to re-place her mother-approved ginger ale with champagne. It was while she was slowly sipping her champagne (to make it last) that she saw him. *Him.* For Ariel, it was one of those moments when the earth stood still. Maybe the other party guests kept moving and talking, but for her, the world stopped revolving. When she saw the man walk into the room, she knew she was seeing her fu-ture. She was seeing the only man she would ever love.

R. J. Brompton. Of course she knew who he was. Sara had sent photos and newspa-per clippings. But photos didn't show what he was really like. You could feel him. Sense him. He had a presence about him, an aura, a charisma such as Ariel had never experi-enced. In all her trips with her mother, she had never seen anyone like R. J. Brompton.

Sara had described him in only bad terms. She said he worked her half to death, and that he had no idea that she should have a life of her own. He called her during the night and asked her where the papers on a land sale were. She would tell him she had put them in his briefcase, then he'd ask where his briefcase was. More than once, she'd had to pull on jeans and a T-shirt and go to his apartment in the middle of the night to find something or to write a letter for him. She said that as far as she could tell, he never slept.

As Ariel stood there watching him shake hands with people, now and then glancing at the blonde on his arm, she knew that someday he'd be hers. She came out of her trance to look into the eyes of the woman with him. She was glaring at Ariel in a way meant to tell her to back off, that R.J. belonged to her. Ariel just smiled. She knew from Sara that R.J. changed women more often than she changed shoes. Next week there would be another mindless blonde— or a redhead, whatever—looking up at him with adoring eyes.

For the whole party, Ariel stayed within viewing distance of R.J. Each time he glanced in her direction, she turned away, as though she'd been looking at someone behind him. But he wasn't fooled. After an hour, he walked toward her. And though she pretended she didn't see him, her heart was pounding so hard she was afraid it would leap out of her chest. If she hadn't had so much inside information from Sara, she would have turned and smiled at R.J. But she knew he was used to that. Sara said that she couldn't see R.J.'s attraction to women, but it was there. She'd told many stories about women making fools of themselves over him. Sara said she'd had to usher each of them out, some of them crying, and later, she always sent them flowers and a nice note that essentially said thanks but no thanks.

Ariel knew better than to rush forward and introduce herself. Instead, she ignored him completely. Sort of. If a person can stalk someone through a three-hour party and still ignore him, that's what Ariel did. She chatted happily with a bunch of old, rich men who kept trying to look down the front of her dress, while she kept an eye on R.J. The second he moved away from whomever he was talking to, she moved away from him. They were playing cat and mouse—and liking it. Toward the end of the party she felt him bearing down on her and she knew she wouldn't be able to escape. She also knew that she'd have only one chance to make a first impression. But she didn't know what he liked. Sweet and simpering? Or cool but smoldering, like Grace Kelly in *To Catch a Thief* ? For him, Ariel would be whatever he wanted. But first she had to find out what would make him want her for more than his usual two weeks.

As he bore down on Ariel, she knew she had to stop him. But how? He was known in the business world as a man who got what he wanted. He'd been called ruthless by more than one source.

Frantically, Ariel looked about the party. Should she go to the ladies' room? But she knew he'd be there when she got out, then that first moment would take place whether she was ready or not. When she saw her mother, she smiled. Ruthless was too mild a word to describe her mother. Knowing that R.J. was watching her, Ariel glided across the room in a manner she hoped was part beauty queen, part seductress, and all cool beauty. When she reached her mother, all she had to do was whisper a few words and she knew that her mother would keep R.J.

away from her better than a pack of wolves could.

Ariel was right.

Just as she entered the ladies' room, she glanced back to see her mother confronting Mr. R. J. Brompton. R. J. looked confused, so Ariel knew she'd won. When she left the restroom fifteen minutes later, R. J. had left the party. Had she missed her one and only chance? No, she had more confidence in herself than that. Ariel smiled the rest of the evening because she had found what she wanted to do with her life: She wanted to marry and raise a family with her cousin's boss.

Life changed after that night as Ariel began planning how to go about getting what she wanted most in the world. First, she had to know her subject, so she went to the library and started researching, spending months reading, cutting out articles, memorizing, and writing her cousin hundreds of letters. The more she wrote, the more Sara wrote back, and Ariel encouraged her cousin to talk about her job and her boss. Ariel would have e-mailed her cousin daily except that her mother didn't believe in the Internet. Ariel thought that her mother feared that her daughter would find out that men and women got naked and had sex and enjoyed it. She was determined to keep Ariel a virgin in both mind and body in anticipation of her wedding night with David—a night Ariel's mother and David's mother had been planning since the babies were born two weeks apart.

As for David, as always, he was Ariel's beast of burden. Since he had contact with the outside world, she had him look up R. J. on the Internet and give her the hundred and fifty pages he printed out. He had daily news flashes about R. J. e-mailed to him, and he gave Ariel copies.

"The media is more interested in his women than they are in what he does for a living," David said, looking at a photo of R. J. "You wouldn't think that a man that old and ugly would be able to get all those babes."

Ariel snatched the photo out of his hand. "He's only forty-two and he is far from ugly," she said, glaring at David.

"Forty-two is old enough to be our father, so—"

"For your information, you and I do not have a joint parent. Anyway, he would have had to be a teenager when he conceived two twenty-four-year-olds like us."

"Conceived," David said, smiling. "What a nice word." He was lounging on her bed, twirling her stuffed duck-billed platypus around his finger. She took it away from him. He'd been back in Arundel since graduating from college two years ago, but he didn't seem in any danger of getting a job. Against his mother's protests, he'd studied horticulture. His mother had spent days with Ariel's mother drinking endless cups of tea while she cried that her beloved son was learning to be a farmer. "Why couldn't he be a doctor or a lawyer? Why a farmer?" she whined. Ariel's opinion was that, with David's money, what did it matter what he studied?

"Don't you have something to do?" she asked, but she knew their mothers had set an obligatory time that they had to spend together. If they missed it, their lives would be made miserable. David and she had made a silent agreement to give them what they wanted, which is why he was now lounging on her bed and nearly tearing the ear off her toy armadillo.

"We could go skinny-dipping in the creek," he said.

"Didn't I hear that you did that two weeks ago with one of the girls who lives by the mill?" The old cotton processing plant hadn't been used in forty years, but it still marked the different parts of town. The tiny houses that had been built for the millworkers were now protected by historical covenants, but that didn't change the fact of where they were.

"Jealous?"

"Of what?" she said as she read through the latest news on R.J. Ariel looked at David. He was stretched across her bed, all long, lean, masculine energy, and she thought that Sara would probably like him. For all of Sara's sarcasm and acting as though she was a tough girl, Ariel thought she was pretty soft. Yes, she thought, Sara and David might get along splendidly.

"Mom wants me to ask you to the dance next Saturday. Shall we do the usual?"

The "usual" was that he'd ask some other girl and Ariel would be his cover. Actually, for the past six months David had been dating just one girl and Ariel was beginning to think he was serious about her. Her name was Britney and she was from the worst side of town that anyone could be from. Her father drove a truck around the U.S. and her mother cleaned people's houses. If David's mother found out about her, she'd probably put herself in the hospital with a panic attack—and stay there until David agreed to give up the girl. He hadn't said so, but Ariel was beginning to think that the real reason David was still in town and hadn't taken a job in another state was because of Britney.

He rolled onto his stomach and looked at her. "So what is it with you and this guy Brompton?"

"I'm going to marry him." David and she had few secrets from each other. They were in prison together, so why shouldn't they be friends?

"Great!" he said. "Told your mother yet?"

"No. I'm going to let you tell your mother, then she can tell mine."

David rolled onto his back and tossed her kangaroo in the air. "How about if you and I get married, move to another state, then get a divorce? If, after living with me, you want a divorce, that is."

Picking up her scrapbook, Ariel sat on the bed beside him. "I know you think I'm joking, but I like this man. Yes, he's older, but he's not too old. The best thing is that he's powerful and rich, so maybe he'll please my mother. If not, he can support me when she disowns me."

"You could get a job, you know."

"What can I do? Clean houses like Britney's mother?"

David gave her a look that let her know she'd crossed the boundary.

"Okay, I apologize. I'm sure Britney is a very nice person, and that you like her for something other than her impressive bra size."

"You can be a nasty little bitch, you know that?"

"Tell your mother that you can't marry someone like me."

Sighing, David turned onto his side and took the scrapbook from her hands to look at pictures of R.J. "You'll have ugly kids—if a man that old can still do it, that is."

"He seems to make women happy."

"He buys them diamonds and they fake orgasms. Not that you would know anything about orgasms. Or do you?"

When she didn't make her usual comeback, he reached out and patted her on the shoulder. "Come on, Ariel, it's not that bad.

I'm not that bad. People in other countries often have arranged marriages. It won't be so bad, I promise."

Ariel glared at him. "Being made to marry someone you don't love is horrible. A lifetime of never hearing bells ring when you kiss! A whole life of never feeling little tingles in your scalp when he looks at you. Years of—"

David yawned. "You've been reading paperbacks again, haven't you? Listen, I'd better go."

"Britney calling you?" she said nastily. In a way, she was jealous. She was jealous that he had someone in his life, while all she had was a scrapbook.

"Yeah," he said, grinning in a lecherous way. "Britney."

Ariel looked away. She wished the man she loved was with her.

David got off the bed and walked toward her. For a moment his arms hung at his side, as though he wasn't quite sure what to do with them. "You hang in there, kid," he said, reaching out to touch her shoulder, but she pulled away. "Ariel," he said softly. "I do understand. You may think I don't, but I do. It's not me who's the problem, it's that you want a choice. You want to choose who you marry."

"Choice," she said. "A concept that is foreign to my existence."

"Maybe you and I could—" He broke off as he stared, wide-eyed, at her scrapbook. Picking it up, he walked to the window and looked closely at the grainy newspaper photo. "You know who this is, don't you?"

"Who is what?" she asked.

He pointed to a woman standing near R. J. She knew the man beside him. He was Charley Dunkirk, an old, rich man who had given R. J. his start in business and was still his best friend. "That's Susie Edwards," David said.

"And just who is Susie Edwards?"

"I forget that you've lived in a tiny world inside the tiny world of Arundel. Her picture is hanging in one of the corridors at the high school. She won every beauty contest in three counties from the time she was three until she left Arundel when she got out of high school. She went to New York, changed her name to Katlyn, and married one of the richest men in the world."

Ariel looked at the picture. The woman was pretty, yes, but in that well-preserved way that meant she'd had half a dozen face-lifts and spent her days in salons. "She's from Arundel and she's the wife of R.J.'s best friend? Hmmm." Ariel's head was whirling with this news. Her intuition told her that this woman was the way she was going to reach R.J. She'd already decided that the less Sara knew about her plans, the better. Unfortunately, this meant she couldn't ask Sara's advice about anything. What Ariel wanted to do was to get R.J. onto *her* territory, into Arundel. If her plan of impersonating her cousin was going to work, Sara needed to be near Ariel while they were pretending to be each other. Ariel knew she'd need help working for R.J., so she wanted Sara close. But how to get R.J.—and Sara went where he did—to tiny Arundel?

Ariel put her hand on David's arm, looked up at him, and gave him her best pleading sigh.

"Oh, no you don't," he said. "I'm not going to help you in this. When you elope with that man, I plan to be the innocent, jilted, almost-bridegroom. I want our mothers to think that I did no wrong. I certainly don't want either of them to think that I helped you."

"David, dear," she said sweetly, "wouldn't you love some tea? We could drink it while we have a nice, long talk."

"I'm going to regret this," he said as he sat down on a chintz-covered chair.

Smiling, Ariel started talking. David was so glad to see her happy again that he stayed the entire afternoon.

In the end, David did help her. Through his girlfriend, Britney, and her connections in "that side of town," he found a man who was sending Susie Edwards—a.k.a. Katlyn Dunkirk—information about Arundel.

David got Mrs. Dunkirk's address and Ariel wrote her a letter asking if they could meet if she ever happened to be in the area. As Ariel hoped, a letter came back soon, giving a time and place in Raleigh.

On the appointed day, with David's help, Ariel managed to escape her mother long enough to meet Mrs. Dunkirk for lunch in Raleigh.

Ariel knew all about the woman the moment she saw her. For all her jewelry (a diamond necklace at lunch?), her careful accent (a sort of French-English concoction), and her five-thousand-dollar suit (in Raleigh?!), Ariel would have known her anywhere. There was an air of the cotton mills around her that no time or money could wipe away. The woman was very nervous and kept smoking cigarettes and talking too much.

In the end, they both got what they wanted. Mrs. Dunkirk said her husband had talked about buying an island and developing it into "a billionaire's playground." It might as well be an island near Arundel. As she said this, she stubbed out a lipstick-tipped cigarette and gave Ariel a look to let her know that in spite of her origins, she'd married into Big Money.

Mrs. Dunkirk said she would direct her husband toward one of the many islands off the coast of North Carolina, if Ariel would get her mother to crown her as Mrs. Arundel at the fall festival. Ariel had to work to refrain from exclaiming at the vulgarity of such a thing, but she knew where Mrs. Dunkirk was coming from. Mill girls were never made Miss Arundel, no matter how pretty they were. Ariel's mother had been Miss Arundel and she had been too. To get my mother to agree to such a low-class display, Ariel thought, I'll have to drug her—or give her what she most wants in life, which is for me to marry David.

As Ariel smiled at Mrs. Dunkirk and agreed, she gave no sign of her inner turmoil. She said she thought it was a delightful idea to have a *Mrs.* Arundel, and who better than someone who had made such a success of her life. Mrs. Dunkirk stubbed out another cigarette and went out to her waiting limo. As she waved good-bye, Ariel thought that breeding always told. Even the one time she'd met Sara in person, when she hadn't had a bath in what looked like weeks, there was an air about her that told who her mother was. Her blood had been diluted by her dissolute father, but the blood of the Ambler family was stronger, and it showed in Sara—just as Mrs. Dunkirk's breeding showed in her.

At these thoughts, Ariel could imagine David telling her she was a snob, but she didn't care. In another era, David would have been a socialist.

By the time Ariel got home, she was ready to go forward in her plan to get the man she loved. But first, she had to tell David what she and Sara were planning to do. He would, of course, protest and tell her that it would never work, but she knew he'd agree to help her. She couldn't pull this off if he didn't help, because David knew her. Really knew her. He wasn't like her mother, who only cared that she was dressed properly and didn't embarrass her.

David was different. One wrong move on Sara's part and he'd know she wasn't who she was pretending to be.

David would help, Ariel knew that. And it was going to work. She knew that too.

Chapter Four

When Sara finally got to Ariel's bedroom, she was so tired that all she wanted to do was crawl under the covers and sleep. But she couldn't because Ariel's bed was covered with a menagerie of weird-looking stuffed animals. Sara vaguely remembered that Ariel had made her memorize some rule about her stuffed animals, but she was too tired to remember it.

The two cousins had spent nearly three weeks together in New York. Ariel had wanted more time, but it was all she could finagle out of her mother. "And I had to lie hugely to get that time," she said. "With David's help, of course. Dear David." When she said this, her mouth turned down at the corners, as though she was bitter about something.

Since the cousins had corresponded for years, Sara would have said that she knew her cousin well, but as she found out that first day, she didn't know her at all. Maybe it was because Ariel had grown up in isolation—homeschooled—but Sara soon found that the things she'd been hoping for didn't happen. There were no girl giggles at night, no schlepping around in their pajamas for hours on Sunday morning.

Sara was sure that Ariel didn't know it, but when she described her mother, she might have been describing herself. It took nearly a week before Sara realized that Ariel knew that she was becoming like her mother and was doing anything she could to prevent it. However, try as she might to avoid it, there was something elegant about Ariel that made people take notice of her.

It took Sara less than twenty-four hours to learn that there were things she just could not talk about, such as her drunken father. Sara was eager to unburden herself, to at last tell the secrets about her life with her father—but alcoholics seemed to be something that Ariel couldn't bear to hear about.

To stop Sara from telling more, Ariel gave her "the look." It was a glance of such coldness that Sara thought that a couple of her toes were going to have to be amputated from frostbite.

Ever the actress, Sara sat in front of a mirror later that night and practiced the look. But what came naturally to Ariel was nearly impossible for Sara. "I think you have to be raised royally to be able to carry off that look," she muttered to herself. The next day she tried it on Ariel. Her hope was that she'd be able to freeze Ariel as she'd done to her cousin. Ariel giggled. "When you do that, you almost look like my mother." Sara was tempted to tell her cousin that she was imitating her, Ariel, but she didn't.

Ariel wanted the two of them to stay in Sara's tiny apartment all day and try to figure out how to be each other. For one thing, Sara was supposed to memorize the entire genealogy of the founding families of Arundel. "It's imperative that you know who belongs to whom."

Sara said it sounded very interesting and she wished she had time to memorize it all, but she *had* to go to work.

The mention of work made Ariel launch

into a hundred thousand questions about R.J. Sara knew Ariel thought she was going to be able to fool R.J., but Sara didn't think he was going to believe the switch for even ten seconds. But there was no reasoning with Ariel. For all that Ariel looked like a lady from the past, all prim and proper and perfectly groomed, Sara soon found that she had a spine of steel. When Ariel set her mind to something, there was no changing it.

It was when R.J. told Sara that he wanted her to go with him on a trip to Arundel, North Carolina, that she saw just how determined Ariel really was. When he told her, Sara was so flabbergasted that she thought her legs were going to collapse. Just minutes before, R.J.'s old friend Charley Dunkirk had been in his office and R.J. had given the man enough whiskey that he was too drunk to walk out on his own. Sara had wanted to give R.J. a piece of her mind about the evils of alcohol, but she'd found out that when she talked to R.J. he twisted her words around, so she'd learned to keep quiet.

For an hour after R.J. told her they were going to Arundel, Sara couldn't speak. She did it! was all she could think. Somehow, Ariel had *done* it. How?! Sara wondered.

Ariel lived in a little, rural town and R.J. was a big-city mover and shaker. He and Donald Trump were buddies. So how had a small-town girl like Ariel made R.J. do what she wanted him to?

Two mornings later Sara was awakened at 4:00 A.M. by the ear-splitting screech of her doorbell. Groggy, she opened the door to see Ariel standing there with the night doorman. Sara was too dumbfounded and too sleepy to say anything as he put Ariel's six suitcases (all vintage Louis Vuitton) inside her apartment.

Ariel took off her gloves (white cotton gloves, like a 1950s model would wear) and looked about the apartment. Sara was still rubbing sleep from her eyes, and she could see that Ariel found all five hundred and fifty square feet of it wanting, but she had decided to be gracious. Smiling, Ariel put her hands on Sara's shoulders and kissed both her cheeks, like in a French movie. Ariel didn't seem to be aware that it was 4:00 A.M. and that her cousin had to go to work later that day.

For Sara, the next three weeks were hell. She had R.J. at the office and Ariel at home. R.J. had explained that the reason he wanted to go to Arundel was to look at some tiny island just off the coast of eastern North Carolina. It was called King's Isle and since it didn't have a beach, it wasn't a tourist spot. But Charley Dunkirk was thinking of buying most of the island and making it into an exclusive resort and he wanted R.J. to scout out the place and give his opinion of its suitability.

Sara asked if he wanted her to do the preliminary research on the island, but R.J. said no, that he'd do it. He wanted her to clear his schedule—which meant he got to sit on a couch and play on the Web, while she had to deal with people who were angry because their appointments had been canceled.

All in all, Sara's workload doubled. Since she had no secretarial skills to speak of, R.J. used Sara as a sort of living appointment book. He expected her to remember where he was to be every second of the day, where everything he owned was, and she was to make everything work. This meant doing things like getting down on her hands and knees with a screwdriver to fix his swivel chair. When he suggested that he keep sitting in it while she worked, she gave him her best imitation of Ariel's icy look. He blinked

at her a couple of times, then got up, chuckling, and went to the other side of the room.
He loved to order electronic gadgets over
the Internet, but he didn't want to bother
reading the instructions, so Sara had to figure out how to work whatever he'd bought,
then show him how to use it. He often
bought a second one of whatever it was and
offered it to her, but she refused to accept it.
Her philosophy was that when someone
gives you a gift, they want something in return. She didn't want to owe R. J. anything.

At home—not that she could still call it
that—she had to deal with Ariel.

For two hours before Sara went to work
and until after midnight every night, they rehearsed. Neither was a better actor than the
other. Sara'd had years of professional
training, but Ariel had had twenty-four years
of lying to her mother, so it amounted to the
same thing.

They began to put on little impromptu
skits in public. They had to put a scarf and
dark glasses over one of them when they
left the building so no one would realize
there were two of them, but once they were
outside, they tried to become each other.
Their favorite pantomime was that Sara was

a rich snot, and Ariel was her overworked personal assistant. They got so good at it that one day Sara said, "Really, Ariel, can't you do anything correctly?" and Ariel looked shocked. She said that Sara had sounded so much like her mother that . . . she couldn't go on. Sara said, "I sounded so much like her that you were overcome with homesickness?"

"Why, no," Ariel said. "You were—" When Ariel realized that Sara was making a joke, she looked at her cousin in astonishment, then they laughed together and Sara began to think that maybe they could carry this off.

Sara had told Ariel that all she really wanted was a break from R.J., but the truth was that what she really and truly wanted was to meet David. Her best acting was when she pretended to be unconcerned and said, "Oh, yes, what about David? Shouldn't you tell me about him?"

Ariel didn't seem to think David was of any importance. He'd been told that they were going to exchange places so he knew everything, but Sara wanted to hear every word about him. She told Ariel that it was the same way that she needed to know everything about R.J. When Ariel was reluctant to talk about David, Sara thought maybe she was jealous, but when Ariel started talking, Sara couldn't stop her.

After days of hearing about him, Sara thought his personality was even better than his looks—if that was possible. He was sweet and kind, thoughtful, intelligent, and willing to help. In other words, he was everything R. J. wasn't. She tried to tell Ariel what a pain R. J. was, but Ariel wouldn't listen to her. For a while Sara thought maybe Ariel's wanting to trade places was because she was one of those superficial women who'd fallen for him, but Sara didn't think so. She thought Ariel wanted to get away from her mother and to see how the normal world lived. As for R. J., if Ariel had any romantic feelings for him after all she'd been told, then she deserved what she got.

Two days before they were to leave for Arundel, Ariel told Sara she wanted her to go to King's Isle too. Ariel's calmness when she mentioned that island showed how far they'd progressed in becoming each other. When Sara first told her R. J.'s friend was thinking about buying a place called King's Isle, Ariel had gone ballistic. "He's crazy if he thinks he can deal with those people!"

Ariel said, starting to pace the room. "Didn't R. J. ask anyone in Arundel what those people are like?" "Anyone" meant the elite of Arundel, the people Sara was to pretend to be one of.

"You don't know them," Ariel said, her voice pleading. "The people on that island are awful. There are terrible stories about them. People who go there disappear. They say they drown, but anyone who lives near Arundel knows the truth."

"Ah," Sara said, suppressing a yawn. Hadn't she seen this on a late-night movie? She hadn't had much sleep since Ariel arrived and she was having trouble concentrating.

It took Ariel a while to calm down and by the time they were about to leave, Sara thought maybe Ariel had given up her childish beliefs about King's Isle, but she hadn't. When it got closer to the time of the exchange, Ariel again started voicing her fear of the little island. She said, "You and David *have* to go with us to that place. You can't leave R. J. and me alone there. You have to persuade R. J. to let you and David go with us."

Sara did *not* want to ask R. J. for a favor.

She talked, she reasoned, she begged, she even cried, but Ariel couldn't be moved. Sara thought about backing out, but by that time she genuinely wanted to do the exchange.

Maybe David and she would get along so well that she could . . . what? Marry him and join the society that her father had so hated? At the thought of her father's hatred of Arundel, she smiled. He'd only hated it because they hadn't let him into it. Sara knew that if her mother's father had welcomed him, given him a house and a job, he would have loved it. He would have had chances in his life, but he'd messed them all up. But Sara didn't want to mess up the one and only opportunity she had of meeting a truly nice man. Her friends at work were trying Internet dating, but so far Sara hadn't seen any good results from that. Ariel had given Sara an opportunity to be part of a society she couldn't otherwise penetrate, and a chance to meet men, David among them, who, in normal circumstances, wouldn't allow people like Sara into their world.

But no matter what she said, Sara couldn't change Ariel's mind about David and her going to the island with her and

R.J. The only way Ariel would continue with the masquerade was if Sara agreed to ask R.J. if she could go with him. "He'll need a guide," Ariel said, "so why not your cousin who lives in Arundel?"

"And her boyfriend?" Sara asked in disbelief.

"Tell him you'll quit if he doesn't take us."

In the end, Sara was too worn down by both Ariel and R.J. to say no to much of anything. Sara was exhausted by the time she and R.J. left for North Carolina. When they got to the beautiful bed-and-breakfast in Arundel that Ariel had recommended, Sara was feeling guilty for what they were about to do to him, but then R.J. started his usual litany of complaints and Sara couldn't stand him again. Who could hate such a beautiful place? She told him she was going to bed, then went to her own room.

Ariel was waiting for her in her room. If she'd been anyone else, Sara would have thought she'd climbed in the window, but she knew that Princess Ariel would never do such a thing.

"He agreed, didn't he?" Ariel asked as she handed Sara the pageboy wig.

Sara didn't know what would have happened if she'd told her no. She said that R. J. had agreed and that tomorrow morning the four of them were heading to King's Isle.

"And may the Lord have mercy on us all," Ariel said. In the next second, she raised a window. "Sorry, but it's the only way you can leave the room and not be seen." Sara started to protest, but then she glanced outside and there in the dark was David, his arms raised upward, as if to catch her. Sara wanted to put on a white dress, stand on the ledge, and fall backward into his arms.

Ariel misunderstood her look. "It's not that bad," she said. "I mean, the part about my house and my mother isn't so bad. King's Isle is horrible, but the rest will be all right. You'll see. Gather your courage and do it."

Ariel meant that Sara was to gather her courage to be able to jump into David's waiting arms. Golly gee, Sara thought. I hope I can do it.

Sara wiped the smile off her face, replaced it with a look of resignation, put the wig on, then fell out the window as gracefully as she could. It would have worked better if her foot hadn't caught on a vine that was devouring the building. She ended up upside down, with one foot in the vine, one flailing about, and the top half of her in David's strong arms.

"Really, Sara!" Ariel hissed from the window. "You're going to wake everyone up."

So much for sympathy from my dear cousin! Sara thought. She wanted to make a snappy comeback, but the sensation of being held by David rendered her incapable of speech. He leaned across her to disentangle her foot, then pulled her more fully into his arms—strong arms—all while apologizing for not catching her properly.

As he carried her to his car, she snuggled her head against his shoulder, and thought that maybe she could forgive him for quite a few things.

"How's your foot?" he asked as he gently set her inside his car. She didn't know what make the vehicle was, but she could smell the leather seats.

"Fine," she said and wished she had on one of Ariel's designer dresses instead of cotton slacks and a polo shirt. David made her feel like a lady.

He smiled and even in the dark she could see his white teeth. He closed the door, then got into the driver's seat and started the car. "So you're Sara."

"Actually, I'm supposed to be Ariel. Maybe once I get her clothes on I'll look more like her. By the way, thank you for helping me back there. I'm not usually quite that clumsy."

"The first thing you'll have to do is stop being so nice. Everyone will know you're not Ariel!"

Sara laughed and relief flowed over her. She knew that Ariel wasn't in love with David, but she'd wondered why a man like him put up with her if he wasn't in love with her. Now she saw that he wasn't and all she felt was relief.

"How about this: 'David! You idiot! If you'd caught me when you should have, I wouldn't have entangled my foot in that vine. Do you think that was poison ivy? Do you think we should go to the hospital?'"

When David laughed again, she wanted to go on all night.

"Are you sure you want to do this?" he asked, his voice full of concern.

"I've never wanted to do it, but . . ." She shrugged to let him know that she had her reasons. "Did Ariel have time to tell you that R. J. agreed to all four of us going to King's Isle tomorrow?"

Sara wasn't sure, but she thought she heard him mutter, "R. J.!"

"So tell me about this King's Isle," she said, smiling. There wasn't another car on the road. "Is it as bad as Ariel says?"

"In Arundel, they don't have the boogie man to scare the kids, they have King's Isle," he said. "Truthfully, the waters around there are full of reefs and there *are* a couple of buried ships. And there've been quite a few wrecks over the centuries. It's tradition around here to make up stories about the islanders luring ships to their deaths."

"Shades of Daphne du Maurier," Sara said, relieved to hear that Ariel's fears were unfounded. She had almost started to believe Ariel's paranoia.

"So how did you get Brompton to agree to let Ariel and me go with you? I mean, let *you* and me go?"

"Confusing, isn't it?" she said and he nodded. "R. J. will give me whatever I want, but I make sure I don't ask for much."

David gave her a sharp look. "Why would your boss give you anything you want?"

"Because he can't run his life without me." Sara could hear her voice rising. "I co-ordinate everything in his life and do everything for him, from programming his cell-phone to buying his underwear. The last time he gave a party, the bartender's three kids came down with measles and I had to serve the drinks. He wanted me to wear a short skirt and a frilly white apron, but I told him he could take his sick fantasies some-where else. You know what he gave me for my birthday? A pair of lovebirds. I gave them to a hospice. I tell you, that man—"

Embarrassed, Sara broke off and looked at David. He was looking straight ahead, his face expressionless. Wow! she thought. He doesn't give anything away, does he? He'd make one heck of a poker player, or a . . .

"Have you ever thought about going into politics?" she asked.

David's beautiful face broke into astonish-ment and he briefly swerved into the next lane. "Found out," he said. "Not even my mother knows my secret ambition. How did you figure it out?"

Sara used all her acting training to keep a straight face. She'd been making a joke—or an insult. He was so stoical that he looked like one of those old presidents on paper money. "You want to save the world?" she asked, trying to sound earnest and not sarcastic.

"More or less." He glanced at her and his eyes were twinkling. "Save the environment, anyway. I've thought about trying to be secretary of the Interior."

"Why not president?" she asked flippantly, but even in the dark car she could see his face turn red.

Turning away, she looked out the windshield. President. This man wanted to be the president of the United States. He was from a good family, had lots of money, an Ivy League education, and he wanted to be president. She looked at his strong arms inside his beautifully ironed shirt and knew that the women would vote for him.

David pulled into a driveway and at last she saw the house she'd dreamed of for so long. He turned off the engine, then picked up her hand and held it. "You'll be okay. When Ariel told me this is what she wanted to do, I said she couldn't pull it off. How could anyone impersonate anyone else? But now that I've seen that you are a woman of great sensitivity and insight, I think you might be able to do it."

When he kissed her hand, Sara felt her

knees turning to jelly. Worse, she felt herself sliding down into the seat. She'd day-dreamed about this man for so long that it would seem natural to have a little make-out session in the car. Besides, she was supposed to be Ariel, so she and David were an item, weren't they?

But then an expression flickered across his eyes and it so reminded her of R. J. that she sat upright and snatched her hand out of his grasp. "David, really!" she said, imitating Ariel. "You're not going to start *that* again, are you?"

Instantly, his expression changed and he sat back in his seat. He blinked at her a few times, then smiled. "You *are* a good actress, aren't you? For a minute there, I thought you were Ariel."

Sara did some blinking of her own because she'd just discovered that what the self-help books told you was true: Men treated you as you allowed them to treat you. When he knew she was Sara, a girl whose father was from the wrong side of the tracks, and she was melting at his touch, he was smirking at her in that way that R. J. smirked at women. But when she became Ariel, aka the Queen of the World, he sat up straight and minded his manners.

"I think that from now on, even in private, we should play our proper roles," Sara said, realizing for the first time that if she ever had a chance of winning this fabulous man, she was going to have to keep him from knowing that she wanted him. Mindful of that revelation, she put her hand on the car door handle. David stopped her.

"You know that Miss Pommy will be waiting up for you, don't you?"

"Ariel's mother? Tonight? But it must be—"

"After two A.M. Yes, I know, but she'll be there. You'll just have to stand your ground." He looked her up and down. "She's going to hate what you have on. Can you brazen it out?"

Sara opened her mouth to say that of course she could, but then her whole body turned the yellow of a coward. "Are Ariel's suitcases in the back?"

"Half of them are. I should have taken the pickup, but Miss Pommy hates it when I drive the truck. 'So common,' she says."

As they got out of the car, Sara wanted to ask if he wore faded denims and a blue shirt when he drove the truck, but that would show the common side of her. "What do you think Ariel would wear on a plane?" she asked.

"Something expensive," he said as he hauled a suitcase out of the trunk, closed the lid silently, then disappeared into the tall shrubbery at the side of the driveway. She followed him and saw an arbor covered with some dense vine. There was a seat on one side. "So this is where you and Ariel sneak away to be alone?"

David snorted. "I spend whole days alone with Ariel in her bedroom, but nothing ever happens."

Sara couldn't tell if he was angry or if that's the way he wanted it to be. He pulled his keys out of his pocket, then turned on a tiny flashlight to look at the numbers on Ariel's suitcase. She had to work to not show her surprise that he knew the combination to her lock.

He put the case on the bench, opened it, then rummaged inside and drew out two pieces of clothing. He handed Sara slacks and a fine-gauge, short-sleeve pink sweater.

As she started to change, she said, "Don't

look." She sounded insincere even to her-self.

Politely, he turned his back to her. She couldn't help thinking that if it had been R.J., he would have folded his arms over his chest and told her to proceed—while he watched. But then, R.J. was a mad sex fiend who came on to anything female.

In seconds, Sara had put on the clothes, which fit perfectly. She could feel the fine texture, and the cost of them, even in the dark. "You can turn around now," she said.

Turning, David looked at her. There wasn't much light, but the moon gave a bit of a glow so they could see each other. "Ariel said that you were . . ." He didn't finish his sentence, but she knew what he was thinking.

"Ariel said I was fat, didn't she?"

He smiled. "Actually, yes. But you're the same size she is."

"I lost the weight I'd gained in college af-ter about four months of working for R.J. Walking in New York while carrying R.J.'s dry cleaning and his steak lunches firmed me up."

"Whatever you did, you look great."

Sara could feel her face turn as rosy as

the sweater and she was glad it was dark so he couldn't see her clearly.

She took a deep breath. This was it. Meeting Ariel's mother was the true test of her acting ability. It was her own private audition for a part that only she could play. "Shall we go?" she said, then followed David to the house. She waited on the big, deep porch with its lovely white-painted wicker chairs and flowered cushions as he hauled four of Ariel's suitcases up the stairs.

Sara wasn't surprised when David inserted a key in the lock of Ariel's house.

The house was as grand and as beautiful as Ariel had told her it was. It had been built in 1832, on top of the foundations of a much older house built by one of Ariel's ancestors. The Weatherly family was even richer then than they were now, so the house was big and lavish. Every surface seemed to have been decorated with a piece of white-painted wood. Every corner had little turned pieces of wood that were fitted into other little turned pieces of wood. Sara was sure that the house was a perfect example of some type of architecture, but it wasn't to her taste.

Standing at the top of the stairs was an

older woman, her shoulders back, her stomach pulled in. She had gray hair piled neatly and intricately on top of her head and she was wearing a lavender chiffon bathrobe over a lavender chiffon nightgown. She looked beautiful and formidable at the same time.

"Ariel," she said in a voice that wasn't quite a shout; still Sara knew that if they were in a theater and the microphones broke, this woman could carry on without them. "You are very late."

"Hello, Miss Pommy," David said from behind her.

Sara saw the woman's face change from stern to sweet in an instant. She gazed at David with love in her eyes. Did Ariel tell me about this? she wondered. If so, she didn't remember it. Or had she heard it and dismissed it, thinking that of course everyone loved David?

"Good morning, David," Mrs. Weatherly said, her voice lowering somewhat. "And how are you on this very early morning?"

"Very well. And you?"

She didn't answer, but looked at Sara. "Ariel, you have a crease in your trousers. And have you been using that face cream I gave you? Your complexion looks like a teenager's. I'll make an appointment for the dermatologist for tomorrow."

Sara could only gape at her. One of her great vanities was her skin. In spite of too much sun and nothing to put on it but soap and water, her skin was one of her best features. Yet this woman . . .

Sara forced herself to smile. "Is that a new gown, Mother? You look beautiful in it."

"Don't be impertinent," Mrs. Weatherly snapped, then turned and started back up the stairs. "David, see that she gets into her room. Ariel, I will see you in the morning and you will be given a chance to explain your unpardonable bad behavior."

Sara stood there, her mouth agape, as she watched her walk up the stairs, then enter a room and close the door. She looked back at David, speechless.

"Translation: She missed you, was worried about you, and she wants to see you first thing in the morning to hear all about your trip."

Chapter Five

The next morning, Sara was waiting on the street corner when David picked her up at 7:00 A.M. She knew it wasn't something that Ariel would have done, but she couldn't bear to face "Miss Pommy." Besides, she told herself, she wanted to see how Ariel and R.J. were getting along. Had he believed the switch?

"Coward," David said pleasantly as she opened the door to his BMW.

"Through and through," she said and laughed. "Have you heard from Ariel?"

"Think your boss threw her out before breakfast?"

"He sleeps naked. I worry that he seduced Ariel."

Sara was only kidding, but when David almost ran into a fire hydrant, she gasped.

"He wouldn't really, would he?" David asked.

Sara was trying to figure out what his concern was. Ariel's last letters said that David was half in love with some "very unsuitable girl" who lived on "the other side" of Arundel. But now Sara was wondering if there was more between them than she'd realized.

As they drove though Arundel, Sara got her first look at the town. It was like a set for a movie about a perfect little town. So this is where I came from, she thought. She hadn't been born in Arundel, but she'd been conceived here. "On top of a Ferris wheel at the county fair," if her father was to be believed.

They passed big, old houses surrounded by beautiful gardens. Huge trees of magnolia and gingko shaded perfect lawns. Flowers bloomed everywhere. Houses had signs in front of them telling the name of the house and the date it was built. She saw the name Ambler, her mother's maiden name, twice. In spite of her refusal to memorize the genealogy of the town's founding families, she remembered Ariel's comments about the Amblers: oldest, richest, most prominent. Her ancestors had walked on these streets, lived in these houses.

She came out of her reverie when David turned beside an enormous Victorian house painted blue and white. It was covered with porches, turrets, and little round windows, all romantic and dreamy.

Looking at her, David smiled. "Built by your great, great, great, et cetera, uncle."

"A man of taste." How good it felt to belong! she thought.

When they got to the parking lot, Ariel and R.J. were outside putting boxes in the trunk of his rented Jaguar. Actually, Ariel was putting in the boxes and R.J. was talking on his cellphone to somebody in Tokyo. Sara fully expected him to start ordering her around as soon as she stepped out of David's car, but he didn't. Instead, she found out what it was like to be on the receiving end of the R.J. treatment, as she'd heard it described. He looked her up and down from head to toe, then back again. When he'd finished that, he looked into her eyes.

For the first time, Sara had an idea of why so many women fell for him. But she knew him and wanted nothing to do with his hot looks. It was easy, almost natural, for her to become Ariel and give him her best imitation of the look. When David reached her, Sara squeezed his arm possessively.

R. J. looked from David to Sara, then back again. There was a knowing little smirk on R. J.'s face, as if to say, This *boy* is no competition for a man like me.

Sara had to fight the urge to tell him what she thought of him, but to do that would give the game away.

"You must be Ariel," R. J. said, at last off the phone. He put himself between her and David, and took her arm to lead her to the front passenger seat.

"And you must be Mr. Brompton," she said, moving her arm out of his.

"Please, call me R. J."

She was tempted to say, "Call me Miss Weatherly," but she just smiled and put more space between them.

"I'm glad Sara asked to bring her cousin along on this trip," he said suggestively.

Sara had to bite her tongue to keep from putting him in his place. She'd seen the way he flirted with women and the way they reacted to him, but she wanted none of it. She looked at David with a plea for help, but he was head-to-head with Ariel and they were whispering.

R.J. still had his eyes on Sara when he shouted for his assistant. "Sara," he called over his shoulder and she almost answered. Luckily, Ariel answered first.

"Yes, sir?" Ariel said, and Sara winced. Never had she called R.J. "sir."

"Did you get my briefcase and my schedule?"

"I . . ."

Sara looked over R.J.'s shoulder to her cousin, who was looking wild-eyed and asking for help. Sara slid away from R.J. and went to Ariel. "I haven't seen my cousin in so long that I think I'll go with her," she said, then led Ariel back into the B and B before R.J. could protest.

"How was it?" Sara asked as soon as they were inside the pretty room.

Ariel collapsed onto the sofa at the foot of the bed, while Sara scurried around and got all the things she knew R.J. would want— which was pretty much everything he'd brought with him except for his clothes.

"He sleeps naked," Ariel said.

"Did I forget to tell you that?"

"Yes, you did. You forgot to tell me a lot of things, like that his computer gets a funny screen on it and he expected *me* to fix it."

"What did you do?"

"Turned it off, then back on. What I know about computers you could put on the head of a pin. Does he walk around naked in front of *you*?"

Sara was putting R.J.'s recharged camera batteries in his case. "Why are you so interested in his naked body?"

"I'm not. It's just that . . ."

Sara looked out the window and saw David and R.J. standing close together. Too close. Rather like dogs circling each other. "We have to get out there," she said. "Here, take this." She thrust a briefcase and camera bag onto Ariel's lap.

"What's wrong?"

"Nothing. It's just that R.J. won't like David."

"Why not?" There was disbelief in Ariel's voice. "David is so boring that everyone likes him."

"Boring?" Sara said, looking at Ariel sharply. A man with the ambition to be president is boring? Not quite. "R.J. had to work his way up from the bottom and David's had everything handed to him. David is the kind of man R. J. despises."

"Does that mean that if R. J. knew who *I* was he'd despise me too?"

"You're too pretty for R. J. to dislike," Sara said.

"Today you're the pretty one. I need about three more hours of sleep and a hairdresser. You, on the other hand, look great. You have on Prada and I'm in . . . what is this?" Ariel asked.

"Liz Claiborne, I think, but I don't memorize the labels in my clothes. Whatever it is, it looks great on you. Really. And the shorter hair suits you. Come on, he'll be blowing the horn in another minute."

"Not really?" Ariel said, and her voice sounded a bit breathless. "He's really an exciting man, isn't he?"

"You're going to find out how exciting he is if you don't get out there immediately."

"What will he do?" Ariel asked.

"Not whatever it is that you seem to think he'll do," Sara said as she piled Ariel's arms full and pushed her out the door. They'd be back by night fall and, if she was lucky, Sara would have a few days alone with David. She smiled at him from behind Ariel and thought about being in the backseat with him on the three-hour drive to King's Isle.

But R. J. thwarted her. "You'll have to sit in front with me since you're to be my navigator, my co-captain," he said. Since this made sense, there was nothing Sara could think of to protest, so she took the seat next to him, while David and Ariel got into the back. They headed east toward North Carolina's notoriously dangerous coast. Hurricanes, shipwrecks, and a long history of pirates overhung the many islands dotting the coast. Some islands were large and well inhabited, and some were just spots of land sticking up in the way of the ships trying to get to the mainland.

"Think we'll see Blackbeard's ghost?" R. J. asked Sara as soon as they were underway.

Since she was pretending to be someone else, she couldn't give him her usual monosyllabic replies, but she wanted to. She didn't like the way he was flirting with the woman he thought she was. "Is it Blackbeard's ghost or his treasure you want to see?" she asked.

"Maybe the ghost would lead me to the treasure."

"I would think that you had enough treasure, Mr. Brompton."

"Everyone wants more, Miss Weatherly. It's called ambition and it's highly prized in this glorious country of ours."

"It's also called greed," she said, but she made herself smile as she said it.

Sara pulled the sun visor down and saw in the little makeup mirror that David and Ariel were head-to-head in the backseat, whispering. I wonder what they're plotting? Sara thought, then put the visor back up.

"Come on, Miss Weatherly—and, by the way, I told you to call me R. J.—hasn't there been something in your life that you wanted so much that you were willing to work hard to get it?"

"It's good to try to better yourself," she said as primly as she could manage. "But when you get to the point where you have too much and still want more, it's time to stop."

"I guess you mean me," he said, smiling. "But, Miss Weatherly, it's not as though you work for me and have to keep your mouth shut. Tell me what you think. Surely Sara has told you some things about me."

"I don't reveal confidences," Sara said as

she glanced over her shoulder. What *were* they talking about?

"So tell me everything about Arundel," R.J. said. "I'm thinking about buying a vacation house there."

"Do you want to know about the people or the land values?"

He laughed. "You know, even if I didn't know you were Sara's cousin, I'd know it. You two sound and act very much alike."

"I couldn't possibly do all that Sara does," she shot back. "Sara is a saint."

"I quite agree," he said quietly, looking in the mirror at the two in the backseat. "On the other hand, she's a terrible secretary. Just the other day, she nearly spilled a pot of hot coffee on me."

Sara had to turn her head away so he wouldn't see the anger in her face. After everything she did for him, all he could remember was that she'd almost spilled some coffee! Right now she wished she could erase the "almost."

"Tell me about the people of Arundel," he said. "Tell me about *your* life there."

Sara put some of her acting training into use and calmed herself. She made herself into Ariel and began talking about all that she'd memorized. She told him about her mother, and her childhood with her home-schooling. She told him about the old families in Arundel, and how they still named their children after the founding fathers. Sara did her best to sound lighthearted, as though she hadn't a care in the world—the way she'd seen Ariel's life until she met that virago who was her mother.

Sara had memorized the way to get to King's Isle, so she gave him directions at every junction.

"What made you choose King's Isle?" she asked.

"Ever hear of a man named Charley Dunkirk?"

"Sara and I have been corresponding for years, so I know a bit more about you and your business than you'd think."

"I can't imagine that Sara ever wrote you a word about *me.* Most of the time she acts like she hates me. The stories I could tell you! Oh, well, where was I?"

Sara narrowed her eyes at him. "Mr. Dunkirk," she said stiffly.

"Oh, yeah. My best friend. Charley has a wife he pretends is a pest to him, but he's mad about her. Former beauty queen." He glanced at Sara. "She grew up in Arundel."

Sara said nothing. What could she say? Ask where the woman lived in town? If Ariel heard the address she'd know if the woman lived above or below the cotton mill.

"Anyway, Charley came to me and said that his wife, Katlyn, wanted him to buy an island off the coast of Arundel and he wanted *me* to take a look at it."

"Why you?"

"I have no idea. Charley didn't know either. At first he thought Kat and I had something going on, but—"

"You wouldn't do that to your best friend, would you?"

"Not unless she—" R.J. was grinning, but at one look at Sara's face, he stopped smiling. "Of course I wouldn't. Code of honor, that sort of thing. Anyway, Charley told me that Kat wanted him to buy an island and open a resort on it. A rich resort. He said . . ."

R.J. sat up a bit straighter and deepened his voice. When he spoke, he sounded very much like Mr. Dunkirk, but Sara as Ariel wasn't supposed to know that, so she had to work to keep from laughing.

" 'No twenty-grand-a-year, Mom-and-Pop-with-the-kids place,' " R.J. said in Charley Dunkirk's voice. " 'I want celebrities. Multimillionaires who crave privacy. This King's Isle is the only island left that hasn't already been exploited. It's like the place has been left for me. It has flat land on one end that could be used for an airstrip. There's no beach, but what's a beach? Sand, right? So we bring in some sand.' "

Sara had to look away again to keep from laughing, but R.J. saw the muscle in her jaw twitching so he went on.

" 'I was thinking of an island in the Caribbean, but Kat wants North Carolina, so that's what I'm gonna give her. Maybe she wants a business to run after I'm gone. Maybe that's it. I don't know why, but she wants *you* to go look at the place for me. You'll do it?' "

R.J. returned to his normal voice. "I told him I'd look at the island and that I'd even take my camera."

" 'Vacation,' " R.J.-as-Charley said. " 'This could be a vacation for you. I'm gonna take one of those one of these days.' Sure you are, I told him. We all are. One of these days."

Sara kept looking out the side window. She remembered the day she'd seen Mr.

Dunkirk half carried out of R.J.'s office. She'd thought then that R.J. had made the old man drunk on purpose, but maybe Charley Dunkirk was just a drinker.

"So you agreed to help an old friend," she said.

"Not without doing a lot of research first. It took a lot of work."

Sara had a vivid vision of R.J. stretched out on the big leather couch in his office, his laptop on his chest. Lot of work, indeed! "Didn't Sara write me about helping you find out about the island?"

R.J. looked in the rearview mirror at David and Ariel, then lowered his voice. "Naw, she was too busy helping me tie up loose ends so I could go. I did the research by myself."

"And who said Hercules had a lot of tasks?"

He laughed. "Yeah, okay, so I dump a lot into her capable hands, but I did find out about King's Isle myself."

"And what did you discover?"

"Nothing that you, as a resident of Arundel, don't know."

"It's always nice to hear an outsider's point of view," she said, smiling. "So enlighten me."

"It's a weird place."

"Everyone in Arundel knows that. But what makes it strange to you?" She was trying to sound as though she knew everything but wanted to hear more.

"Nothing important, but I think it might have great money-making potential."

"The most important thing."

"Have to feed the bottom line, but, tourist-wise, that island does have an interesting history. Apparently, the inhabitants refused to take part in either the Revolutionary or the Civil War. When the patriots won, they refused to change the name of their island to what the new government suggested, Freedom Island. And when soldiers in the War Between the States landed, no matter what side they were on, the King's Isle people burned their war boats, then put the soldiers in rowboats and sent them back to the mainland. When President Lincoln heard of it, he said that if all the states did that there wouldn't be a war. He didn't allow his troops to waste ammunition blowing up the island, as many people wanted to do."

"Too bad everybody didn't do that," Sara said.

"Yeah, too bad. By the early 1890s King's

Isle was poverty-stricken, with just a few hundred people living there. Then natural hot springs were discovered bubbling up from the rocky center of the island and a year later, King's Isle was *the* place to be. The rich went there to play and to lounge in the waters. They built big summer houses, put in roads, and almost overnight, King's Isle became rich."

"It isn't rich now, so what happened? The spring dry up?"

"Sort of. Around the turn of the century there was an explosion—nobody knows what caused it—and in an instant, the springs were gone. Since then, the island has declined and now there are only about two hundred and fifty inhabitants on its five square miles. The big old houses are still there, but the Internet sites said they're rotting into the ground, and the current residents have become squatters. The kid who delivers groceries might be living in two rooms of a ten-thousand-square-foot house that has crumbling marble floors. A lot of the residents pay no rent."

Sara could see the possibilities. If there was anything that newly rich people liked, it was making people think they'd been rich for a long time. Old mansions would do that. "Why hasn't someone fixed up the old buildings and made the island into a resort before now?"

"From what I could find out, quite a few people have tried, but every businessman has been sent away. It seems that the current residents are just as inhospitable as their ancestors."

"You'll do it," Sara said before she thought.

"Think so?" R.J. said.

"Sara's told me that you're very persuasive."

"Did she?" R.J. asked, smiling. "I hope she's right. I'd like to get that island for Charley. I was thinking that with modern mining methods, maybe the springs could be uncovered. Charley was right that most people like the caché of going to a tropical island, but a place off the coast of the U.S. with hot springs? That has enormous possibilities. Maybe an ad campaign could make people believe the waters had healing powers."

Sara liked everything that R.J. had told her—except, of course, for the lie about advertising the waters as having healing powers. Maybe she could persuade him to let *her* work on the project. She could live in Arundel and work on King's Isle. Doing what? she wondered.

"There it is," R.J. said and she looked ahead. In front of them was the water, a huge dock jutting out from it, and in the distance was the island. There was no ferry. R.J. pulled the car to the side of the road and cut the engine. "Anyone hungry?" he asked.

"Heavens no!" Ariel-as-Sara said from the back. "After the breakfast at the inn, I may never eat again. You should have seen it! Thick slices of bread stuffed with cream cheese and soaked in syrup. I think I gained three pounds."

"I had a big breakfast too," David said.

Sara didn't turn to look at R.J., but she doubted if he'd eaten that big breakfast at the B and B. About two months ago, he had been on his fourth Danish one morning and she couldn't resist saying, "I see you're turning in your six-pack for a keg." As far as she knew, he hadn't eaten a doughnut or a Danish since. "I'm hungry," she said.

"Thanks," he murmured, but she wouldn't look at him.

He started the car, turned it around, and drove back to a little mom-and-pop restaurant about a mile down the road.

"So, Mr. Brompton," David said as soon as they'd ordered, "what's your purpose for going to King's Isle? Other than to exploit the people, that is." David was smiling as though he was making a joke, but it fell flat. "That's what you do for a living, isn't it?"

R.J. leveled his eyes at David. "Of course it is. That's what all of us working-class stiffs do. We use up the world's resources. So, tell me—what was your name again, sonny?—what have *you* done in the world?"

"Studied how to save it."

When Sara saw the two men looking at each other like clashing elks, she wanted to walk out and never return. What were they so angry at each other about? She looked at Ariel to see if she had any answers, but then saw that Ariel was leaning toward R.J. in a way Sara had seen many times. He seemed to fascinate some women. R.J. was ruggedly handsome, with that brash, aggressive, pulled-himself-up-by-his-bootstraps look, while David had a clean-cut, never-had-to-work look about him.

This has to stop, Sara thought.

"My money's on the old one," she said

loudly. "He's older, but he has a ruthless-ness that young one has never had. It's my guess that this man would stop at nothing to get what he wanted, while the kid has a conscience and scruples. Those are great ideals, but they aren't needed in the business world. And if these two take their juvenile whose-is-bigger fight into the alley, I believe the old one will win. What about you?" she asked Ariel.

"The younger one, definitely," Ariel said. "He can be quite persevering when he wants something. He doesn't quit. Nothing makes him stop. When your old man is worn out, the kid'll still be fighting. He might have broken bones and missing teeth, but he'll keep on fighting. David doesn't give up."

Sara glanced at R. J. and saw that he was thoroughly enjoying every word of what the lovely young women were saying, but David was red to his ears. Whatever the men were thinking, Sara had successfully shut them up.

After they finished their lunch, they went back to the car, where R. J. smiled at Sara in a conspiratorial way, as though he were a prizefighter and she'd just bet on him to win over a kid half his age.

By the time they got back to the dock, the ferry was there. It was a fairly modern thing, able to carry four cars. R.J. mumbled that he'd expected a man with a raft and a pole. Sara nudged Ariel to pay the five-dollar charge—that's what the assistant does, after all—and R.J. drove the car onto the steel surface. Theirs was the only car on the ferry; they were the only people going to King's Isle.

Once the ferry was underway, they all got out of the car and walked to the end of the rail to look out across the water toward the little island in the distance. After a while, Ariel and David moved away, talking in low voices about something urgent.

"Think Sara will marry him?" R.J. asked quietly.

"I beg your pardon," Sara said.

"Him. The jock. Think she'll marry him?"

Sara had no idea what to say, but she knew that R.J. was up to something, so she let him talk. "I guess Sara's told you that she's always saying she wants to quit her job. I should let her. I should give her a big severance bonus, then let her go do whatever it is that she wants to with her life. From the way she was looking at that jock at lunch, I think they're already half-engaged. She could live in a big, old Victorian monstrosity in Arundel and grow prize-winning roses. Why she wants that kind of life, I'll never know. I guess you know that she trained to be an actress."

"Not a very good one," Sara said.

"Are you kidding? She was on Broadway in a play and she was really good."

"How do you know this about her?" Sara asked softly. She wouldn't have thought that R. J. could shock her, but this did.

He shrugged. "I typed her name on the Internet one day and it came up that she had a bit part in a Broadway play. I went to see it three nights in a row. She only had a walk-on part and three lines of dialogue, but I thought she was great. She was the heroine's daughter's best friend, and she wore one of those thin, white dresses that always makes you wonder what's underneath."

Sara was so stunned she could hardly speak. When had he taken time out of his a-woman-every-night schedule to see her in a play? She started to say something, but he moved away to the far end of the ferry to look back at the mainland. He left Sara frowning in puzzlement over what he'd said.

Finally, they reached the island. It was a perfect vision of yesteryear, and Sara knew that R.J. wouldn't be disappointed. King's Isle was run-down in a way that some people would think was romantic, but a businessman would know was anything but. Every house in view, every water-front building, needed repair, and if they didn't get it soon, they were going to fall down. R.J. was right, Sara thought. There's no money here. And, worse, there was an air about the place that spoke of a failure to preserve what the place had once been. She didn't think he was going to have much trouble buying the entire island.

When she turned around, she saw that R.J. was staring at her, and she wondered what he was thinking. David and Ariel were standing by the rail, shoulder to shoulder, and they looked as though they were half-afraid of the island, half-hypnotized by it.

When the ferry stopped, they got into the car and drove onto the island. Everyone was silent. Sara saw R.J. look in the rearview mirror several times. When she glanced back, Ariel and David were staring out the car windows with wide eyes. Sara was sitting straight up, looking ahead.

There were no people around. No one at all. R.J. drove slowly down the street, looking at the run-down buildings. There was absolutely no one in sight.

"Where are all the people?" Sara whispered.

"Maybe it's an island holiday," David said. "St. Somebody's birthday or something and they're having a picnic."

No one said anything to that. Sara glanced at R.J. and thought that even he looked a bit unsettled. What could bother *him?*

"I thought I'd drive around the island, have a good look at it, then we could go back," R.J. said. "When's the next ferry run?" He looked in the rearview mirror at Ariel, but Sara knew that she hadn't looked at the schedule. But then, neither had Sara. Talking to R.J. as a person and not being ordered about by him had so unsettled her that she hadn't thought of things that usually would be second nature to her.

R.J. drove past two residential streets before coming to what was obviously the heart of the town, then he took a right and drove down the main street. It was deserted, completely empty of people. There were no traffic lights and no stop signs. Leaning forward, R.J. looked at the buildings.

"What do you think?" Sara asked quietly.

"This town is dead," he said. "I think they'd welcome some money."

"Where are the people?" Ariel asked from the back.

No one had a reply.

R.J. glanced at the car clock. It was 1:30. "How soon do you think we can leave this place and get back to the mainland? Didn't anyone see when the next ferry ran?"

"I don't like this place," Sara whispered.

R.J. took a left at the end of the street and entered a tree-lined residential area. There was one huge, old Victorian house after another. Each one needed painting and a lot of repairs. Some had windows with paper taped over them. Fallen trees had been left where they hit the ground.

On the corner was an especially big house. It was brick, with dark green shutters that had been recently painted. There was a faded sign in the window: ROOMS TO LET.

"Shall we spend the night?" R.J. asked, trying to dispel the gloom in the car.

Silence was his answer. So much for humor, Sara thought. The hairs on her forearms were standing upright.

All of them were looking at the houses so hard that no one was watching the road carefully. Sara yelled, "Look out!" and R.J. swerved to miss the dog that was lying in the middle of the road. He ran the car up onto the sidewalk and winced when he heard it scrape the bottom on the flaking concrete curb.

Sara jumped out of the car before he'd turned the engine off and ran toward the dog. R.J. followed her, with Ariel and David on his heels. Sara was crouched down by the dog when they got there.

"It's been dead a while," she said, looking up at R.J.

"And wasn't well cared for while it was alive," David said in disgust. "The poor thing looks as though it was starved to death."

Ariel said nothing. Too frightened to move, she stood close to David, her eyes downcast.

"Yeah," R.J. said, looking about the place. The silence in the town was eerie. All they heard were birds chirping. No cars, trucks, no planes, not even any boats.

"Do you think anyone lives in these houses?" Sara whispered into the silence.

"Not people I'd want to know if they'd treat a dog like this," David said.

"Maybe it was old and—" R.J. began.

David cut him off. "Look at it! That dog isn't more than a year old, if that. I don't think it's even fully grown, but it's been so mistreated that—"

Ariel took David's hand in hers and he calmed down.

"I think we should go," Sara said. "This place gives me the creeps."

"How about if we take some photos, then leave?" R.J. said.

"Yes," Ariel whispered, still holding David's hand. She looked as though she was standing in the middle of a haunted house.

Sara, seeming to forget her disguise, silently held out her hand to R.J. for the keys, then went to the car and got his camera out of the trunk. She was soon clicking away as fast as a digital camera could go, making a circle of the street. "Done," she said. "So let's go find out when the next ferry runs to take us out of here."

Everyone nodded in agreement.

But David held back. "We can't leave the

dog where it is. We have to at least move it out of the road." He started to pick it up by himself, but R.J. took one end of it and they set it on the far sidewalk, out of the way.

"I think I should tell someone about the dog," David said as he started toward the nearest house.

"I think we should get the girls out of here," R.J. said loudly.

For a moment David seemed torn between his sense of chivalry and his love of animals. But then he looked at Ariel's white face, and she won.

No one said anything as they got back into the car.

R.J. drove slowly back through the town, pausing now and then so Sara could snap photos out of the window. "I'll have a lot to show Charley," he said, forcing cheerfulness into his voice, but no one answered him.

He went down two more residential streets, but they still saw no people. The houses were big and showed that King's Isle had once been rich, but was now faded and poor. "I'll report to Charley that I think he can buy the entire place for about ten dollars," R.J. said to Sara.

"Do you think he *should* buy this place?" she whispered back.

R.J. drove down the main street again and they looked at the shops. Most of them were empty.

"There's fresh produce in that store," Sara said, almost with excitement in her voice. "There *are* people here."

There was what looked to be a café and a hardware store. But since there were no people, they couldn't tell what was open and what wasn't. R.J. started to turn back to the ferry, but at the end of the street was a big building. "I think I saw somebody," he said and kept going straight.

When he didn't make the turn, David said, "You missed the road!"

But Sara saw the big building at the end of the street and knew what was in R.J.'s mind. They'd come there for a purpose and R.J. meant to do his job. Maybe the big building could be turned into the clubhouse for a golf course, she thought. When he glanced at Sara and nodded toward the building, she knew they were in agreement.

It was a courthouse and, unlike the other buildings in town, it was in excellent repair. In fact, it was beautiful. It was two stories and looked much earlier than the Victorian houses in town. "Charley will like this," R.J. said.

"*I* like it," Sara said, then they both got out. Ariel and David stayed in the car.

Sara took photos of the courthouse and the street leading up to it, while R.J. walked around and looked at the building. "Yeah," he said, "Charley could make something out of this town. He could repair the houses, bring in some businesses, and make it into the resort his wife wants."

R.J. was smiling at the thought of telling Charley the good news when all hell broke loose. Out of nowhere came two police cars, one from the right and one from the left. The cars slammed on the brakes, just missing the sides of the rented Jag, and out jumped four armed policemen. Both Sara and R.J. stood where they were, too stunned to move. All four of the men surrounded R.J., as though they thought he was going to try to run for it.

"Are you the driver of this vehicle?" asked a tall, broad-shouldered man, his face serious.

"Yes, I am," R.J. said, smiling, trying to ingratiate himself to them.

What do they want? Sara thought. A donation?

To her horror, the policeman said, "Read him his rights," and in the next second R.J. was being handcuffed while someone Mirandized him.

Sara came out of her stupor. "What do you think you're doing?" she said loudly as she tried to move into the middle of the men.

"Get back!" R.J. said, but Sara didn't obey. When one of the cops pushed her aside, R.J. started to struggle and one of the policemen knocked him to the ground. He groaned when his knee hit the pavement. His lip was bleeding and he couldn't wipe the blood away because his hands were cuffed behind him. When a second cop pulled him upright, R.J.'s shoulder was wrenched half out of its socket.

"What's he charged with?" Sara asked, again trying to put herself between the cops and R.J.

"He killed John Nezbit's dog. Malicious homicide."

"What?!" Sara and R.J. shouted in unison.

A cop grabbed R.J.'s arm and started pulling him toward the courthouse door.

"You can't do this!" Sara shouted. "That dog was dead when we saw it."

"That's not what Mr. Nezbit says. He says he saw you swerve onto the sidewalk just so you could hit his dog."

"Sir!" David said to the policeman, and Sara was glad to see him. Even though R.J. ran a big corporation, he had a look about him of a street fighter. David was clean-cut personified. If anyone would be listened to, he would be. "Mr. Brompton saw the dog lying in the street and swerved onto the sidewalk to miss it. The dog was already dead— and had been for a long time. We moved it to the side of the street."

"That's not what Mr. Nezbit said," the policeman shot back, his fingers digging into R.J.'s arm. "He said you hit the dog so hard that your car went one way and the dog went the other. He said the four of you got out and laughed about it."

This was so absurd that all three of them—Ariel was still in the car—were stunned into momentary silence.

"That's not true," Sara gasped.

"Tell it to the judge," the policeman said, then pulled R. J. toward the courthouse.

"Sara, call my lawyer," R. J. shouted over his shoulder as they pulled him toward the door.

Relieved that the short-lived masquerade was over, Sara pulled off the wig and ran to the car to get her cellphone.

"At least this got you to stop lying to me," R. J. called as he disappeared into the courthouse. He was trying to inject some humor into the horrible situation.

Chapter Six

No signal.

Sara tossed the useless cellphone into the car and looked at David. Ariel was cringing in the backseat, saying nothing.

David turned to Sara and said, "Get in the car with Ariel and go back to the ferry. If the ferry isn't there, hire a boat. If you have to swim back to the mainland, do so, but I want the two of you off this island immediately."

Sara took a breath. "I'm sure that what you're saying would have sounded good in a 1950s Western, but this is the twenty-first century. You and Ariel go back. I'm going to get R.J. out of there." She started toward the courthouse, but David grabbed her arm.

"Where do you think you're going?"

"To find a telephone," she said, shaking off his grasp. "This seems to be the only building that has people in it, so I'm going in there to use their telephone."

"I'm sure this is all a mistake," David said. "Someone else must have seen us with that dog. In all those huge houses, there must have been someone who saw us."

Sara started to say something as she put her hand on the big brass door handle, but Ariel stopped her.

"Don't leave me alone," Ariel whispered. Her face was white with terror.

David put his arm around her shoulders. "Let me do the talking," he said to Sara as he opened the courthouse door. When she started to protest, he said, "This isn't about women's rights, this is just logic. Sara, you sound like a Yankee, and, Ariel, you're scared out of your mind, so who knows what you'd say? By default, that leaves me."

"I hope they don't throw me in jail because of my accent," Sara muttered. She thought she was being sarcastic, saying something that couldn't possibly happen.

But, in the end, that's just what did happen. The chief of the King's Isle police department put all four of them in jail. There were two cells that shared a wall of iron bars. Ariel and Sara were in one, David and R. J. in the other.

As soon as he saw them, R. J. looked at Sara and said, "What the hell have you done?!" It was a whisper that was a shout.

David, his hands manacled behind him, gave Sara a look over his shoulder that was intended to singe her hair.

Ariel and she weren't handcuffed and Sara knew that was because of Ariel's gracious manners. Even when she was being arrested, Ariel said "please" and "thank you" and never raised her voice.

When the policeman had removed David's handcuffs, then shut the doors on them, Ariel sat on the end of the bed, her back rigid, and looked straight ahead. She was in such a state of trauma that Sara didn't think she was capable of speech.

R. J. walked to the shared wall of bars and glared at Sara. "What did you do?"

She sat down on the opposite end of the bed from Ariel and tried to smile. "Did we ever fool you with our disguise?"

"Not for a second," R. J. said in dismissal. "I want to know why all of you are in here. Did you call my lawyer?"

"No signal," Sara said, looking down at her hands. She was trying to think how long it would be before R. J. was missed. No one would miss her until her rent was due, but R. J. was a different matter. How many of his adoring secretaries knew where he was going this weekend? The answer was that only she knew R. J.'s schedule.

"Sara," R. J. said quietly. "I'm waiting."

Before she could come up with a reply, David said, "She told the chief of police that you were a very important man and that you'd bring so many lawyers into this two-bit town that World War Two would look like a picnic."

"I see," R. J. said and when she glanced up at him she saw a twinkle in his eye. She knew he was thinking that she'd said exactly what he would have said if they'd given him time to talk. He put on a fake frown to cover his smile, then turned to David. "Not what she should have said, right?"

"No." David's face was stern, and he kept looking at Ariel, who seemed to be in a state of near catatonia.

Before R. J. could say anything else, the door that led into the cell opened and in came a man who had the air of a lawyer.

Lawyers came and went in R.J.'s office so often that Sara knew she could have picked them out naked (them naked, that is, not her). They had a certain walk and an arrogance that not even doctors could match.

The man was wearing a cheap, dark green summer suit. He was tall and thin, no lips at all, small eyes and a pointed nose, and he was chewing gum. In spite of the fact that he looked like a rat, he had a big smile and an attitude that said all of life was a laugh.

"Hi!" he said, as though the four people in the two cells were his long-long friends. "I heard you were in a predicament so I came right over to see if I could help. Now, which one of you is Sara?" As he said this he looked from her to Ariel, then back again. He stopped at Sara, as though he guessed she was the one with the big mouth.

"You have to apologize," he said, and when she nodded, he looked at R.J. "You the dog killer?"

R.J.'s face turned red and Sara could see that it was all he could do to keep from telling the man off.

David stepped between the two men—

behind the bars, that is. "I am David Allenton Tredwell," he said. "Of Arundel."

"Arundel, huh?" the man said. "Tea party people."

Sara looked at R.J. in question and he shrugged. What tea party? they wanted to know. Sara got up and moved closer to the bars.

David smiled. "Yes, sir, I am," he said proudly. "One of my ancestors—"

Rudely, the man turned away. "We're still loyal to the king around here and we drink tea, not coffee."

Sara started to laugh, but then she saw the look on the man's face. He was serious.

"I'm Lawrence Lassiter," he said, "and I'm an attorney. Unfortunately, there's only one attorney in town and I happen to be defending Mr. Nezbit. He's the man whose dog you killed."

"I didn't kill any dog," R.J. said softly, but in a voice that carried weight.

Lassiter stepped closer to the bar and narrowed his eyes at R.J. "I've known John Nezbit all my life and I know that he has responsibilities that would weigh heavy on any man. He has a wife and six children, all of whom he struggles to support. That dog of his . . ." The man paused and swiped at his eyes as though wiping away a tear. "He raised that dog from a puppy and it was a companion to his children and to him. That dog guarded his family from danger and watched over them while they slept. That you mainland people would maliciously run over that dear animal again and again, all while hanging out of the windows and laughing, is beyond anything we've ever heard of about you people."

When David started to say something, Sara saw R. J. put his hand on the younger man's arm. R. J. was watching the lawyer with narrowed eyes. Sara had seen that expression on R. J.'s face only twice before. Both times the recipient learned why R. J. Brompton was called "ruthless."

"That poor dog," the lawyer said, then pulled a handkerchief from his back pocket and wiped his nose. He lifted his chin and gave a little smile, as though he was smiling through his tears. "Oh, well, all we can do is warn our children about you people and hope that the stories will make them stay at home where they belong. So! Now it's done and you must pay the price."

"And how much would that be?" R. J.

asked in a voice that made the hairs on Sara's neck stand on end.

"I have no idea," Lassiter said, his eyebrows raised, as though R. J. had asked him an odd question. "That's up to the judge to decide. How much is the safety of a man's family worth?"

"We'll buy him a new dog," David said. "A trained guard dog. A rottweiler. Or a Doberman."

"I guess if it had been one of his children you'd buy him a new kid too, right?" Lassiter said as he looked at Ariel, who was staring at him, her face flushed, her eyes wide. "Or maybe you'd let one of these beautiful young ladies have a baby with him to replace the child you killed."

David grabbed the bars. "Is that the case you're going to present to the judge? That we might as well have killed a *child?!*"

"When do we see the judge?" R. J. asked quickly.

"Monday morning," Lassiter answered.

All four of them gasped. "Do you mean we have to spend three nights in here?" Sara asked. When she felt Ariel take her hand, Sara clung to it.

R. J. moved closer to the bars. "If your

case with Nezbit doesn't start until Monday, that means you're free to help *us* now. For a proper attorney's fee, that is."

"Wish I could help you there, but I can't," Lassiter said, chewing on his gum. "You see, everything you brought with you, including that fancy car, has been impounded by the independent government of King's Isle. The way things stand now, you only have the clothes on your backs, so how could you pay me?" Again, he looked at Ariel.

"I can have money wired to you," Sara said.

"Wired?" Lassiter chuckled. "Like Western Union? You know what happened the last time I tried to help some tourists that were in a similar situation to yours? They gave me a check, but when they got back to the mainland, they canceled it. I called them, but you know what they did? They changed their phone number. When I went over to the mainland, I found out that they'd moved and left no forwarding address. Can you imagine that?"

For a moment they were all silent as they thought about what he'd said. To get away from him—or was it to get away from King's Isle?—people had had to leave their home.

"If we could get you money, cash," R.J. said, "could you get us out of here?"

"Sure. It's not like you can go anywhere, is it? There's no ferry until Monday afternoon and no one in town is gonna help you. Not after what you did to Fenny's poor dog."

"Fenny?" R.J. asked. "I thought his name was John."

"John Fenwick Nezbit. Good old name." He looked at David with a sneer. "Of course it's not like the names in Arundel that carry old money with them, is it?"

For the first time, Ariel moved close to the bars and smiled at the lawyer. "Personally, I hate coffee," she said in the sweetest voice anyone had ever heard. "And, Mr. Lassiter, I understand your reluctance to trust people who didn't grow up on your beautiful island. Perhaps this would persuade you to help us." She pulled off her ring and handed it to him. It was small but exquisite: a sapphire surrounded by diamonds. Sara guessed that the ring was worth at least twelve grand. Smiling in a gracious way, Ariel handed the ring through the bars to the lawyer.

Sara held her breath. She could believe that he'd take the ring and they'd never see him again. But he smiled at Ariel, then yelled,

"Ike!," and a policeman came through the door and unlocked the cells. Sara knew she'd never heard anything in her life as good as the key turning in that lock!

As soon as the door swung open, Sara wanted to run out into the sunshine, but R. J. and David held back, so Ariel and she stayed with them. "If you represent Nezbit, who represents *us* on Monday morning?" R. J. asked.

The man looked David up and down, his upper lip sneering. "He looks like a lawyer in the making. Let him defend you. As for the rest of you, an apology and a fine should do it."

"What did Ariel do?" David asked.

"Illegally parked," the lawyer said quickly. "She was in a car that was parked on the courthouse steps. The whole town saw it. Well, that's all the help I can give you for now. Just show up Monday morning."

"Where can we stay?" Ariel asked. "Sir. I mean . . ."

He smiled at her. "There's no hotel here, if that's what you mean, but there is a boarding-house. But the landlady wants money and yours is being kept for the moment." He shrugged.

"That's illegal!" David said, taking a step toward the lawyer. Again R.J. caught his arm.

"Let me give you some advice, Mr. Rich Kid from Snooty Arundel: Keep your mouth shut. Don't ask any questions of anybody. You know how to mow a lawn? Paint a house? Then get a job and let people pay you in food and a bed. Come Monday morning, show up here at nine A.M. sharp and say 'yes, sir' and 'no, sir' to the judge. Pay your fine, then get off King's Isle, and never come back. You understand me?"

"Yes, sir, he does," Ariel said quickly. "We all understand you and we're going to do just what you said. Aren't we, David?"

Sara could see the conflict on David's beautiful face. She doubted if he'd had much bad happen to him in his life, so he believed in the goodness of people. He probably believed that if you talked to a person and explained the situation, he'd see your point of view. Sara wanted to put her arms around him and comfort him.

When she glanced at R.J., she could see that he was trying not to look at the lawyer with hostility as that would only hurt them. "Is there any possibility of a sentence other than a fine?" he asked the lawyer, who was at the door.

When Lassiter turned, his face showed his gloating. He loves this! Sara thought. "Yeah, sure. You could get six to eight months in jail. Depends on the judge's mood. And how good a case against you I present, of course."

"You can't—" Sara began.

Lassiter cut her off. "Can't what, little New York missy?" His eyes were angry, full of hate. "Can't send a rich man to jail? I can assure you, missy, that our courts here may be small, but they're legal. For all that we protest, we pay taxes to your American government so we are, on paper, part of it. By the time your lawyers prepare a case and by the time our one and only judge who, by the way, is Fenny Nezbit's uncle, has time to hear the case, your sentence will be up. Tell me, Mr. Rich and Powerful"—he looked at R. J.—"do you think we're so stupid that we can't delay a hearing a whole eight months and keep you in jail that entire time?"

When R. J. didn't answer, the lawyer left the jail area laughing.

David, R. J., and Sara stood where they were, staring at the closed door with their mouths open, their brains in a state of shock. Eight months in a jail cell!

It was Ariel who started toward the door and the rest of them followed her. What had to be the entire police force of King's Isle was in the outer office and smirking in triumph. They held their heads high and walked out without a word. Once they were outside, they looked at one another, then without a word, they grabbed hands and started running.

They ran down the main street of the island toward the narrow road that led to the ferry. Sara didn't know what they were thinking. That maybe the ferry would be there and they'd jump on it, sail away, and forget that this ever happened?

But when they got to the ferry landing, the dock was empty. They separated, feeling a bit embarrassed about holding hands and acting so childish, and each person found a place on the dock to be alone and to collect him/herself. They were in a state of shock. They had no car, no money, and they had to appear before a judge in two and a half days.

Chapter Seven

"Why were you so afraid of this island?" Sara asked Ariel.

"Afraid of the place?" R. J. asked, looking from Sara and Ariel. "Who was afraid of it?"

Sara nodded toward Ariel. "In New York she told me she was terrified of it and didn't want to go."

R. J. stood up and looked out toward the water, as though he might be able to see the ferry. There was nothing, not so much as a fishing boat in sight. He looked back at Sara. "When you two were in New York and planning this charade to dupe me into believing that you weren't who you were, is that when she told you information that you could have passed on to me?"

"I'm sure that if I'd told you that my cousin said King's Isle was a bad place, you would have called off your plans to go." When R. J. said nothing, Sara looked at him harder. "You knew, didn't you? You researched this place by yourself. You don't do anything by yourself, but you researched this island without me." Standing, she advanced on him. "What did you see that you didn't want *me* to see? And why didn't you tell me there was a possibility of problems?"

R. J. looked at David and Ariel as though for support, but they were looking at him with interest. "A few websites mentioned that past visitors had had some problems here, but it wasn't something that I concerned myself with."

"You were concerned enough that you hid them from me," Sara said, still advancing on him. "Why didn't you tell me?"

"Why didn't you tell *me* that you wanted to get away from me so much that you were willing to treat me like a fool and wear that stupid wig and those clothes? Who made that jacket?"

"Chanel," Ariel said. "Don't blame Sara, it was all my idea."

"But she went along with it. Is this why

you were so tired for the last weeks? You and your cousin figuring out how to make me look like an idiot? Is that what you think I am, Sara?"

"Don't you turn this on me!" Sara said. "Ariel and I did this—" She waved her hand in dismissal. "Why we did it doesn't matter now. The point is that you kept vital information from us and that's why we're in this situation now."

"You wouldn't have listened to me," he said. "Since when have you been interested in scary stories?"

"He's right," Ariel said. "*I* tried to warn you, but you wouldn't listen to me either."

Sara sat down on a piling and looked out at the water. "I guess everything is my fault." When no one spoke, she looked up at them. Ariel and R. J. seemed to agree with her, but David was frowning.

"I'd say it was Ariel's fault," he said. "After all, she was the one who got Mrs. Dunkirk to get her husband to—"

"What?!" R. J. shouted. "How could *you* manipulate a man like Charley Dunkirk?" He stopped talking and looked at Ariel in speculation.

She, in turn, only looked at her hands.

David stepped forward and looked at R. J. "Blaming people isn't going to help. We need to think about how we're going to live for the next few days. We're in a hostile town, with no money, and no outside communication. And as for Ariel, yes, she warned us."

"But no one said anything to me," R. J. said, sounding sulky and left out.

"And you told no one what you knew," Sara snapped back at him.

"I think I liked it better when you didn't talk to me," he said.

"You should be so lucky."

"Could you two stop arguing for a minute?" Ariel said. "We need a place to spend the night. What about that house we saw with the sign in the window? Maybe we can bargain for a room."

"Let's pool our resources and see what we have," R. J. said.

"I have a watch," Sara said as she unfastened the little gold band and placed it on top of the piling. She looked at R. J. "It was a gift so I don't know how much it's worth."

"Ten grand," he said, taking off his own watch and putting it beside hers. "My watch is worth about thirty-nine dollars. Or was worth that when I bought it five years ago."

Sara was glaring at him. "You gave me a ten-thousand-dollar watch as a Christmas gift?" she said to R.J. "That's not what you're supposed to give to your employees."

"It's my money so I'll do what I want with it. You," he said, nodding to David, "what do you have?"

David reached inside his shirt and pulled out a gold chain. "This is worth a few hundred," he said as he added it to the pile.

"I didn't know you wore a necklace," Ariel said, looking at David.

"Believe it or not, there are a lot of things you don't know about me."

"I doubt that," Ariel said as she removed her earrings. "Diamonds. Worth about five thousand. The necklace is valued at twelve thousand," she said as she started to unfasten the clasp. When David reached out to help her, Ariel turned to R.J. "Would you, Mr. Brompton?"

"Sure, honey," he said, undoing the clasp to her necklace.

"Don't let him touch you," Sara said, still glaring at R.J. "I want to know why you gave me a ten-thousand-dollar watch for Christmas. That is not an appropriate gift."

"You like it, don't you?" R.J. said. "It

keeps good time, doesn't it? And you've worn it every day since you got it, so what's the problem?"

"The problem is that I work for you and you shouldn't give such an expensive gift to an employee. You give a watch like this to your girlfriend."

"Good heavens, Ariel!" David said as she put her fourth piece of jewelry on top of the piling. "How much jewelry are you wearing?"

"Counting the ring in my navel?"

All three of them looked at her in astonishment.

Ariel smiled sweetly. "What I have or do not have in my navel is no one's business."

"Good for you," Sara said. "Don't let them boss you around."

"You know," R.J. said slowly, looking at Ariel, "you looked just like Sara when you said that. It's that haughty, I'm-better-than-you look that she gives me when she doesn't want to be bothered."

"Which is pretty much all the time," David said.

"Exactly." R.J. tipped his chin back and lowered his lashes. " 'Leave me alone. I'm divine and you're not.'"

David laughed. "Perfect. Even if they

didn't look alike, I'd know they were related. Tell me, does Sara let you know that only *she* can do it correctly, whatever 'it' is?"

"All the time. My only defense is to pile work on her. 'Here, if you're so good at managing the world, I'll let you do it.' If only she could type . . ."

"Yeah, Ariel too."

Both men were laughing. They were sitting on opposite sides of the weathered piling, their legs crossed, the women sitting on either side of them.

Ariel grabbed the pile of jewelry, leaving behind the two pieces the men had contributed and giving Sara back her watch. Without a word between them, the two women stood, locked arms, and started down the road into town.

"I hate both of them," Sara said.

"Me too," Ariel said, then sighed. "Sara, as much as I love this female bonding, what are we going to *do*? We need to make arrangements about eating and sleeping, that sort of thing."

"I don't know what to do, but let's not tell the men that." She glanced over her shoulder, disappointed that the men hadn't come after them.

Ariel slowed her pace, still holding onto her cousin's arm. "I don't think that what they did to R.J. today was unusual. I've heard that these islanders accuse people of a crime they didn't commit in order to get money from them."

"I've already figured that out, but don't worry, R.J. will fix it. By tomorrow he'll have helicopters here and more lawyers than can fill an ocean. He'll call Charley Dunkirk and he'll fix everything. I think we should find a place to spend the night, get some food, then—"

"Look! I hear people!"

They were standing near the junction to the main street of King's Isle and they could hear people talking, as though a crowd was moving toward them.

Sara held onto her cousin's arm. "Do you think it's a lynch mob coming for us?"

"I don't know how you can make jokes after what happened."

For a long moment, Sara and Ariel stood still, arm in arm, looking at the street that earlier had been like a ghost town. Perfectly ordinary-looking people, dressed in perfectly ordinary clothes, were milling about. Some were opening shops and some were walking down the street. There were a few children running, throwing dirt and being yelled at by their mothers. Girls, boys, men, and women, all moving about, laughing, talking. Ordinary, except that not one of them glanced at them.

At last the men caught up with them. "It's like the curtain going up on a play," David said. "One minute the stage is bare and quiet, then the curtain goes up and there are lots of people."

"It's *too much* like a stage set for my taste," R. J. said, looking hard at the people in front of them. "Do you think they don't see us? Or have they been told to ignore us?"

"I vote that we go to that place where we saw the sign, ROOMS TO LET, and see if we can get some accommodation for the night," Ariel said as she held up a gold necklace with four pearls on it. "Do you think this will buy us a couple of rooms for a night? Or two?"

"One night is all we need," R. J. said. "Tomorrow I'll find a telephone and get us out of here. What say you, my lords and ladies, that we join this play?"

Ariel grimaced. "What I want to know is, is it a tragedy or a comedy?"

"Life is what we make of it," David said. His tone was so exaggeratedly happy that Sara and R.J. groaned. "Okay, so maybe in this place we have to work a little harder to be able to see the good." He wiped his hands over his eyes. "I could almost believe that none of what happened did. Are we really to appear in court on Monday morning to answer a charge of killing a dog?"

"No," R.J. said firmly. "Once I get hold of my lawyer, he'll send half a dozen men down here and drown the entire police force in paper. There won't be any court hearing on Monday." He glanced at Sara and gave a little smile to let her know that his plan was exactly what she'd told the cops would happen.

Sara had to turn away so R.J. wouldn't see her smile. She knew how his mind worked. So maybe she'd been wrong to try to strong-arm the police here on little King's Isle, but it was the way she'd learned from watching R.J. He had power and he knew how to use it. She had every confidence in the world that R.J. would get them out of this ridiculous situation.

"Shall we go to the rooming house?" Sara asked. "We might as well enjoy our time here," she said, then her stomach gave a growl. "Sorry."

"My stomach thinks my throat's been cut," R.J. said, making Sara look at him in surprise. Usually he was careful to not show his country upbringing, so he never used old sayings like that one.

"Do you think they sell cosmetics in this town?" Ariel asked. "Lancôme or Estée Lauder, maybe."

"Maybe Maybelline," Sara said as they walked down the main street and headed toward where they'd seen the house with the sign.

People smiled at them as they walked, but no one stared. It all seemed so normal that with every step they took, it was harder to remember the events of earlier that day.

"Were we really in jail?" Sara asked softly. "Or did we make that up?"

Ariel looked at her cousin as though she'd lost her mind. "We have no car and no money. We have to spend the night here, but we have no luggage. How can you think that we made anything up?"

"It just seems so . . . I don't know . . . normal, I guess."

"It doesn't seem normal at all," Ariel said.

"One minute the town is empty and the next it's full of people who are doing their best not to look at us."

"She's right," R.J. said. "The sooner we get out of here, the better."

"I agree," David said.

Sara sighed. "I'm just so glad to get away from work for a few days that—" Breaking off, she glanced at R.J. "Sorry."

"No need to be," he said. "I'm glad to get away from work too." They could see the house with the faded sign just ahead of them. R.J. looked at David. "At work, I have an assistant who is quite efficient—"

"Except that she can't type or take shorthand," Sara said.

"Right. But she can remember things. She's better than any of those talking machines that you have to type things into."

"So what's wrong with her?" David asked, opening the little gate in front of the house.

"She hates me. Pure and simple hates me. Most of the time when I ask her a question she won't even answer."

As David let the others go through the gate, he looked at Sara. "Is that true? Does his assistant hate him?"

Sara gave him a little smile, but when she

didn't answer, R.J. laughed. "See what I mean?"

They walked up the stairs to the porch of the big old house and R.J. knocked on the front door. They heard nothing.

"The owner's probably in the streets with the other residents pretending to be something he's not," Ariel said.

Sara raised her hand to knock again, but the door was opened by a woman—and the four of them were shocked into speechlessness. She was tall, good-looking, in her early forties, and dressed in cotton trousers and a shirt. It would have been an ordinary outfit if it hadn't been so tight. Buttons bulged over her large breasts. She'd tied the tail of the shirt around her waist so there was an inch of trim, tanned flesh showing. Her trousers were tightly belted and so snug around her hips that if she'd had a tattoo you probably could have read it.

But it was her expression that was the most lascivious. She looked greedy as she smiled warmly at the two men. The women stepped back and the men stepped forward.

"Hello," David and R.J. said in unison. They were in front of Sara and Ariel, blocking their view. "We've come about—" Again, they said the words together.

The woman laughed. "I know who you are and I can guess why you're here. Come in, please, but don't mind the way I look. I've been painting the back hallway."

David and R.J. stepped through the doorway, their eyes on the woman and hers on them.

Ariel looked at Sara as though to ask if they should dare enter the house. "As long as she doesn't try to get in the bathtub with me, I don't care what she looks like," Sara said, following the men into the house.

When the four of them were inside, the woman said, "I'm Phyllis Vancurren and welcome to King's Isle, although I imagine you wish you'd never set foot on the place." Turning, she started down the hall, motioning for them to follow. "I just made some tea. Would you like some?"

David and R.J. practically ran after her, but Sara and Ariel held back. "I like Larry Lassiter the lawyer more than I do her," Ariel said.

"I'm sure she's a fine person and has nothing on her mind except giving us food and a place to stay."

When Ariel looked at Sara with wide eyes, Sara grinned. "If they're casting a play for the woman who looks in the mirror to see if she's the most beautiful, then kills the girl who's prettier than she is, there she is."

"Come along, girls," Phyllis called over her shoulder. "By the time you two slow-pokes get to the kitchen the tea will be all gone."

"Who do you think she wants?" Sara asked under her breath.

"David," Ariel said instantly. "She wants David."

"I don't see why. R. J. is smarter."

"You don't think about smart when you want to go to bed with someone."

"True, but the morning *does* come," Sara said.

The two women walked into the kitchen to see R. J. and David sitting at a big oak table drinking iced tea out of tall glasses.

"I was beginning to think that the two of you got lost," Phyllis said, her voice a sort of purr.

"Do you have a telephone?" Sara asked.

"I already told R. J. that no one on the island has a working phone right now. And we won't have any for about ten more days. A trawler hit the underground cable and cut it in half." Phyllis filled more glasses with ice and tea. "Usually we're quite modern here on King's Isle. We have telephones and even the Internet, but right now we're in the dark ages. The dark ages with electricity and flush toilets, that is." She looked at R.J. and David as though she'd made a very funny joke. They laughed as though she had.

"Do you have rooms to rent?" Ariel asked.

"Honey, as you can see, that's all I do have. I have rooms and rooms and more rooms. They all need painting and fixing up, but I do have them."

Again the men laughed as though she'd said something witty.

Sara gave a fake smile. "So how much do you charge?"

"Whatever you have. Or you can send me a check when you get back to the mainland. I'm flexible." She looked at R.J. with lowered lashes. "You look like a man who pays his bills."

"Yeah," R.J. said in a husky voice. "Actually, Sara pays them, but I put the money in the bank."

Phyllis looked at Sara. "So you *work* for him. I thought maybe you were couples."

She looked at David. "What about you? Married?"

"He's engaged to me," Ariel said too loudly.

Phyllis looked Ariel up and down. "Interesting. You two girls certainly look alike. I can hardly tell you apart. I guess you're sisters."

"Cousins," Ariel said. "Is there somewhere I can freshen up?"

"You want the toilet, don't you? There's no use being fancy around here."

Ariel's face turned red as she gave Phyllis the look, but the older woman didn't seem to notice.

"Come on," Phyllis said, "I'll show you your rooms. I've put you in the nanny's suite. I hope that's all right. The man who built this house had eight kids and he didn't want to see or hear any of them, so he made a whole suite in the attic. There're a couple of air conditioners up there so you won't be hot. It's two bedrooms, a big bathroom that you'll have to share, and a little sitting room. Come along. Follow me."

Ariel and Sara were the first ones out of the kitchen, but the men stepped in front of them to follow behind Phyllis. When she went up the wide staircase, her hips swayed from one side to the other so much that she almost hit the wall and the railing. Behind her, with their eyes glued to her backside, came R. J. and David. The Pied Piper didn't have such mesmerized followers.

Ariel caught David's arm. "She said, 'I've put you in the nanny's suite.' "

"So?" he asked.

"She was telling us that she knew we were coming. She's putting us up there for a reason."

"Ariel," David said with exaggerated patience, "I know that what's happened to us has been awful, but I don't think this entire island could be as bad as you think it is. If this were the nineteenth century, maybe, but not now."

"You're so right, David. What was I thinking? Nowadays there is no murder or crime of horrific proportions. All the serial killers have been caught. All the criminals put away. And, besides, you've been to college while I stayed behind in our sleepy little town, so what could I possibly know?" She stepped in front of him and went up the stairs.

Behind her, David threw up his hands in exasperation, then followed Ariel.

Chapter Eight

On the way up the stairs, R.J. whispered to Sara, "You two need to stop glowering. Get on her good side."

"Like you and David are doing?" she said as she moved beside Ariel. "So how much do you hate her?"

"Scale of one to ten? About a thousand."

"Me? A million."

"Look at them," Ariel said. "They're like cartoon characters drooling over her." Phyllis Vancurren was bulging out of her shirt and trousers and the men were doing their best to see all that wasn't showing—which wasn't much.

"Wonder why she put us way up at the top of the house?" Sara asked. Then, stepping on a creaking floorboard, said, "Better than an alarm system."

On the second floor, Phyllis pointed out her own bedroom. It was a huge room, with a four-poster bed that was draped in a fine cotton-and-silk blend.

"That fabric costs at least two hundred dollars a yard," Ariel whispered to Sara, "and in the hall I saw what looked to be three genuine Hepplewhite chairs with new upholstery."

"If she doesn't need money, then why is she taking in roomers?"

Ariel nodded toward David.

"You think she wants David?" Sara gasped.

Ahead of them, Phyllis and the men had stopped chatting.

"My goodness!" Ms. Vancurren said, looking at Ariel as they entered the sitting room. "What a look!"

"Don't mind Ariel, she's just nervous about Monday," R.J. said. Behind Phyllis's back, he gave Ariel a warning look to be nice.

"Ah, yes, that," Ms. Vancurren said. She sat down on one of the two little sofas in the sitting room and spread her arms across the back, which made her breasts even more prominent. David and R.J., eyes glazed, sat on the sofa across from her. "I guess you want to know about that."

Sara and Ariel sat on chairs that had been upholstered with fabric adorned with a bunny rabbit pattern and they all listened to what the woman was saying. As she talked, Sara looked about the room. There were bars on the windows—to keep children from falling out, or to keep them in? Had they left prison to return to prison?

First, Ms. Vancurren told them about herself, saying that she wasn't from King's Isle. She'd married an older man who lived in Pennsylvania, and when he died she was horrified to find out that he'd left everything to his first wife. All she got was an old house on the island where his father had grown up, and a tiny insurance policy. It was enough to live on, but not enough to have any fun with. "If you know what I mean," she said. Both men nodded vigorously.

Sara and Ariel exchanged looks. They didn't believe a word of it. Next, Phyllis told them that Fenny Nezbit was a loser and a liar, but he was the judge's relative, and the Nezbit family had lived on the island for centuries. "So what I'm saying is that it could go either way on Monday."

"Why was the town empty today?" Sara asked.

"Annual Whale Day," she said, smiling. "We're a small island and we all know one another, so we tend to do things together. You can imagine our surprise when we got back and heard all that had gone on."

"Lassiter said there were witnesses who would testify that we had . . ." R.J. couldn't seem to go on.

"Maybe there are witnesses, but did you ask the sheriff's men about them?" Phyllis seemed to be hinting that the witnesses wouldn't be all they were supposed to be.

"Actually, we didn't really get a chance to talk to anyone," David said.

"If I were you," Phyllis said with an air of conspiracy, "I wouldn't worry too much. I'm sure Judge Proctor will throw out everything on Monday morning. And I'm sure that the entire police force knows that you didn't kill a dog. It's just that in the past we've had some problems with outsiders, so the police tend to be careful."

"What happened to make the police suspicious of outsiders?" Sara asked quickly.

Phyllis waved her hand as though that wasn't important, then looked at Ariel and smiled. "I can see that you've heard some of those outrageous stories about us. We are truly wicked people." She said this as though it couldn't possibly be true.

"What stories?" R.J. asked, at last leaning back against the couch. He was a man of the world so he'd seen lots of women with the raw sex appeal that this woman had, but David was watching her with his mouth slightly open.

"Oh, you know," Ms. Vancurren said, then moved on the couch in a way that made her breasts jiggle.

"No, I don't know." R.J. narrowed his eyes as he looked at her. Sara wanted to hug him! Was he beginning to look past what he was being told and see underneath? Underneath something besides her clothes, that is.

The woman glanced at Sara, then at Ariel. "You mean you haven't heard how we kidnap mainlanders?" She gave a smile that was supposed to make her look innocent, but it lost its effect since two-thirds of her breasts were exposed. "According to the mainlanders, we arrest tourists and keep them in jail for absolutely years."

R.J. raised an eyebrow at her. "And you don't?"

She shrugged in a way that almost made her right breast pop out of her shirt. When she moved, Sara saw the front of her bra and she was sure it was Aubade. If she was broke, how did she afford French underwear? "I have some work I must do and I know that you have things you want to do." She gave the men a leering look, as though she knew all of them were going to jump into an orgy as soon as she left.

When she stood up, R.J. and David jumped to their feet, and Sara was afraid they were going to ask the woman to stay.

"I'll leave you to it then," Phyllis said. "Sorry about your luggage being impounded, but you'll get it back."

"And the car and all our cash?" Sara asked.

"Is there somewhere we could get dinner?" R.J. asked.

"Oh, you poor babies," she said, purring toward the men—and not answering Sara's question. "If I could cook, I'd make you a fabulous meal." She gave a little look that said she may not be able to cook but that she had, well . . . other talents. "Go to the pub and tell them to put your meal on my account."

As she left the room, the two men fell all over themselves thanking her for her generosity.

Ten minutes later, the four of them were heading down the stairs, but Sara was hanging back.

"What are you doing?" Ariel whispered.

"Counting steps and seeing which ones make noise. If we want to get out of this place, we need silence, and a way to avoid this old-house alarm."

"Good thinking. Cover me," Ariel said. "I need to do something."

"You—?" Sara began, but Ariel had already tiptoed back up the stairs.

As soon as the three of them were outside, David said, "Where is she?"

"Bathroom," Sara answered.

"Ariel is snooping, isn't she?" David said.

"I really have no idea. I wonder why the people here call an American restaurant a 'public house' as they do in England?" she said, trying to change the subject.

Five minutes later, Ariel came out the front

door and Sara went to her. "What did you do?" she whispered.

"I wanted to try the telephone that I saw in her bedroom. It was dead. I didn't have time to see if the problem was that it was unplugged before I heard her coming."

"I wish you'd be more careful. I don't trust that woman," Sara said. "And where did you learn to sneak around like that?"

"When you have a mother like mine, you learn to sneak—and lie. I'm good at both. Wait up!" she called to the men and hurried ahead.

R.J. stopped walking and held out his arm to Sara. She took it.

"We'll fix this," David said. "After a good dinner—"

" 'Eat, drink, and be merry,' " R.J. quoted.

" 'For tomorrow we die,' " Sara finished.

Chapter Nine

When they reached the restaurant the locals called a pub, all four of them smiled. The interior did indeed look like an English pub, down to the horse brasses hanging around the huge walk-in fireplace. It was warm weather so the fire wasn't lit, but it was easy to imagine that it was lovely when it was.

The waitress treated them as though she was used to strangers. None of the other patrons so much as glanced at them as they were shown to their booth. Ariel and Sara sat beside each other, the men across from them.

The waitress passed out menus, photo-copied sheets inserted into those old-fashioned black-trimmed plastic holders.

The men ordered beers, Sara ordered a gin and tonic, while Ariel asked for sparkling water with a slice of lime.

"I think we should try to enjoy our time on the island," David said when the waitress was gone.

"Should we enjoy the 'no money' part first or the 'coming trial' part first?" Sara asked.

David acted like she hadn't spoken. "We've met someone good, we have a charge account, and we'll get off the island on Monday. Someday we'll look back on all this as an adventure."

The waitress gave them their drinks and as soon as she was out of earshot, Sara said, "I don't trust that Vancurren woman," then the women laughed because Ariel had said the same thing at the same time.

"Boo, hissss," R.J. said, sipping his beer. "Both of you are jealous."

"Of what?!" Ariel and Sara demanded, then laughed again, because again, they'd said the same thing together.

"We were good at exchanging places," Sara said.

"You were abysmal," R.J. said. "Although I like your new clothes, and what did you do with that wig? Do they make it in red?"

"That doesn't matter," Sara said, "and don't start another argument. Ariel and I don't trust her and we don't like her."

"And every word she spoke was a lie," Ariel said.

R.J. looked at David. "Did she talk? I didn't notice that she could talk, did you?"

"I thought she was a deaf mute," David said. "Never said a word, but the hand gestures were nice."

"Both of you are despicable," Sara said.

"I agree," Ariel said. "Any woman could dress like that and look like that, but a lady—"

She cut herself off because both David and R.J. pointedly looked at her breasts. Neither Ariel nor Sara was flat-chested by any means, but neither were they burdened with breasts the size of cantaloupes.

Ariel was unperturbed. "Wherever do you think she found a surgeon on this island?" she asked in mock innocence.

"She could have had them done in California," Sara said. "You know, back when they were pioneering implants. I wonder what they're full of? Some poisonous gel? Maybe she should have them checked."

"Okay, you two," R.J. said, grinning. "Have you decided what you want to eat?"

"Seafood," Sara said.

"Yes, definitely seafood," David said, then he and Sara smiled at each other. They were making a joke because there was nothing but seafood on the menu.

"Let's see," Sara said, thoroughly pleased to have David's attention, "they have fried seafood, steamed seafood, or grilled seafood. Or, they mix seafood with other seafood, then they fry it or steam it, or they put it all together in a little dish and bake it." David was smiling more broadly with every word she spoke.

"Could you just say what you want to eat without the editorial?" R.J. snapped.

With David's laughing eyes on her, Sara put her finger on the menu, ran it down the page, stopped, then looked. "Number eight. Fried clams, flounder, and shrimp." When David did the same thing, she said, "What did you get?"

"Oysters," he said in a low, seductive voice that suggested the long-held belief that oysters give a person sexual appetite. Sara laughed suggestively right back at him. R.J.'s glare was making her feel good—and after the events of the day, she needed whatever could make her feel good. "Oysters . . ." she said. "Oh, yes. Let's have oysters."

The waitress's arrival stopped Sara from saying more and they gave their orders. As soon as she left, Sara looked at David to let him know she was ready to continue the teasing, but R. J. leaned across the table to Ariel and said, "I want to hear everything you know about this island."

Ariel looked around the restaurant as though she thought the other people in the restaurant were listening. "I've been told that they do what was done to us," she said.

"Anything else?" he asked.

"That isn't enough?"

"I guess it is," R. J. said. "The Internet sites say the same thing. I just thought you might know something more."

The food came and as they ate, they tried to talk of something other than their predicament, but it was difficult.

The waitress returned for their dessert order. Sara was full, but wondered if this would be their last meal. They had yet to tell the waitress they were charging everything to Ms. Vancurren. Was her credit good? Or would they be washing dishes? she wondered.

When the waitress handed the men their plates of apple pie and put the bill on the table, R.J. told her that the meal was to be put on the account of Phyllis Vancurren. For a moment Sara thought the young woman was going to take the desserts back. She pursed her lips and frowned, then said that they could charge a meal one time, but never again. She went away in a huff, and for the first time, the other people in the restaurant looked at them. Sara wanted to slide down the seat in embarrassment.

For a moment the four of them were quiet. Sara picked up a fork and began to share a piece of pie with David.

"I wish I'd ordered another drink before I told her," R.J. muttered and Sara smiled.

"I'm just glad we didn't tell her before we ate," David said and Sara smiled more.

"What are we going to do for food tomorrow?" Ariel asked.

Again they were quiet, but then R.J. took the pen out of the plastic folder the waitress had left and pulled a napkin out of the metal holder. "Let's make a list of useful things that we can do. Maybe we can get enough work to feed ourselves for a few days."

"We'll work for food and a bed, just as Lassiter said," David said, and for once Sara was glad for his gung-ho attitude.

"I can mow lawns," Sara said. "In fact, I might be the best at mowing lawns of any other person on the planet. I can even mow them in patterns. I once wrote a kid's initials in the grass."

When she finished, the others were looking at her in a way that she couldn't read.

"Lawn mowing," R.J. wrote, but no one could read his writing so Sara took the napkin and pen away from him and wrote "lawn mowing" legibly.

She looked at R.J. "You can lay brick."

R.J. grimaced and she knew that his pride was hurt. He could make multimillion-dollar deals, but she didn't think there would be any call for those on King's Isle. Suddenly, the seriousness of everything hit her. She looked at the napkin and saw the two items. How had they come to this? What had they done to deserve this? What would happen to them if the judge decided that R.J. was guilty?

It was David who lightened the air. "Sara,"

he said seriously, "have you no pity? Maybe your boss used to lay bricks when he was younger, but he can't do it now, not with the extra weight he's carrying."

Sara looked up at David with her mouth open in shock. Was he trying to start a fight? Did he want R.J. to drag him out into the alley? But then David winked at her and she understood.

"Listen, kid," R.J. said, "I can still do a day's work and this so-called weight I'm carrying is dormant muscle."

That made them laugh. Dormant muscle!

When R.J. looked at Sara, she knew he was aware that David had purposely saved them from depression and R.J. was grateful. "Put me down there for brick laying or any kind of construction." He looked at David. "And what can a blue-eyed darlin' like Jock here do?"

"Put on your list that I could be a style consultant," Ariel said.

"For what?" Sara said. "Are you going to help them decide between the Dolce and Gabbana or the Armani for the gala?"

Ariel didn't smile. "I'm going to teach Phyllis Vancurren to dress her age."

Sara laughed. She'd been topped.

At that moment a man walked past their table, bumped into it, then caught himself before he fell. David reached out to catch him but the man righted himself. He was short, thin, ugly, had a beer in one hand, and the unmistakable look of a long-term drunk.

Sara moved the napkin with the list away from the man's hand before he knocked it off the table.

"Yeah, that's it," the man said, slurring his words. "Move away from me, missy. High-class goods like you can't be near some-body like me."

Sara kept her head down.

"You want to get away from her?" she heard R.J. say and there was fight in his voice.

When she looked at R.J., she saw that he was about to get out of his seat and go af-ter the man, but David was doing his best to keep R.J. pinned in place against the wall.

The drunken man stood at the end of the table for a moment, blinking to clear his vi-sion. He looked from Ariel to Sara, then back again, then shook his head. Sara knew that with her Ariel wig on they looked enough alike to be twins.

She could feel the tension of the two men at the table and she was afraid they were going to do something rash. She looked back toward the bar, intending to summon help, but everyone in there and at the tables was studiously looking down and ignoring them.

She was just about to get up and see if she could coax the man away from their table when he stood up straight. He stumbled to get his balance, then walked toward the bar.

Everyone let out a sigh of relief when he was gone. Sara made a quick glance about the room and saw that the patrons had started eating again. They made her angry. It was as though they thought that anything bad happened to them was deserved. R. J. caught her eye and they exchanged looks. He too had seen the lack of reaction from the other patrons.

"Only centuries of inbreeding can create something like that," R. J. said and they all smiled. The man had indeed been ugly: skinny, with big, stand-out ears. His skin was sallow, his cheeks shrunken and covered with bristles of gray.

"How old do you think he is?" David

asked. "I have an idea he's no more than forty-five, but he looks much older. Hard island life, I guess."

In the next moment the front door opened and a man came in. His face was red, as though he'd just come in from being on a boat. As David and Sara watched—the other two couldn't see over the backs of the benches—the man went to the bar, ordered a beer, then slapped the drunk on the back. "Got a new dog yet, Fenny?" he asked loudly. A hush fell over the restaurant and the bartender nodded toward their booth. When the man saw David and Sara, his face turned an ugly shade of purple and he hurried out of the restaurant before he was served his beer.

The four of them fell back against the tall backs of the booth. To say it was silent in the restaurant was an understatement. Sara was sure she could hear the linoleum cracking. In the next moment noises came from the bar, but she didn't turn around to see what was happening. They knew that the drunk, a.k.a. John Fenwick Nezbit, was being ushered out of the building.

Sara glanced at David and saw that even he had lost his smile. "That's what we're up against?" he whispered. "A judge might believe *him* over *us?*"

"Come on," R.J. said, "let's get out of here."

They kept their heads high and their eyes straight ahead as they walked out of the restaurant. Sara could feel the people around them working hard not to stare.

Once outside, they slowly walked toward the boardinghouse.

"If they took everything away from us on the word of a man like that . . ." Ariel said, but couldn't finish her sentence.

"Then there's no doubt that this is a put-up job," R.J. said.

Sara glanced at him and saw that his eyes were glassy, but she couldn't tell if it was fear or anger. He was the one being accused of the crime. He was the one who stood to lose the most if . . . if. . . . She couldn't bring herself to think about what could happen.

"Tomorrow," Sara said, "we're going to do whatever it takes to get ourselves off this island. We're not going to be here for that court date. Is everyone agreed on that?"

"You trying out for cheerleader?" R.J. asked, but he was smiling.

"That's David's job," Sara joked.

"I tried Ms. Vancurren's phone and it was dead," Ariel said.

The men looked at her.

Ariel shrugged. "I did it just before we left for the restaurant. I would have hidden myself and found out more, but I heard her on the stairs."

Sara looked at David. "Does she often snoop . . . successfully?"

David gave a rueful smile. "I can't tell you the number of times I've had to pretend that I was talking to her when I had no idea where she was. If her mother was doing something she didn't want Ariel to know about, you can bet that Ariel was there hiding in the ferns and listening."

"Interesting," R.J. said, looking at Ariel with admiration.

"I vote that we get a good night's sleep, then in the morning try to find jobs of any kind that we can," Sara said. "With all the seafood eaten around here, they must have a lot of fishing boats going out."

"We could hijack one," R.J. said.

"Excellent idea," David said. "I think that tomorrow we should separate and each of us should find out what we can do to get to the mainland. Or even just to call. Surely there's a radio or something on this island."

"I'm sure there are telephones in every house," Ariel said, "but they're not going to let *us* near one of them. If I could call one person, I'd call my mother. She'd have the U.S. Army here in minutes. And the FBI."

"I'd call my lawyer," R.J. said. "As much as I pay him, he'd show up with the navy."

"I'm with Ariel," David said. "I'd call her mother. She'd call in UFOs if she had to."

They were smiling, laughing even, and they turned to Sara in question. Who would she call? What could she say? That she'd call her boss? She looked away from them and said, "Look, her ladyship has left the porch light on."

"Is it red?" Ariel asked, deadpan, and they laughed.

When Sara glanced at R.J., he seemed to be in serious thought. David and Ariel hurried toward the house, which was beginning to seem like a haven in a storm, but R.J. caught Sara's hand. "I've let you down," he said softly.

"Of course not," she said, pulling away from his grasp. "You're in more trouble than we are."

"But I'm the one who wanted to come to the island in the first place. I'm the one—"

Sara was embarrassed by his words and wasn't sure what to say.

"Sara—" he began, but she turned away just as Ms. Vancurren opened the front door. She was wearing a filmy green negligee and matching robe, and she was yawning and acting as though she was unaware of her sexiness. "I didn't expect you to stay out so late," she said.

As soon as they were inside the house, David said to Ms. Vancurren, "We met the man Nezbit."

"I was afraid that would happen," she said. "He frequents the pub rather often."

Sara was watching her closely and saw that she showed no surprise that they'd met Nezbit. Someone had already told her. How? she wondered. Was there a private telephone system on the island? Or had someone run over here as fast as possible to tell her? That she'd been told made Sara sure the woman was in on everything. Would she get a split of the money R.J. would be charged on Monday?

R.J. stepped forward. "I don't think the

testimony of a man like that will hold up in court."

"Don't underestimate him," Phyllis said. "His family's been on King's Isle for generations and he's rich."

"Rich?" Ariel said. "He doesn't look rich."

Ms. Vancurren gave Ariel a look up and down, then smiled. "He doesn't wear designer clothes, but he's got money."

"So how did he get it?" R.J. asked. "More dogs, more tourists?"

Phyllis gave a little smile. "Now you've hit on one of the great mysteries of this island. Fenny hasn't worked a day since his thirty-second birthday. All he does is make babies, but he's always got money. I could tell you stories that—" She cut herself off to give a yawn that nearly made her come out of the top of her nightgown. "You'll have to forgive me, but I'm exhausted. I must get to bed." With that, she went up the stairs to her bedroom and closed the door.

"What a rude woman!" Ariel said in a tone that made it sound as though rudeness was the worst condemnation in the world.

Sara didn't know about the others, but she was so tired she could have stretched out on the stairs and fallen asleep.

David smiled at her. "After you."

Upstairs, they stood for a moment looking at the bedrooms, but didn't move. "My kingdom for a toothbrush," Sara said.

"Should I ask to borrow one from Phyllis?" R.J. asked.

"You enter that woman's bedroom and you won't come out alive," Ariel said in absolute seriousness.

"Sounds good to me," R.J. said.

Sara was too tired to care about the men's lusting after that dreadful woman and took a step toward the bathroom, but Ariel beat her to it. She slipped into the room and shut the door before Sara could take a step. She leaned against the door and sighed.

"So how do we split the bedrooms?" R.J. asked.

David looked puzzled, but Sara knew what R.J. meant. "Boys in one, girls in the other," she said.

"Darn!" R.J. said, and Sara smiled.

The three of them were standing just outside the bathroom door so they could hear everything that Ariel was doing inside. Water running, toilet flushing. Sara stepped away from the door. "Remind me to be extra quiet when I'm in there."

In the next second, they heard a loud thump from inside the bathroom. It sounded as though Ariel had fallen.

"Ariel?" Sara said through the door. "Are you all right?" There was no answer. "Ariel?" Still no answer. She tried the doorknob. Locked. She rattled the door handle.

R. J. stepped forward. "I don't think we should wake our landlady." He turned the doorknob hard, but it didn't open. He looked at her. "Sometimes in these old houses, the same key works on all the locks."

He didn't have to say more. Seconds later, Sara was back with a key taken from one of the bedroom doors and he inserted it into the lock. It wouldn't go in. Squatting, he looked through the keyhole. "The key's in the lock on the inside. I need to get it out."

"Let me try," David said. He had taken a wire coat hanger out of a closet and twisted it open. Kneeling beside R. J., he worked the wire into the lock, and seconds later they heard the key hit the tile floor inside the bathroom. To their ears it sounded very loud and all three of them held their breath. Would Ms. Vancurren hear?

When they heard nothing from downstairs, R.J. looked through the keyhole. Whatever he saw made his shoulders tighten and the back of his neck redden.

"What is it?" Sara whispered.

R.J. stood up while David put the bedroom key in the bathroom door lock. "Let's get it open as fast as we can," R.J. said and Sara knew that something was wrong with Ariel. A sense of panic came over her. If something was wrong, who could they call for help? The King's Isle police?

The key worked and David opened the bathroom door. Lying on the floor, clothed only in her underwear, was Ariel. She was curled into a ball, her back to them, facing the tub. David reached her first and pulled her into his arms. "Ariel, baby," he whispered.

Sara's back was to the tub and the curtain was drawn across it. When she looked up at R.J. she saw that all the color had left his face. He was looking down into the tub, his eyes wide, his skin bloodless.

As Sara turned her head, R.J. said, "No!" but it was too late. Lying in the tub, half-hidden behind the curtain, was John Fenwick Nezbit. His eyes were open and he was as ugly as when they'd seen him in the bar, but he had a hole in his forehead. He was dead.

Sara was standing there, looking at that odious man and thinking what seemed to be rational thoughts, when R.J. grabbed her under the arms and pulled her upward. Without knowing it, she'd been sinking down toward the floor. Three more seconds and she would have been lying beside Ariel in a faint.

David looked up when R.J. moved so swiftly, and R.J. nodded toward the end of the tub. Whatever David felt, he stayed calm. He looked at the dead man, then turned his attention back to Ariel, who was just coming to.

"I'm fine," Sara said, but when she tried to take a step, her knees gave way. R.J. swept her into his arms, carried her into the sitting room, and put her on one of the couches. There was no liquor in the rooms, but he got her a glass of water. Behind him came David, carrying Ariel. He set her on the couch across from Sara.

"Stay," R.J. said to both of the women, but they didn't need the order. He and David went back into the bathroom and closed the door.

Ariel looked at Sara and she looked back, but they said nothing. Sara reached across the coffee table and handed Ariel the glass of water. She sipped, then put the glass down on the table.

They sat in silence, listening, but there were no sounds. If the men were talking, they were doing it so quietly that they couldn't be heard.

After what seemed like an eternity, David and R. J. came back into the room and took the chairs at the ends of the couches. Both of them looked older than they had an hour ago.

"He's dead," R. J. said. "Shot through the head."

"It couldn't have been us," Sara said. "The whole town saw us at dinner."

"And they saw him," R. J. said. "He was in the bar when we left so that means he was killed while we were walking back. Alone. Just the four of us. No outside witnesses."

"He was killed then carried up the stairs of that woman's house," Ariel said, sitting up. "She knows he's here and she's downstairs waiting for our screams."

They looked at her, blinking at the venom in her voice.

"There aren't going to be any screams," R. J. said calmly. "There will be no screams and no hysterics. We're going to treat this like it was a business deal." He looked at them as though they might protest, but Sara knew that if there was one thing R. J. was good at, it was business.

"How do we do that?" Ariel asked softly.

"For one thing, we don't let the enemy know what's in our heads. And we don't do what they expect us to. Right now it's my guess that there are people hiding in the bushes outside, waiting for us to do something dramatic."

"Such as?" David asked. He was trying to sound cool and calm, but Sara could tell that he was as scared as the rest of them. Except R. J., that is. He didn't seem afraid at all. He seemed angry.

Chapter Ten

"Don't fade out on me now, Johnson," R.J. said softly.

He and Sara were in the bathroom, looking down at the body of John Fenwick Nezbit. They weren't touching him, just looking, as though they couldn't really believe what they were seeing.

"I'm—" Sara began.

"Scared out of your mind?"

She nodded.

"I am too."

"You?"

"That surprises you?" R.J. asked.

"Shocks me," she said. "You go into deals that terrify other people, but you're always calm."

He shrugged. "Money. What does it matter? You win, good; you lose, okay. But this . . ." He nodded toward Nezbit's body. "This was planted here with the intention of our taking the rap, and the rap leads to prison, even to execution."

She was getting more scared now. "We couldn't just tell someone, could we?"

"What do you think?"

"Not an option," she surmised.

He sat down on the closed toilet and motioned for her to close the door. "Look," he said softly, "I figure that it's you and me in this. Those two . . ."

Ariel and David were in the sitting room, close to each other on the sofa, neither of them saying anything. R.J. had called Sara into the bathroom with him—and "Fenny."

"She's in on it," Sara said, motioning toward the door and meaning Phyllis Vancurren. "I know you and David think she's beautiful, but I wish you could see her clearly."

"Give me a break. You've seen the women I date. Do you think I'd fall for some overused hag like Phyllis Vancurren? I knew she was up to something the minute I saw her."

"Ariel says there are some very expensive things in this house."

"More than you know. Your cousin isn't the only one who can snoop. I opened a few cabinets. Looks like she knew we were coming far enough in advance that she hid some items of jade, porcelain, and the odd Ming vase."

"They're making a fortune here, aren't they?"

"Someone is, and I agree that Vancurren is in on it, although I can't figure out how much. One thing for sure is that they were waiting for us. They knew we were coming."

Sara's head came up. "The ferry."

"Right," R.J. said, smiling. "I didn't tell anyone, but I looked for a schedule, but there wasn't one. When we got to the water on the other side, there was no ferry in sight, but after we had lunch—"

"And we'd told the waitress we were going to King's Isle for the day—"

"The ferry magically appeared."

"For your Jaguar. With that car, you might as well have put a sign on your head: I am rich." Sara sat down on the end of the tub. The curtain hid the body from her. "And we were told that the ferry wouldn't return until

after the trial. Which could now be for murder," she added.

"I don't think that was part of it. The websites I read reported more than one tourist
complaint, but nothing could be done because it was their word against the King's
Isle police and the judge."

"And then there's the story about the couple who had to move to get away from Larry
Lassiter. Do you think that was true?"

"I don't know, but when I get out of here,
I'll find out."

Sara looked at her watch—the one she
now knew cost ten grand. It was just after
midnight. "How do we get out of this?"

"I have no idea. You're the clever one, so
what do you think?"

"My first thought is to get rid of the body,
but how? We can't carry it outside or we'll
be seen. I think you're right when you said
people are out there watching us."

"They're probably expecting us to walk
down those creaky stairs carrying a rolled-up
carpet."

"Three, six, eight," Sara said.

"What?"

"Those are the numbers of the stairs that
creak: three, six, eight."

"If I didn't think you'd slap me, I'd kiss you for that."

"You told David I was a bad secretary. You said—"

"Come on," R. J. said, "let's see if the others have calmed down now." He got up and held the door open for her.

Ariel and David were sitting close together on one of the sofas. David was holding her hand.

"I don't know how you can stand to be in there with that . . . that body," Ariel said.

"We're trying to figure out what to do," Sara answered.

"Any luck?" David asked.

"Only that we have to get rid of the body, tell no one, and that Sara here"—he patted her thigh—"knows which steps creak. I think we can get the body down the stairs without Phyllis hearing," R. J. said.

"She wouldn't hear us anyway," Ariel said. "She's drunk."

"How do you know that?"

"When I tried the telephone, I opened the cabinet by her bed. It was full of bottles of vodka. And I smelled it on her breath when we came back."

"You can't smell vodka," R. J. said.

"I can," Ariel said and gave him the look.

"I've seen you before, haven't I?" R. J. said, staring at Ariel.

"Anyone have any ideas what to do? Besides call the police, that is?" Sara asked, meaning to distract R. J.

"Do you think the police will come bursting in on us if we don't do something soon?" Ariel asked.

"Yes," R. J. answered. He looked at his watch. "It's been . . ." He looked at Sara.

"Twenty-three minutes."

"Yes, it's been twenty-three minutes since we found the body. They'll be expecting us to do something soon."

"There's a chest freezer in the basement," David said and the others looked at him, wide-eyed. "Remember?" he asked R. J. "She told us."

"Right," R. J. said, smiling. "On the stairs. She said her first apartment wasn't as big as the freezer in her basement."

For a moment, the four of them looked at one another.

"If the body is gone in the morning," Ariel said, "they'll know it's in the house."

"Not unless they see us take it out," Sara said, looking at R. J. "Remember when you got Mr. Dunkirk so drunk he had to be carried out?"

"I didn't get Charley drunk," R.J. said. "He does it to himself every day. He—"

"What are you thinking?" Ariel asked her cousin.

Sara looked at R.J. "Could we fake it?"

For a moment he just looked at her, then a slow smile crept over his face. "Two of us take the body downstairs, while two more make the people who put it there think we're hauling the body out of the house."

"That's exactly what's in my mind," Sara said.

"We always were a good team," R.J. said softly.

"We should all stay together," Ariel said firmly. "We shouldn't separate."

"Ariel," R.J. said, "I want you to go into Phyllis's room and get something of hers to put on the body. Something identifiable. Maybe monogrammed. If the body is found I want it to look like Vancurren did it. It won't fool anyone for long, but we need all the time we can get."

Ariel swallowed. It was one thing to snoop around her mother's house, but quite an-

other to snoop in a stranger's bedroom—
with the owner in it.

Sara stood up. "Let's get going. I fear
we'll be spending the night in—"

"Don't say it," David said, standing up.
"No one is to touch that body. No hair, no
body fluids, nothing."

Sara looked at David and saw that there
were little white lines beside his mouth, and
there were circles under his eyes. If his ambition was to have a political career, it could
be ending right now. She wanted to go to
him and comfort him, but R. J. stepped between them. "Ariel, you go . . ."

Sara could see that Ariel was scared to
death. She walked with her to the door that
opened on the stairs.

"What if she's awake?" Ariel whispered.
She was glad there was a light over the
stairs.

"My guess is she wants to be asleep so
she can't be accused of knowing anything,"
Sara said.

"Or maybe she has a conscience," Ariel
said to Sara, then they looked at each other
and shook their heads no. "Maybe her bedroom door is locked." Again, they shook
their heads no. The last door in the house to

be locked would be Phyllis Vancurren's bedroom.

"Three, six, eight down, backwards coming up," Sara whispered as she opened the door.

"How am I supposed to count that?" Ariel said, then she looked at the wallpaper and smiled.

Sara smiled back. "Roses," she whispered. "Count the roses."

Ariel took a deep breath, then started down the steps. At the third step, she held onto the rail and stepped past it. No creak. Smiling, she looked up at Sara, who smiled in return, then Ariel looked at the roses on the wallpaper. One of the roses above the creaky step had been painted blue. It was something you wouldn't notice unless you were studying the wallpaper, but it was there.

Ariel pointed at the blue rose and motioned to Sara, but she didn't understand. Ariel slowly went down the stairs, noting the blue rose each time there was a stair she was to skip. When she was outside Phyllis's room, she looked up at Sara, still standing in the doorway, smiling encouragement.

Slowly, carefully, silently, Ariel opened the

bedroom door and breathed a sigh of relief when she saw the tiny night-light in the wall. When her eyes adjusted, she saw Phyllis Vancurren sprawled across the bed, snoring softly. Ariel thought she might be able to fire a shot and not wake her, but she didn't want to chance it. She tiptoed over the carpet—antique Persian, she thought, and at least ten grand—and went to the woman's chest of drawers. As she'd hoped, there was a hairbrush. Ariel took a tissue from the box, removed some hair from the brush, and put it in her pocket. Glancing in the mirror above the dresser, she looked at Phyllis, then Ariel silently opened a top drawer. Junk. Old hair clips, business cards, broken combs, a small box of cheap jewelry. She closed the drawer.

The next drawer held underwear. Ariel couldn't have been more pleased if she'd found gold. *Clean* underwear! She jammed the front of her shirt with half a dozen pairs of lacy underpants. The bras were, of course, useless to her and Sara, so she left them.

The next drawer held a stack of night-gowns, all French-made, all nearly transparent. Ariel was tempted to take a couple of those, but she didn't.

In the bottom drawer, she hit pay dirt. There were monogrammed handkerchiefs and a handwritten card. *I will love you forever. Phyllis,* it read. She slipped a handkerchief and the card into the waistband of her trousers.

As she shut the drawer, she noticed a tiny red beam in the mirror, like a light on something electronic. Turning, she scanned the room but saw nothing. She looked back in the mirror and there it was again, a red spot, but now she realized she was seeing it through a gap in the curtains. It was outside.

With her back against the wall, not daring to touch the curtains, Ariel looked through the tiny gap and waited. In a few moments the red showed again. It was the tip of a burning cigarette. Just as R. J. said, someone was hiding in the shadows, smoking and watching.

Ariel tiptoed across the carpet, left the room, and went back up the stairs.

"What took you so long?" Sara said. "I was beginning to worry!"

"Look what I got." Ariel pulled the underpants out of her shirt, the two monogrammed handkerchiefs, and finally the card.

"Clean underwear," Sara said in awe. "The greatest luxury in life."

"Where are they—and him? It?"

"They left just after you and took it downstairs to try to find the freezer. I was left here to make these." She stepped aside to show Ariel two long lumps of sheets and pillows, both of them tied together with burlap twine, into roughly the shape and size of Fenny Nezbit.

"That's very good. It's—" Ariel broke off as the men came into the room. They hadn't made a sound as they came up the stairs.

"Did you find it?" Sara asked.

"Yes," David said, his face even paler than before. "This goes against everything I've ever believed in. We just hid a dead body—"

"Yeah, and we had to take the frozen food out. It'll thaw, then stink," R. J. said. He was looking at Ariel. "Did you do okay?"

"Brilliant," Sara said. "She stole us some clean underwear."

When the men just blinked at that, Sara shrugged. "It's a girl thing. But Ariel also got some evidence you can use to incriminate that woman."

"We'll drop it off when we go out," R. J. said, then looked at Sara. "How'd you do?"

She stepped back to show the stuffed figures she'd made.

"Excellent," R. J. said, his eyes sparkling. "You always could put together anything."

"I saw a lit cigarette," Ariel said. "Someone is standing at the back of the house and smoking."

"No police cars?" R. J. asked.

"I had half an inch between the curtain and the wall so I couldn't see much," Ariel said. "Would you mind telling me the plan?"

Sara spoke first. "If the police are involved in this and are watching, we figure they'll stop us as soon as we leave the house with a big roll across our shoulders. But if it's an individual who's watching—"

"Or two," David said.

"Yes, if a few people are watching, they'll follow us and see us dispose of what I hope will look like a body," R. J. said. "Sara and I are to go one way, you and Jock here the other way."

No one moved. They just stood there glaring at R. J.

"Okay. David," R. J. said. "Ariel, you and *David* will go a second way."

"We found some useful things," Sara said to Ariel. "There's a treasure trove of stuff under the eaves." She nodded to the little doors in the bottom of the slanting attic walls.

"Ready?" R.J. asked.

"I think it would be better if I went with *you* instead of David," Ariel said to R.J.

When Sara looked at David, his face turned red. So *that's* what this whole thing is about, she thought in disgust. Another woman who wanted R.J. "I think that's a great idea," Sara said, stepping closer to David.

The men looked at each other in silent, mutual agreement, then they traded places so they were back to where they had been.

"Sara and I know each other," R.J. said in a way that meant there'd be no more discussion of the matter.

"So do Ariel and I," David said, sounding as though R.J. had been the one who'd asked Ariel to go with him.

R.J. turned to Ariel. "When we go out, play it suspicious, as though you're doing something bad."

"We are!" David said. "We should have—"

Breaking off, he looked at them. "Called the police" was not an option.

Ten minutes later, they were ready. Over David's shoulder was one of Sara's dummies wrapped in a small rug. He was bending his knees to look as though whatever was inside the rug was very heavy.

Sara had dressed the other dummy in clothes she'd found in a box under the eaves. She'd put a broomstick inside the dummy to make it stay somewhat upright, and they'd put the Ariel wig askew on its head. She and R. J. were going to try to walk the dummy out, as though they were carrying a drunken person between them.

As they started down the stairs, Ariel silently pointed out the roses marked with blue to show the squeaky steps. It looked as though other people had stayed in the rooms with the barred windows, and they too had heard people sneaking upstairs.

At the front door, they paused and waited while R. J. went down the basement steps to deposit incriminating evidence on the body. He was back in a moment. He turned off the porch light, then cautiously opened the front door.

"It's showtime!" R.J. said.

Chapter Eleven

"I can't go on with this," R.J. said quietly to Sara. "I want you and the kids to stay in the house and do whatever it is you need to to survive, but I have to . . ." He waved his hand to indicate that he had some ideas that he was going to keep to himself.

Sara was struggling with the limp dummy between them, trying to keep the floppy thing upright. If it weren't so dark outside, and if R.J. weren't leading them into an even darker forest, she'd never believe that anyone watching them would believe they were carrying a dead body. "I have no idea what you're talking about," she said. "We need to—"

"Get this body thrown over the cliff on the

east side of the island. Yeah, I know that, but . . ."

"So help me, if you start keeping secrets, I'll drop this thing and start screaming." She could feel R. J. laughing.

"I think I liked it better when you didn't speak to me. Was I really such a terrible boss?"

"The worst. You rule and no one else is allowed to have any input."

"But it's my company."

"Then run it all by yourself."

"You *do* hate me, don't you?"

"Could we talk about this later? Right now I'd like to keep us out of jail."

"Which brings us back to the beginning," R. J. said. "I think there's more to this than meets the eye. I'm beginning to think all this has to do with my work."

Sara hesitated, but she didn't stop walking. The dummy's feet were dragging and they had to shift its weight often. R. J. had put some rocks in the coat pockets and down the front so it weighed quite a bit, but it wasn't enough. "What have you done at work that would make someone want to frame you for murder?" she asked.

"Nothing specific, but I wonder if this has

to do with . . ." He trailed off and she could feel him shrug.

"For once in your life, I'd like to hear the truth out of you. What is really going on?" She could feel his smile and he took most of the weight of the dummy onto his own arms, giving Sara a break.

"Kids!" R.J. said. "They talk you to death, don't they? It's a good thing both of them are rich or they'd starve to death."

She knew he'd changed the subject and hadn't answered her question, but then that's what he always did. "I assume you mean Ariel and David."

"Exactly," R.J. said.

"So what are you planning to do about them?"

"I left them a note saying I wasn't returning, that I'd see them in court on Monday— unless they could find a way to escape this place. I think that whoever planted this body on us, is after *me,* so I'm going to do my best to find out who did it."

"On your own?" Sara asked.

"On my own. Just the way I run my company."

"I see," Sara said.

"Here," R.J. said, turning into some trees.

"You seem to know this place well. Have you been here before?"

"Never, but I spent quite a bit of time reading about it on the Internet, remember?"

Sara swung around with the dummy and they walked into the dark, dense forest. "Does this lead anywhere?" she whispered. She wanted to talk, wanted to get angry at R. J., for the reality of the situation might make her collapse. Someone had killed Fenny Nezbit and that person was still out there. If he—or she—thought that R. J. and Sara were carrying a dead body, why shouldn't he/she shoot them too?

Sara and R. J. walked in silence for a few minutes and Sara began to think about the truth of their situation. She could be accused of being an accessory to murder. Or would she be accused directly? Did they execute two people for one murder?

"I want to drop this body off the east side of the island," R. J. said softly. "There's a cliff there. When I read about it I thought of hang gliding, not using it to discard a body, even a fake one."

Sara didn't smile. She was thinking about what R. J. had said about going off on his own to find the truth. She didn't want to admit it, but she too wanted to get away from Ariel and David. How could that be? she wondered. Her whole reason for being on the trip had been to be near David.

"I'm going with you," she whispered, then prepared herself for the fight she knew was to come. She'd have to argue with R. J. that she wasn't a "kid" like David and Ariel, that she could be of some use to him. But R. J. didn't say a word. When he didn't try to argue her out of it, she knew that he had something in mind.

"If all you want is a chance to try to seduce me—" She broke off at his suppressed laugh.

"You never give up, do you, Johnson? What have I done to make you think I'm the lowest of the low?"

"The women you seduce then abandon."

"What should I do? Marry them? Do you think I don't know what they want from me? They want money, that's all. If I didn't have money, they wouldn't give a short, ugly, old guy like me a second look. All those gorgeous young females would go out with gorgeous young males. Money is what gives old men like me a chance." He stopped walking. "Let's toss him over here. Let's make a production of it, then when he's gone, you can pretend to cry and I'll comfort you."

Sara ignored the last of his statement as she took the legs of the dummy and R.J. took the shoulders. They swung it back and forth several times over an edge that Sara hadn't even seen. She'd been listening so hard to what R.J. was saying that she hadn't even realized they were at the edge of a drop-off into the sea.

"Now," R.J. said, and they let the body go.

She could see it fall down and down until it hit the rocks below. "Why didn't the killer just do that to the body in the first place?"

"That's what I want to know," R.J. said, reaching out his arms for her.

Sara pulled back. "What are you doing?"

"Comforting you for a moment."

"Even in a mess like this, you never stop coming on to a woman. I must say that you had me going there for a moment with your sad little story about being rich and unloved."

"You didn't believe me?"

"Not a word of it."

"So I don't get a good-bye kiss?"

"I told you, I'm not going back. I'm staying with you, but before you get any ideas, I want to know what you're up to."

"Let's get out of here," he said, looking around the dark forest. They could see no one and the only sound was of frogs and mosquitoes. "I think that whoever is watching has seen all he needs to."

"You feel it too?" Sara asked, rubbing her arms as the hairs were standing on end. It was probably eighty-five degrees but she felt cold. When R. J. started to put his arm around her, she pulled away. "I want to know what you're planning to do." She didn't look at him but she knew that he was in a dilemma. For all that he called her, fifty times a day sometimes, he was still a very private man. For the first few months she worked for him, she thought that there wasn't anything in his life that she didn't know about. But then he'd announced a merger with another company and she realized that she'd never heard a word about it. He'd done all the research and the paperwork by himself. If she knew nothing else about R. J. Brompton, it was that he was a man of many secrets. Now he was trying to decide whether or not to share his secrets.

Sara was silent as they walked back toward the town. She knew better than to try to force him to tell her what he was planning to do—or even to persuade him. He had to make up his own mind.

"I'm going to visit Mrs. Nezbit," R.J. said at last.

"You're going to seduce the widow?" Sara asked, aghast.

"Could you get your mind above the belt for a few minutes?" R.J. snapped. "She'll know something. If nothing else, she'll know his enemies. Who hated him enough to kill him?"

Sara remembered the man's angry hostility when they'd seen him in the bar. "Based on my experience, I think maybe several people wanted to kill him. Even Ms. Vancurren said he was a liar and a thief."

"A liar and a loser," R.J. said quietly. "Are you slipping on me that you didn't remember that?"

"I remembered. Maybe it was something else that made me think he was a thief."

"Could it have been the twenty-thousand-dollar watch he was wearing?"

"I didn't notice that."

"I did and I think you did subliminally. Phyllis said he was rich."

Sara stopped walking. "You want to find out how he got rich, don't you? Maybe he was blackmailing someone and his victim got fed up and murdered him."

"And we happened along and they tried to pin it on us," R. J. added.

"What's going to happen when there is no body found?"

He started walking again. "I thought about that. How can we be accused with no body? That freezer was plugged in but the food in it was old. I don't think it's been opened in a long time, certainly not on a daily basis. It could be a while before they find the body in there."

"But then the killer will be looking for it over the side of the cliff."

"And wherever the kids tossed their dummy."

"Why do you keep calling them 'kids'? Ariel is the same age as I am."

"I've heard that great emotion is what makes you grow up. If that's true, *are* you and Ariel the same age?"

"I think that with my dad I may be about a hundred and fifty."

"And I'm a thousand."

"You?" she asked. "Since when do *you* have any emotion? I've seen you dump women without a backward glance."

"Their tears were over losing my bank account."

"Not all of them. What about Tiffany?"

"She ran up accounts at Bergdorf's and Barney's in the six figures, all on the prospect that I was going to marry her. After I got rid of her, Harry Winston's called me and asked if I wanted to continue holding the ten-carat pink diamond ring."

"Ah," Sara said. They had reached the Vancurren house and she felt R. J. take a step backward. She turned to him, her eyes pleading. "You're not going in, are you?"

"No, and you can't go with me. This is something I need to do alone. I don't need a committee meeting every time I want to get something done."

Sara looked up at the top floor of the old Victorian mansion and saw a light behind the curtain, then a shadow. David and Ariel were back. Sara knew that what R. J. was saying was correct. It had taken as much time to get David and Ariel calmed down about the body as it had to try to deal with it. Part of her wanted to go back to them. This would be her chance to get to know David better. She'd show him that she was calm under stress, that she could handle things. R.J. was the natural leader of the four because he was the oldest and more experienced, but with R.J. out of the picture, maybe Sara could take over.

Yes, she thought, she'd take over and David would hate her for it. Ariel would swoon in his manly arms and David would sweep her up and carry her to the altar. And Sara would be left behind. Strong, capable Sara would be left behind.

"I'm going with you," she said more firmly, bracing herself for the coming argument with R.J.

"You'd miss your chance with Mr. Politician."

"What makes you think he wants a political career?"

"I listen and I watch people. You thought you might be in love with him, didn't you?"

"Yes. No. I don't know. It's complicated. He belongs to my mother's family and I'd like to be a part of them." She glanced up at the window. "But I think I inherited all my genes from my father's sharecropper family."

R.J. looked around. They were on the edge of the town, hidden under some trees, and Sara could feel that he had something to say, but he didn't say it. "Are you sure you want to go with me?" he asked. "I could use your help."

She waited, her breath held. It seemed that she'd never wanted anything as much as she wanted to stay with R. J. If there was any way for them to get out of this mess, he would find it.

"Okay," he said at last and started walking rapidly. "But you do what I tell you."

"I always do."

"Actually, you don't," he said softly. "In fact, you've never taken me up on any offer I've ever made you."

Sara didn't want to talk about them. She was having trouble following him in the dark at the rocky edge of the road. Ariel's expensive Italian sandals weren't made for actual walking. "How can you plan something with Nezbit's wife when you haven't even met her? Maybe she's as much beneath your standards as the beautiful Phyllis Vancurren."

"You twist everything around, don't you? If I like a woman, that proves I'm a leacher. If I don't like her, that makes me a snob."

"Just so we understand each other," Sara said.

R. J. laughed. "Come on, let's get some sleep."

"Where?"

"How about a front porch? I've seen a lot of those what-do-you-call-'ems with cushions on them."

"Chaises. Daybeds. Lounges. I guess we better not try to break into a house."

"No, I think not," R.J. said. "You up for a night of mosquitoes?"

"Sure. Mosquitoes aren't as bad as bullets. Do you know anything about Nezbit's widow?"

"I know that if she knows she's a widow, then she's in on it. My plan is not, as you seem to think it is, to seduce her. I mean to seduce her six children."

"What?! You can't—"

"You always believe the worst of me, don't you?" he said, putting his hand on her elbow and steering her toward a dark house with a huge porch. There were half a dozen pieces of furniture on the porch. "When you were a kid, was there anything that your father did that you didn't know about?"

"No," Sara said slowly, walking up the stairs of the porch. She smiled as she thought about what R.J. was saying. To get information out of an adult would take a long time, but they had only days. But what child didn't blab everything they knew to anyone who asked?

Still smiling, she sat down on one of the two cushioned daybeds on the porch. The cushions were musty and she could feel torn places in them. If she saw them in daylight she'd probably be horrified. Were there mouse nests in them? Bugs? What about snakes?

"Come on, Johnson," R.J. said softly, reaching across the distance until he felt her hand. "The worst is over. If the police knew about the death, by now they would have arrested all four of us. My guess is that, at the most, two people know about Nezbit's death."

"One is Phyllis Vancurren."

"I'm not so sure of that. Whoever put the body in the bathtub may know she drinks herself to sleep every night. And the creaking stairs are marked."

She was quiet a moment, looking up at the stars and trying to relax. It wasn't easy since she feared that at any moment police cars would arrive, sirens blaring, and arrest them. "Ariel will be frightened if I'm not there."

"Don't kid yourself," R.J. said, his voice

sleepy. "That girl is made of steel. She may be stronger than you and me put together."

"You're wrong. Her mother—"

"Her mother! *That's* where I saw her before. In New York. I was at a party with Tiffany. It was just before we broke up and she knew it was coming, so she was putting on a great show of jealousy. There was a pretty girl there and she kept staring at me. But every time I took a step toward her, she ran away. It was an interesting game but I got tired of it fast. Then, out of the blue, this woman comes up to me and tells me that if I so much as touch her virginal daughter she'll have me arrested. The whole thing was too much. Tiffany was on the verge of making a scene, some girl was flirting with me then running away, then some woman nearly accuses me of being a rapist. I left the party."

In spite of her fear, Sara could feel herself relaxing. "How many of your hundreds did you leave them?" she murmured.

"What hundreds?"

Sara was too tired to argue. "The ones in your shoes. Each pair you own has a hundred-dollar bill folded under the insole. Two shoes, two one hundreds."

"Both of them," R.J. said sleepily. "Do you mind?"

"No. They need them."

"They have each other. I'll bet you fifty grand that by Monday your little cousin will no longer be a virgin."

"You touch her and—"

"Keep your knickers on. Mr. President is going to do it, not me."

"How did you know about him, about his . . . wanting . . ." She was more asleep than awake.

"To be president? You told me. You're no good at keeping secrets."

"Secrets about the man I love," Sara whispered, then fell asleep.

R.J. lay awake for a few minutes, looking at the stars over his head. There was a hole in the porch roof. Yeah, he thought, Charley better get here soon before the old houses rot into a pile. He glanced at Sara, looking at her profile in the dim light. I know who you love, but *you* don't know, he whispered. Smiling, he went to sleep.

In the bushes, their every movement was watched.

Chapter Twelve

"I hear fishing boats," R.J. said, his face close to hers. "I want you on one of them. I want you off this island."

Sara opened an eye enough to see that it wasn't quite daylight, which meant that they'd had maybe two hours' sleep.

She was tired, hungry, and dirty—but she still knew a trick when she heard one. R.J. was trying to get rid of her. "And let you have all the glory of solving the mystery?" She hadn't quite opened her eyes, but she heard him chuckle as he stood up.

"Today I'll talk to some of the fishermen and make arrangements for the lot of you to return to the mainland. Are you going to lie there all day?"

"Maybe," she said, stretching, her eyes still closed. It was cool and pleasant in the early morning on the porch and she didn't want to face reality.

"Sara," R. J. said in a tone she'd never heard before, "if you don't get up, I'm going to join you on that couch. Think we'll put on a show for the neighbors?"

She refused to let him bully her. "Naw," she said lazily, "they only look out the windows to see dead dogs."

When she heard him chuckle again, she opened her eyes. He was looking down at her in the way she'd seen him look at several women, but she didn't react as they did. She knew what happened to women who fell for that come-to-me look. Sighing, she sat up and looked out at King's Isle. There was no one in sight, just a lot of empty-looking old houses.

As she remembered Fenny Nezbit's dead body and all that the four of them had done to conceal it, Sara had to fight down the fear that rose in her throat. She ran her hand through her slightly greasy hair, and her tongue over teeth that felt as though they had green stuff growing on them. "Does prison have a bathroom?" she asked. "I need a bath, some deodorant, and clean clothes."

R. J. didn't seem to have heard her as he looked out at what they could see of the town. For all their ordeal, he didn't seem to have changed much. How was it that men could sleep in their clothes and wake up with them unwrinkled? And why did the stubble on his cheeks only make him look more rugged? If he stepped onto a fishing boat right now, he'd look like one of them.

Reluctantly, she got up. Minutes later, she was following him along the same road they'd been down the night before. Each step took them farther away from Phyllis Vancurren's house, farther away from Ariel and David. "Think they'll be all right?" Sara asked.

"I think they'll be ecstatic. They have enough money to live on for a few days, so they can do what people like them are so good at doing: nothing."

"You don't like them much, do you?"

"Who was it who came up with that idiot scheme of trying to make me think the two of you were each other?"

"It wasn't about you," Sara said, but then thought better of it. As far as she could piece together, Ariel had seen R.J. at a party in New York, thought she was in love with him, and so had asked Sara to change places with her. And because Ariel thought she needed Sara with her, she'd arranged for the four of them to go to King's Isle together.

"If it wasn't about me, then who was it about?" R.J. persisted. "You and the prez? You wanted to be part of his snobby little set so much that you tried to make a fool of me?"

Sara was too tired to put up with his accusations—and she wasn't about to try to defend herself. "Did you forget to take your arthritis medicine this morning, old man? Is that why you're so cranky?"

"No," he said slowly. "I'm trying to be unpleasant enough that you'll go back to your friends."

"Won't work," she said, giving a huge yawn. "I'm used to your bad temper. Besides, who said they *can* go back? If anyone is going to get us out of this mess it's you, so I'll stick with the winner."

"I'd think that was a compliment, but that would mean the world is ending, so I know it can't be."

"Where are you taking us?"

"To breakfast. That sound good?"

"And how do you plan to pay for it? Washing dishes?"

R.J. held up a folded hundred-dollar bill.

"Does that mean you gave Ariel and David only one bill?"

"Nope," he said. He was walking so fast she was having trouble keeping up with him.

"You lied to me, didn't you?"

"Nope."

"When we get out of this I'm going to quit working for you."

Turning back, R.J. smiled. "Belt."

"What?"

"You think you know all about me because you snooped in my closet and found out that I keep emergency money inside my shoes. But you didn't find out that all my belts are custom made and they have money in them too."

"I have *never* snooped in your closet! If you remember, you told me—" She cut herself off. What did it matter now? "How much do you have?"

"Humph!" R.J. said as an answer. "There's

the restaurant for the fishermen. It opened at four A.M. Ready?"

Sara was still thinking about how to defend herself from his accusation of snooping in his closet when she saw the fishermen leaving the open restaurant. She then realized that maybe they could leave the island after all. If R.J. had a few hundred, maybe it would be enough of a down payment for an escape.

"You can go," R.J. said softly, looking at her. "I'm sure I can work out a deal."

The vision of Fenny Nezbit dead in the bathtub sat down in front of her eyes. If she left the island, she could get help. She could return with a whole herd of lawyers. She could . . . she glanced up at R.J. If she left, she'd be leaving him here alone at the mercy of the police. "I think you should send Ariel and David," she said. And if they left the island, what would the police do to her and R.J.?

"I've thought better of the whole idea. We're being watched and I think we're expected to try to leave on a fishing boat, and if we did try, they'd put all of us in jail. Minutes later, they'd find the body and we'd never get out of here alive. I think it's better for us to stay in sight, so we can keep our freedom, such as it is. Everything we do that we shouldn't do needs to be done in absolute secrecy."

"I agree," Sara said, relieved that she wasn't going to have to choose between staying and leaving.

He held the door to the restaurant open to her and as they entered, silence fell over the customers. There were eight Formica-clad tables, all but one full of men wearing heavy trousers and boots, ready to go out on their boats. Sara looked at the clock. It wasn't 5:00 A.M. yet. She gave as much of a smile as she could manage to the men in the restaurant and to the waitress behind the counter. No one smiled back. The men looked down at their food in silence and the waitress turned to the coffeepot.

They sat at the empty table and R.J. picked up the menu that was stuck between the napkin holder and the ketchup bottle. "I think I'll have the special," he said in a normal tone of voice, as though they weren't sitting in a silent restaurant.

Sara had to work to focus on the menu. The special was two fried eggs, two pieces of bacon, two link sausages, a biscuit, three pancakes, orange juice, and coffee. Before she thought about where she was, she said, "I can see you're sticking to your diet."

Two tables away, a couple of men gave little guffaws of laughter. She looked at R. J. in surprise and he smiled at her, pleased.

"And what are you going to have?" he asked. "Your usual bowl of sticks and twigs?"

There was more laughter, a bit louder this time.

"Sticks and twigs describes your last girl-friend's figure," she said with her teeth clenched, as though she were angry with him. "I'm going to have scrambled eggs and plain toast, that is if you don't mind that Phyllis doesn't cook them."

"Leave her out of this!" R. J. said, but loud enough for everyone in the restaurant to hear. He leaned toward her. "If it weren't for her, we'd—"

"What?" Sara said, leaning forward so their noses were almost touching. "Be sleeping on outdoor porches? What I want to know is why you didn't take her up on her offer last night."

"And leave you to wander around outside by yourself? All of us were looking everywhere for you. And all because you'd had a jealous fit over a very nice woman who—"

"Nice! I know exactly what part of her *you* think is 'nice.' She—" Sara broke off because she realized that the people around them had started talking again. The men were chuckling and she could hear the name "Phyllis" now and then.

"Good," R. J. whispered. "Very good. I think that acting training of yours paid off."

"Who was acting?" she said, looking down at the menu. When she looked back at him, he was staring at her with wide eyes. "Don't kid yourself. I'm not in the least jealous of your women." When he started to say something, Sara nodded toward the approaching waitress.

"So what will you two be having this morning?" she asked, her face serious.

"Phyllis Vancurren on a platter," Sara said sweetly.

The waitress didn't miss a beat. "And you?" she asked R. J.

"I'll have the same," he said, his eyes on Sara.

"Okay, that's two ham sandwiches with a side of gravy," the waitress said.

Everyone in the restaurant, including Sara and R.J., burst into spontaneous laughter.

When they left the restaurant, the fishermen waved at Sara and R.J. as though they were one of them, as though the men understood what was going on between the two. When Sara paid the check—she was, after all, still R.J.'s assistant—she'd asked the waitress where the Nezbits lived. "We want to apologize about the dog," Sara said, her eyes downcast.

When she looked up, the waitress was looking at Sara as though she didn't know if she was lying or crazy. It came to Sara that if the town was in on what was being done to them, it was because they were being threatened. By whom? With what? she wondered.

The waitress gave her directions. "It's about three miles," she said, but she didn't offer transportation.

Outside, R.J. was waiting for her. "Three miles, right?"

"Yes," she said. "Did you ask?"

"I asked directions and that took some doing, as all of the men wanted to run away from me. Someone has warned them not to give us a ride off the island. Can you walk in those shoes?"

"Not well. Toothbrush and toothpaste, of course, and a decent pair of shoes that I can walk in. They head my list of wants."

R. J. looked down the main street of town. There wasn't a store open yet. When he saw Sara was taking off her shoes to go barefoot, he smiled. "Good idea. I think I'll do the same." He untied his leather brogues— no sandals for him—stuffed his socks inside, tied the shoes together, then took her sandals from her and tied his laces around them. "Together at last," he said, holding up the four shoes.

"You're incorrigible," Sara said, but she was smiling.

"No, actually, I'm the world's greatest lover."

"You wish. Stop that and tell me what you found out."

"Nothing."

"Nothing really, or nothing you're going to tell me?"

"What do you think Fenny's wife is like?"

Sara knew she was going to get nothing more out of R. J., but she trusted him. She thought he had managed the fake argument in the restaurant deftly. If anyone had seen them outside last night, R. J. had covered it. He said that Sara had run out in a jealous fit and they'd all had to look for her.

"I don't think anyone knows that Nezbit is dead," R. J. said.

"Or that he's missing." They were on an old, pot-holed road, surrounded by over-hanging trees and there seemed to be no one around, but she still lowered her voice. "What do you think they're afraid of?"

"The judge. The police. Maybe Lassiter. One thing for sure is that no one is willing to help *us.*"

"You'd think there would be at least one rebel among them," Sara said. "One person who was willing to stand up to them."

"He'd have to have no family who could be threatened, and he'd have to not care if he lived or died. It's my guess that the residents like it here and don't want it to change. They have rent-free housing, plentiful food, friends. What more is there in life?"

"Toothpaste," Sara said and R. J. laughed.

"You think that's the road?" he asked, nodding toward a dirt road that turned off to the right.

"I hope so. My feet are bruised and raw," Sara said.

"I'll kiss them to make them better."

"I'd rather have a pair of sneakers."

"Where's your watch?"

"Now that I know how much it costs I'm afraid to wear it. It's safe inside my— It's safe."

"Mind if I look and see what time it is?"

She shook her head at him, but he was making her feel better. His jokes were making her forget the seriousness of the situation they were in. While they were in the restaurant, she'd had a vision of those fishermen carrying a noose, coming to lynch her and R.J. for killing their dear friend Fenny Nezbit.

After a while, they came to a narrow road with a beat-up, old mailbox at the end of it. In barely discernible letters, they saw the name Nezbit.

Sara hesitated.

"I want you to go back to Ariel," R.J. said quietly. "Just go down this road, take a left and—"

"I know the way," Sara said, her hand shielding her eyes from the sun. "Do you think she'll meet us with a shotgun? Do you

think—" She broke off because she saw a
pickup truck coming toward them. It looked
to be traveling at the speed of light, with
gravel flying behind it in a storm, and the tail
end skidding back and forth.

"Get down!" R.J. yelled, then pushed
Sara into a deep ditch. He jumped in beside
her, put his arm over her head, and ducked
down.

"Do you think they saw us?" she whispered.

"I hope not," R.J. said, but in the next
second the truck came to a skidding halt in
front of them. R.J.'s body was nearly over
Sara's in protection.

"What you doin' down there?" came a
woman's voice. "I thought you was gonna
come see me."

They looked up to see a thin woman, with
her head half out of the truck window, looking down at them. She had on haphazardly
applied makeup and hoop earrings that
reached her shoulders. Her face was so sun
damaged that she could have been anywhere from thirty-five to fifty.

"Well?" she said, "you comin' to my
house or not?"

"You're Mrs. Nezbit?" R.J. asked, standing up in the ditch, reaching down his hand to help Sara up.

"That's the burden the good Lord put on me and I bear it as best I can. You gonna stop hidin' in the ditch with the snakes or are you gonna come to my house?"

"With you!" Sara said, jumping out of the ditch and onto the road.

R.J. was beginning to recover himself and he started toward the other side of the truck. "This is very kind of you to invite us to your house and especially to pick us up."

"I didn't come to get you. I'm on my way into town. That girl that come with you is givin' New York makeovers, clothes and all. I'm on her list so I gotta go. You two can take care of my young 'uns while I'm in town. I think it's the least you can do after what you done to my poor dog. That was a good animal." She wiped at her eye and managed to smear a full inch of black eyeliner across her temple.

"Mrs. Nezbit," Sara began, "I really don't think we can—"

"Now don't you go gettin' uppity with me, or are you jealous of your sister? Just because she has the talent don't mean you don't have some somewhere. That's all the time I got to stay here helpin' you. Go ask Effie what to do. She's as smart as any of Fenny's kids are. See ya someday," she said with a cackle of laughter, then took off in a flurry of gravel and dirt.

When Sara stopped coughing, she looked at R. J. "Ariel is . . ."

"Making over the entire island," R. J. said in wonder.

"As you said, my cousin has a backbone of steel." There was pride in Sara's voice, and wonder. Ariel had said she could be a style consultant, but Sara had laughed at her.

"You can go into town if you want," R. J. said softly.

"And hand Ariel the eyeshadow brushes? No thanks. Let David do that. But you're going to owe Ariel. Thanks to her, it looks like you're going to be able to spend time alone with all six of the Nezbit kids."

"Do you think any of them will be in diapers?" There was fear in his voice.

"At least two. You know, don't you, that some kids stay in diapers until they're four years old. That means she could have several in diapers. Cloth diapers that have to be washed. Wonder if she has a washer, or does she wash them in the creek?"

"You have an ugly sense of humor."

"I developed it while working for my boss. Someday I'll have to tell you about him."

"Not today. I've had enough for today."

Sara pulled the front of her shirt out and glanced down. "And it's not even seven A.M. yet." She laughed when she saw the little spark in his eyes. "Obviously, you're not dead yet. Come on." She started walking down the driveway.

"If there are diapers, I'll give you a ten percent raise to change them," he said.

Sara shook her head. "Not enough. How about the corporate apartment by MoMA?"

"Do you know how much that thing is worth?" he asked, aghast.

"I hope they're cloth diapers."

"A twenty percent raise."

"I'll think about it," she said, smiling. It was nice to think about being off that island and home in safe New York.

They didn't see the house until they were above it, looking down on its long, narrow roof. A stone hillside had been cut away and the back wall of the one-story house had been built to fit against the rock. The front of the house faced the water—and the most spectacular view either R. J. or Sara had yet seen.

"Wow," Sara said, looking across the roof to the water. In the distance she could see three other islands, their forms misty and beautiful. There was a narrow expanse of beach in the front, the honey-colored sand meeting the water. Trees shaded the house but didn't block its view.

"Who do you think built this?" Sara asked.

"Nezbit," R. J. answered, and Sara couldn't help laughing.

"Another stolen house," she said. "But this one . . . I've never seen anything like it before. Have you?"

When R. J. said nothing, she looked at him. He was frowning in a way that made her sure he knew something.

"What is it?"

"When I was in college, I saw a plan for a building a lot like this one," he said.

"Do you think they stole the idea?"

"I don't know."

Sara wanted to kick him because she was sure he was keeping something from her. But in the next moment they heard a shot and in an instant, R.J. had pushed Sara to the ground again.

"Don't be scared," said a small voice from beside them.

They turned and saw two children, a boy and a girl, standing there. They were both about four years old, had brown curly hair, and, despite being grubby from head to toe, were two of the loveliest children Sara had ever seen. They didn't look as though they could possibly be the product of a union of Fenny Nezbit and his sun-wrinkled wife.

Chapter Thirteen

"Are you Nezbit children?" Sara asked, standing up slowly so as not to frighten them, but they didn't look scared. Whoever had fired the shot hadn't frightened them.

The girl nodded.

"Do you have a gun?" R. J. asked.

Sara started to tell him not to be absurd, but the children giggled. They were very dirty, their pretty faces darkened with what looked like weeks of not bathing. Their clothes were raggedy and drab-colored. Their feet were bare, calloused, and in-grained with grime.

"You didn't think we were elephants and you took a shot at us, did you?" R. J. asked and the children giggled more.

She'd never seen R.J. around children before, and she smiled.

"So who did fire that shot?" he asked.

"Gideon," the boy said. "For rabbits."

"For supper," the girl said.

"You don't eat what your mother gets at the grocery?" Sara asked.

"Sometimes," the little girl said, then in the next minute, they ran off into the woods.

"Rabbits for dinner," Sara said. "They're living wild."

"I'm not so sure." R.J. turned back to look at the house. "Shall we go down and meet the rest of the family?"

"Only if we must," Sara said, but she followed him down the path to the front of the house.

When they got to the bottom of the hill, they saw that the house was in need of repair. But in spite of gutters hanging down, cobwebs as big as towels, and piles of trash, underneath it all, the house was beautiful. "With some paint . . ." Sara began.

"And a crew of carpenters," R.J. said as he knocked on the front door.

In a few seconds it was opened by a girl, about twelve, who was obviously Fenny

Nezbit's daughter. She was as skinny as her parents, and she had ears that stuck straight out, parting her lank, blonde hair on both sides. Her nose was long, her eyes drooped at the corners, and her mouth was in what looked to be a perpetual downward bend.

"You the baby-sitter?" the girl asked in a voice that said she knew all about everything and was sick of it all.

"I guess so," Sara said tentatively and glanced at R.J. She'd really like to know how information traveled so quickly around the island.

"Then come in," the girl said, "but don't touch anything. My dad finds out you stole anything and he'll get you in court."

Behind the girl's back, R.J. raised his eyebrows.

Inside, the house was cool and shady, enough so that Sara didn't think there was any need for an air conditioner. As they followed the girl to the back of the house, they looked around. To the left was a big living room, with worn furniture facing an enormous TV that must have cost thousands. A stereo with speakers that a rock band would envy was on the wall opposite the big windows. On the back wall was a built-in cabinet with glass shelves. It looked as though it hadn't been dusted in years, but it held porcelain flowers that Sara knew were expensive. In the corners she saw stacks of boxes with the names of the TV shopping channels. It didn't look as though the boxes had been opened.

When Sara nudged R.J. to look at them, he nodded toward the right and she looked toward a hallway that contained more un-opened boxes. At the end of the hall was an open door and inside was a huge bed that looked as though it was carved into the shape of a shell. It wasn't to Sara's taste, but she recognized that it cost a lot of money.

When the girl stopped, they were in the kitchen. Before them, sitting at a small round table, were two more girls who looked just like the first one: stringy hair, skinny bodies, ears sticking out. They looked up at Sara and R.J. without curios-ity, then down again at their empty plates.

Smoking on the stove was a big cast-iron skillet with about half a pound of bacon fry-ing. The tallest girl cracked half a dozen eggs into the skillet on top of the bacon grease.

"Are you Effie?" Sara asked, taking a step forward. "Your mother told us about you. She said—"

"Don't come no closer," the girl at the stove said, her face turned into a snarl. "Yeah, I'm Effie, but no matter what you try to butter me up with, you ain't gettin' none of this food."

"We had breakfast, thank you," Sara said stiffly.

"Yeah, I bet you did," the girl said, smirking. "I know you ain't got nothin' to eat." This idea seemed to please her so much that she smiled as she used a spatula to place eggs and bacon onto three plates.

Sara looked at R.J. as though to ask for help, but he was looking around the house.

"Who built this place?" he asked.

"Nobody you ever heard of," Effie said nastily.

Sara rolled her eyes. "Mind if I use your restroom?" she asked as she turned toward the hallway.

"No!" one of the other girls shouted. "Use the outdoors."

"I beg your pardon," Sara said.

The three girls were looking at her, their faces wearing identical expressions of hostility.

Sara stopped walking.

"Who are the two little kids outside?" R. J. asked.

"Twins," one of the girls said, her mouth full, her lips glistening with grease.

When Sara looked at R. J., she saw that his face was flooding with red. He looked as though he were angry enough to kill someone. Without thinking, she put her arm in his. "I think we should go outside," she said loudly. "Your mother wants us to look after you, but you girls seem to be all right by yourself. I think she must have meant the twins. Maybe I should give them a bath."

"Not in here, you won't," Effie said. "Creek's good enough for them."

"You—" R. J. began, but Sara tightened her grip on his arm and started moving backward toward the door.

"Creek," Sara said. "Right. I'll bathe them in the creek."

One of the other girls spoke. "Daddy says they're too pretty anyway, so it's better if they're dirty. It'll keep 'em from gettin' too fond of themselves."

"Your father sounds like a man of great wisdom," Sara said, holding tightly onto R.J.'s arm, her eyes begging him to say nothing.

"You makin' fun of me?" the girl said, her small eyes narrowed. "My daddy'll get you back. On Monday he's gonna make you pay for what you did to the dog."

"I'm sure he will," Sara said, still backing up. "By the way, where is your father?"

"Don't know and it ain't none of your business anyway."

"Of course not," Sara said. "It's just that someone called your mother and—"

"There ain't no telephones. The cable's out." All three girls were looking at Sara as though she was trying to pry information out of them, which she was.

"Oh, right," Sara said. "It must have been the cellphone then."

"Cellphones don't work here."

"Then how did she know about the . . . ?"

"Makeovers?" Effie asked.

"Yes," Sara said, holding tightly onto R.J.'s arm.

"Same way she knows ever' thing. Gideon."

"And who is he?" R.J. asked, and there

was as much hostility in his voice as there was in the girls'.

"That's for me to know and you to find out," the oldest girl said, smirking.

Before R.J. could say anything, Sara pulled him through the door, shut it behind them, then led him to the shade of a big tree. "What was wrong with you?" she hissed. "We're supposed to find out information, not antagonize them."

R.J. leaned against the tree and looked out at the water. "That's like what I grew up in," he said quietly. "My sisters . . ." He didn't finish, but just stood there looking at the water.

If it hadn't been for the blood vein throbbing in his neck, she wouldn't have known how agitated he was. She sat down on a big tree root by his feet. "I would imagine those children have been abused," she said. "At least neglected. I doubt that they've had a chance to be anything except what their parents made them into."

"Why is it that two children can grow up in the same household, suffer the same abuse, but one turns out to be a murderer and the other one helps people?"

"I think they've been trying to answer that since Cain killed Abel."

R.J. sat down beside her. "I think that under the dirt on those little kids are bruises." He looked away, his eyes focused on something inside himself.

She wanted to sit there and listen to what R.J. needed to tell someone. She knew him well enough to know that he confided in no one, not his friends, not anyone. But Sara knew that they didn't have time for listening to anything right now. Maybe it was just now hitting R.J. what he was up against, what they were all up against. A dead man was a great deal different from a dead dog.

"At least you had sisters," she said. "My old man took out everything on *me.* Just me. For seventeen years I heard how my sainted mother had been killed by 'them.' He meant the people in Arundel. I thought they'd sent a hit man. You know what I found out after he died? That my father had been driving the car when she was killed and that he was drunk. I also found out that my mother's family paid for the lawyer that kept my father out of jail. I wondered if they'd done me a favor by that. If he'd been sent to prison, would I have been sent to live with one of them? Would I have grown up as Ariel did, with her trips to New York to have clothes made for her? Would I have a boyfriend like David?"

When she finished her speech, she looked at R.J. and saw that his eyes were no longer angry. He was smiling at her. "They did you a favor," he said softly. "If you were like Ariel, I wouldn't like you."

She wanted to make a smart-aleck retort to that, and a week ago she would have, but now she was pleased by the compliment. "Are you making a pass at me?"

"You haven't looked in a mirror for a long time, have you?" he asked, but he was chuckling. He got up, then held out his hands to her. When she came up, she was standing on a tree root and nearly as tall as he was. Their faces were close together.

There was something about the moment, about their shared backgrounds, that made her feel different toward him.

"If you fall in love with me I'll have to get a new secretary," R.J. said softly.

"Good," she said, moving away from him. "Then I'll get a good severance and move to L.A. and become a movie star."

She expected him to say something negative, that she was too old, or might be in jail for the rest of her life, but he didn't. Turning away, he said, "I'm sure you'll make it. You certainly have enough talent."

She followed him, smiling, but a few minutes later, she wondered if what he'd said was a compliment or not. Was he telling her that she was usually acting? That she wasn't a sincere, honest person?

"You want to tell me what you meant by that crack?" she asked, moving beside him. When she saw that he was smiling, she knew she was right. "What a rat fink you are! Here I was feeling sorry for you, but you say something nasty to me in return. You—"

She broke off because he put his arm around her waist, pulled her against him, and kissed her. It wasn't a light kiss, but the deep, hard kiss of a man who was at last getting something he'd wanted for a very long time. Sara felt herself melting against him, collapsing against him as though she was trying to draw strength from him. In the last horrible days, her world had been turned upside down, but she had stamped down her fears, and with them, she had buried her needs for reassurance. Now, in

R.J.'s strong arms, she hugged him back; she kissed him back.

When he moved his face from hers, she was ashamed to find that there were tears on her cheeks. "Sssssh," he said, caressing her hair, holding her against him. "It'll be all right. I'll see to that. I'm sorry I got angry back there. It won't happen again."

"It's okay," she said, sniffing and pulling away from him. She turned away so he couldn't see her face. When he was silent, she saw he was looking at her strangely. "I'm not going back to Ariel, if that's what you're thinking."

"No, I wasn't thinking that at all," he said softly. "About this . . ." He waved his hand to mean the kissing. "It was just one of those spur-of-the-moment things. I . . ." He trailed off and looked away. He seemed to be puzzled by something. "How about if we go find this kid Gideon?"

Sara was embarrassed about the way she'd kissed him back, about the way she'd held onto him. He'd never made a physical pass at her before. He'd made a thousand little sex jokes, pretending to want to make love to her, to want to— She looked up at him, but he was looking at the pathway in

front of them. It led up a steep hill and into
the dark woods. "I can't imagine how dumb
he is," Sara said at last, breaking the awkward silence.

"Because Effie is the smart one?" R.J.
said, and seemed to be glad for something
else to talk about.

"Exactly," she said.

"It's the firearm that worries me," R.J.
said. "Stay behind me and—"

"Let you get shot first?"

"It would solve a lot of problems," he said
in a joking way, but Sara didn't laugh. She
followed him up the hill and at the top, the
path turned right, leading into deep woods.
They walked for a while on soft pine nee-
dles, unable to see more than a few feet in
front of them because of the density of the
trees. It was very quiet in the woods, as
though they were the only people on earth.

When they came to the end, both of them
stood still for a moment and stared. Before
them was a small cabin, with a porch and
stone fireplace, a deer skin and a washtub
nailed to the side. It had been built on the
tip of a rock cliff that jutted out toward the
ocean. For all that the house below them

had a great view, the cabin had a better one.

There was smoke coming out of the chimney, but no one was around.

"If I didn't know where I was, I'd think I was on the set of a pioneer movie," Sara said. "This *is* the age of the Internet and space travel, isn't it?"

Stepping onto the porch, R.J. looked closely at the benches and the enameled pots. "Most of this stuff is handmade, and it's not for decoration. It's being used daily."

"By me," said a voice to their left, and they looked toward the end of the porch to see a tall, handsome boy with dark blond hair and deep blue eyes. He had a long string of fish in his hand. "Want some breakfast?"

"We just had—" Sara began.

"We'd love to!" R.J. said with enthusiasm. "Mind if I help you clean those?"

"If you know how to clean fish, you can move in," the boy said, smiling, showing perfect white teeth. "I'm Gideon."

"I'm—"

"I know who you are. Everyone does. You're the latest patsy." He looked at Sara. "And you must be the secretary."

"Assistant," she said, smiling. "I don't type very well, as I've been told many times."

"Too bad," Gideon said. "I have some briefs that need editing."

Both R. J. and Sara looked at him in consternation.

"Just kidding," he said. "No briefs. Nothing that needs editing. Just fish that need to be cleaned, then cooked." He walked around the front of the porch and they saw that he was at least six feet two. He was wearing clean jeans and a T-shirt, but both were faded and nearly worn-out. His feet were encased in worn moccasins.

For all that he was no more than sixteen, seventeen at the most, there was something about the boy that made a person relax around him.

"It didn't take you long to find me," he said over his shoulder as he went to a big rock protruding out of the ground in front of the cabin. R. J. practically ran down the steps to stand beside him.

Sara watched in amusement as R. J. eagerly took the fish from the boy and started to clean them. She'd had no idea he knew anything about the outdoors. "Do you have a restroom?" she asked.

"Not inside," Gideon said, smiling. "The girls refuse to let you use theirs?"

"Yeah," R. J. said as his knife expertly split a fish in half. "Real sweethearts."

"They're as mean as their father," Gideon said matter-of-factly, but with no animosity. He looked back at Sara. "Sorry, but all I have is an outhouse and the creek."

"I'll wait," she said as she sat down on a bench and watched the two men clean the fish. She was quiet for a few moments, but she couldn't stand it any longer. "So who are you and why do you live here in this cabin and who are the twins?"

Gideon laughed softly as he put the cleaned fish on a slab of wood and started toward the house. "Come inside," he said. "I need to get the twins fed."

Gideon held open the door and R. J. let Sara go in first. Inside, it was one room, with a big bed in the corner, a fireplace in one wall, an old-fashioned cookstove beside it, and a few pieces of old furniture with heavy rugs draped over them. It was cozy and homey, smelled of wood smoke, and Sara felt comfortable for the first time since Ariel

had arrived at her apartment in New York.
She sat down on the couch and propped
her feet on the pine coffee table.

"Put you through it, have they?" Gideon
said as he took a chair across from her. R. J.
was at the cookstove and he seemed to
know exactly what to do as he lifted the iron
disk and put in small branches taken from a
box on the floor.

"Bad enough that we'll do most anything
to get off this island," R. J. said.

Sara knew he was telling the young man
that he'd pay a lot for transportation, but
Gideon just looked straight ahead. He
wants something, she thought. Whatever he
tells us isn't going to be for free. And until
he gets what he wants, he's not going to
help us get out of here. She looked at
Gideon. "Are you as nice as you seem or are
you an illusion? Are you going to turn us
over to the sheriff for trespassing?"

"You know, don't you, that you're not in
any real trouble?" Gideon said.

"No," R. J. said, "we don't know that at
all." He gave Sara a look of warning that she
wasn't to get too comfortable and she
wasn't to trust too much. This young man

may seem nice, but he was the son of the dead man.

"The island was alerted that something big might be happening," Gideon said. "The office of billionaire Charles Dunkirk called a realtor in Arundel, and soon after that we heard that the illustrious R. J. Brompton was checking out every website about the island."

When Sara looked at R.J., he raised an eyebrow. She knew what he was thinking: good detective work.

"Someone from the island called your office in New York," Gideon continued, "and asked when the meeting on King's Isle was. He gave the wrong date. 'The eighteenth, right?' Something like that. Your secretary said that Mr. Brompton wouldn't be on King's Isle until the twenty-second, so we knew when you were arriving."

"And your plan was to put us in jail?" Sara asked, eyes wide.

"Not my plan," Gideon said. "I had nothing to do with it. I have nothing to do with any of them, but that doesn't keep me from knowing what's going on."

R.J. was heating a skillet full of oil, about to put the fish in. "Why would they want to make me hate this place? If they went to all that trouble to find out I was coming, they must have known I was thinking of buying land here. Or is it that they like this place just as it is and don't want to sell?"

"They very much want to sell. We're a dying society. The fishing is bad and all we have is a hope of tourism. But people never return to King's Isle," Gideon said. "There's nothing here. There're no beaches, no hot springs. The idea was to force you to stay here for a few days so you could look around and really get to know the place. They thought that if you spent time here, you'd come to like it."

"They scared us half to death," Sara said. "That man Lassiter—"

"He's a real sleaze, isn't he?" Gideon said. "Fenny's best friend. The island wasn't expecting four of you and that threw them off a bit. They were told it was just going to be the fabulously wealthy R. J. Brompton and his secretary. The truth is that the majority of the population had no idea what was going on. We were told to go spend two hours on the west side of the island and anybody who didn't would be fined a thousand dollars."

"That's a lot of money," Sara said.

"The day before you arrived, the underground telephone cable was cut."

"Did *you* go to the west side of the island?" R.J. asked.

"I never do anything anybody tells me to do," Gideon said and for the first time the humor was gone from his voice. "Tell me, Mr. Brompton, what were you going to do about King's Isle?"

"Tell Charley Dunkirk not to buy anything here."

Sara looked at him in astonishment. "You'd already made up your mind before . . . ?"

"Before we were arrested on a made-up charge? Yeah. I didn't like the place the second we got off the ferry."

"Right," Gideon said. "There are too many people here, too many houses involved. It's easier to start from scratch."

"Smart kid," R.J. said. "You want to work for me?"

His remark was meant as a joke, but Gideon didn't take it as such. "Yes," he said seriously. "Anywhere, anytime. As you said, I'll do anything to get off this island."

R.J. slid six perfectly fried fish onto a

platter. "Why don't you just leave? You look big enough."

"I'm underage and Nezbit would come after me."

"Nezbit? Your father?"

"I have no proof of it, but I'm sure he's not my biological father, and the law says he is so I have to stay. Besides . . ."

"The twins," Sara said softly. "Whose are they?"

"I don't know. The old man brought them home one day like he'd found puppies."

"Didn't Social Services—?"

"Here? Nobody on King's Isle will go up against the Unholy Trio."

"Nezbit, Lassiter, and the judge," R.J. said.

"Right on."

R.J. smiled. "So what happens now?"

"They'll fine you over that dog Nezbit used to torture. Poor thing was probably glad to die."

"How is Phyllis Vancurren involved in all this?" R.J. asked.

Gideon shrugged. "She was told to be very nice to R. J. Brompton. They wanted to put him—you—in the jail upstairs in her house so you couldn't escape. She was told that Brompton was known to be 'a great cocksman,' so she was allowed to seduce him."

Sara gave R. J. an I-told-you-so look, but he ignored her as he put the platter of fish on the table.

It was when young Gideon got up from the chair that Sara saw the scars on the back of his legs. His trouser leg had caught on the bottom of the chair and ridden up to expose a few inches of skin. When he saw Sara looking, he brushed his trousers down.

"I have to get the twins," Gideon said, then quickly went out the door.

"Did you see?" Sara whispered to R. J.

"Yeah, I saw. Don't mistake his niceness. There's enough hatred in that young man to start a war."

"Or to kill someone?"

"Easily."

"But he stays here to take care of the little kids."

"Yeah, maybe. But if Nezbit was out of the way, he'd be free to leave the island and take the twins with him—if that's what he wants to do. I'm not so sure." He looked at the door when he heard voices.

"I like him and I vote that we tell him

about Nezbit being dead," Sara said. "Gideon is the first person on this island that I've thought couldn't possibly be a murderer. The rest of them . . ." She rubbed her arms as she thought of the people they'd met so far. "We need help and we need it quickly. We don't have much time. I expect sirens to go off any second because they've found the body and they're searching for us."

"I'm sure everyone on this island knows exactly where we are."

"That's reassuring." When the door opened and Gideon came in with the twins, Sara stopped talking. Both she and R. J. watched the young man with the children. The love he had for them was evident. He sat them at the table, with big pillows on the chairs so they were high enough, then carefully pulled every bite off the fish to make sure there were no bones.

Sara watched the four of them at the table for about five minutes, then that's all she could stand. All of them were nibbling on the remains of a few fish, but nothing else. To the right of the cookstove was a tall cabinet with a cotton curtain hanging across it. She could see a bag of flour peeping out of a corner and next to it was a can of baking powder. Getting up, she went to the cabinet and, without asking permission, she flung back the curtain. Everything she needed was there.

"Peel a dozen of these," she said to R.J. as she handed him a bag of store-bought apples. She was glad she wasn't going to have to deal with the hindquarters of some recently slaughtered wild animal.

"And, Gideon, take those children and a bar of soap outside. They don't sit down to my table until they're clean."

"Yes, ma'am," he said, then grabbed a child under each arm and hurried to the door.

"Heterosexual," Sara said, staring at the closed door.

"What?" R.J. whispered.

"Gideon is heterosexual. The way you tell for sure is to say, 'If you'll go outside and set yourself on fire, I'll cook.' Straight men will say, 'Where are the matches?' Gay men— Hey! Are you listening to me?" R.J. had a glazed expression on his face that she'd never seen before.

"You can cook?"

"I had to if I wanted anything to eat. Are

you just going to sit there or are you going to help me?"

"Do with me what you will," he said, and in the next second he was peeling apples. "Wow, you can cook," he kept saying.

She pointed a long knife at him. "When we get back to New York, if you ever expect me to cook anything for you, I'll—"

He grabbed her hand and quickly kissed the back of it. "Never. I promise. Never." For a full minute, he was silent as he peeled apples, then he said, "What kind of things can you cook?"

"If you fall in love with me I'll have to get a new boss," she said, mimicking his earlier phrase, then they looked at each other and laughed.

Chapter Fourteen

"So how did Nezbit make his money?" R.J. asked, leaning back in his chair on two legs, a toothpick in his mouth. Sara thought all that was needed was for Charlie Daniels to be playing in the background.

"That's the great mystery of the island," Gideon said, pushing away his plate. He had eaten some of everything Sara had made: fried apples, biscuits, scrambled eggs, bacon, and little pancakes with smiley faces on them. The twins had run outside ten minutes before, probably to get the clean off them. "How old are you?" Gideon asked Sara.

"Too old for you," R.J. said quickly. "So how do you think your dad—Sorry, Nezbit— makes his money?"

"And who's the TV shopper?" Sara nodded toward the house below them.

"His wife," Gideon said, shrugging.

Sara looked at R.J. Gideon didn't call either of them mother or father.

"I don't trust any of this," R.J. said to
Gideon and Sara could hear the caution in
his voice. "I don't think any of this is as innocent as you think it is. I think someone
means to harm us."

Gideon looked from one to the other of
them. "What's happened?"

Sara sat down at the table with them.
"You need to tell him," she said to R.J. "We
have today and tomorrow and that's it. If
someone opens that— You know what I
mean. We have to trust *someone.*"

Gideon looked at R.J. "I can understand
that you don't trust me since I live here on
this godforsaken island. When I said I'd do
anything to get off it, I was telling the truth.
Fenny Nezbit has used me as a pack horse
since I was six years old. I don't know
where I came from, but I suspect my ances-
try has something to do with that house he
lives in and with this cabin."

Getting up, he went to an old cabinet
against a wall, pulled out a tattered sketch

book, and tossed it on the table. "I drew those."

R.J. took the book and began flipping pages as Sara looked over his shoulder. There were beautiful drawings of buildings that seemed to rise out of the sea, others that were set back into cliffs so they looked to be part of the landscape. There were pages of drawings of seashells and clams, then the shapes were transformed into houses.

"You have talent," R.J. said.

"Which proves I'm not Fenny Nezbit's son." Gideon sat back down at the table. "He made me quit high school when I turned sixteen. He said too much education 'waren't good for a man.' I was going to run away then. I was going to stow away on that damned ferry boat and leave this island forever."

There was so much anger in his voice that Sara reached out and put her hand over his. "That's when he brought the twins home, isn't it?"

"Yes. He knew me. He said he'd throw the kids out to sea if I left."

"What about their parents?" R.J. asked.

Gideon shrugged. "I have no idea. Boat

wreck, probably. I tried to find out, but couldn't."

Sara felt her heart breaking at what the beautiful boy had gone through, but R.J. was sitting back in his seat and watching him. She got the feeling that he didn't trust Gideon, but she wasn't sure why. Did he think the boy was lying?

"He's dead," R.J. said after a while.

"What?"

"John Fenwick Nezbit is dead. We found him shot through the head and lying in the bathtub in Phyllis Vancurren's house."

Gideon's handsome face turned pale.

"Are you all right?" Sara asked.

"It's over," he whispered. "The twins and I are free. We can leave and no one will come after us. Thank you."

"Wait a minute!" R.J. said. "We didn't kill him."

"Then who did?" Gideon asked, then smiled a bit. "Right, you think I should know that." He got up from the table and went to the front window to look out. "It could have been a hundred people, including Phyllis. Fenny used to pester her until she threatened him with death. Everyone knew she'd been the mistress of some rich man, so

Fenny thought she was a whore and should put out for him."

"Who else?" R.J. asked.

"The other two."

"Lassiter and the judge?"

"My money's on Lassiter," Sara said. "He's the slimiest man I've ever met. He made my skin crawl."

"Who came up with the idea of arresting us?" R.J. asked. "And who cut the cable?"

"I don't know," Gideon said. "They don't tell me anything. The twins like to listen at doors and they tell me what they hear. I take that and what I know of Fenny and put it all together."

"What do you think will happen if some-one finds Nezbit's body?" Sara asked.

"Where is it?"

R.J. and Sara looked at each other, weighing whether or not they could trust this young man this much. R.J. made a de-cision. "It's in the freezer in Phyllis's base-ment."

"Good," Gideon said. "She'll never find it there. She never uses that freezer."

"You sound like you know her well."

Gideon gave Sara a sheepish grin. "All the young men on the island know lots about

Phyllis Vancurren and her house. Did you see the blue roses?"

"Yes," Sara said, smiling, "but I'd already counted steps so we didn't need them."

"Counted steps?"

"Sara remembers things," R.J. said before she could reply. "What will happen if they find the body before the hearing on Monday?"

"It won't be good," Gideon said. "Judge Proctor and Nezbit are—"

"Related," R.J. said. "Yeah, we've been told."

"Who really, really wanted Nezbit dead?" Sara asked. "Besides us, that is?"

"And me," Gideon said. "My guess is it was whoever wanted the money but couldn't find it."

"Ah," R.J. said. "Now we get back to that. What money?"

"Thirty-two years old," Sara said softly. "Phyllis said Fenny Nezbit hasn't worked since he was thirty-two years old."

"That implies that he worked before he was thirty-two," Gideon said, then waved his hand. "I would imagine he found a shipwreck. Not a big ship, but something from

Florida, rich, retired people, maybe. Boats wreck around here often."

"Very often?" R. J. asked.

"More often than is probably normal," Gideon said, but looked away as he said it.

Sara knew what R. J. was thinking. Could it be possible that the islanders were supplementing their income with what they made by making ships wreck? How were they doing it?

"What we need to do is find out where Nezbit was getting his money, who wanted it enough to kill him, and to do it in less than two days."

" 'Bout sums it up," Gideon said, his eyes laughing at the absurdity of that idea. "Two days to solve something that others on this island have been trying to find out for over ten years. Every three months Fenny leaves—or left, I guess—the island and returned with cash. He and his wife spent the money to the bone, then Nezbit went off to the mainland again and returned with more cash."

"What does he do just before he leaves?"

"Goes to the middle of the island and disappears for about six hours."

"And of course you followed him," R. J. said.

"When ol' Fenny left town it looked like the Pied Piper the way people followed him, but he always managed to give them the slip. I can attest to the fact that he vanished into thin air. Poof! He was gone."

"But you've looked over that area when he wasn't there, haven't you?"

"Many, many times," Gideon said seriously. "I used to fantasize about finding the money and running away with it. But then, I think that's the dream of every man, woman, and child on this island. 'Fenny's gold,' we call it."

"The man was an alcoholic," Sara said. "So was my father, and he couldn't keep a secret." Even as she said it, she knew it wasn't true. No matter how drunk her father got or how often, he'd never told her the truth about the night her mother died.

"You name it and it's been tried," Gideon said, "but no one could pry a word from Fenny. His wife used to tell him that if he died, the money would be lost. Fenny said, 'Then you'll miss me, won't you?' He didn't tell anyone anything. He enjoyed the people following him, and he liked to lead them on wild-goose chases. He grew up on this island and knew every inch of it well. His father drank and Fenny used to stay in the hills for weeks at a time. He knew all about living off the land."

"Like you do," R.J. said, looking around the cabin.

"Like I've had to learn," Gideon said, his eyes defensive. "As soon as I was taller than Nezbit, I moved out of that house and into here. I think that whoever built that house lived in this cabin while it was being built—and I think I'm connected to him."

"Couldn't you check the deeds to find out who built it?" Sara asked.

"For all that Nezbit looks stupid, he isn't," Gideon said. "His name is on the deed as the original owner. There's no record that I can find of who built the house. The old-timers say, 'Some man from the mainland.' He stayed to himself and met no one here."

"Smart man," R.J. said.

"Where were the hot springs?" Sara asked.

"You can't go up there," Gideon said quickly. "The ground is loose and there are cave-ins."

"From the explosion?" R.J. asked.

"From the dynamite," Gideon answered. "The hot springs that made this town rich weren't real. Way up on top is a natural stone reservoir. Back in the 1890s some men put big iron cauldrons in the middle of it and heated the water, then piped it down the hillside into little tubs that were also heated. For some unknown reason, somebody dynamited the reservoir and put a hole in it. That was the end of the phony hot springs."

"Maybe we could package this island as the most notorious—" R. J. began.

"Most wicked," Sara said.

"Yes, most wicked island in the U.S. 'Come see where the Victorians duped the unsuspecting rich.' "

"And where the islanders made the boats wreck on the rocks so they could steal their riches," said Sara.

"And babies," Gideon said.

Sobering, R. J. and Sara looked at him.

"I had to have come from somewhere and those twins don't belong to anybody on this island," Gideon said.

R. J. and Sara looked at each other, then got up from the table. "You ready?" he asked.

She knew what he was talking about without his having to say it, and she was glad that they weren't going to have an argument about her going. "I need some hiking boots."

"You can't go up there," Gideon said. "It really is dangerous, and besides, the whole place has been combed by every resident on this island. You'll never find Fenny's gold—if it exists. He hadn't been off the island in six months. Maybe he took all there was."

"Can you get her some shoes?" R.J. asked Gideon.

The young man shook his head in disbelief, then smiled. "Been nice knowing the both of you," he said. "For a minute there, I had some hope of getting off this island."

"If I do, you will," R.J. said. "And that's a promise."

"With the twins," Sara said. "We'll even try to find out who their parents are."

For a moment, the emotion in Gideon's eyes was almost more than Sara could bear.

"What size shoe do you wear?" he asked.

"Six," Sara said.

"Same as Effie," Gideon said. "This will be easy. You need anything else?"

"A backpack, water bottles, socks of course, a good moisturizer, flashlights, and—"

"And a cellphone," R.J. said. "Get us what you can. I just want to see where the hot springs were."

"And a toothbrush and paste," Sara said. "Shampoo and a portable shower, or maybe a big claw-foot bathtub would be nice. And a—"

"A map," Gideon said. "Wait here while I tell the kids what to get, then I'll go start a fight with Effie while the kids raid the house. We'll be back in ten minutes."

Chapter Fifteen

"Tell me again why we're doing this?" Sara asked as soon as Gideon left the cabin.

"I don't believe what I'm being told." He was looking out the window. "You think that kid has gone to the police?"

"No. Why don't you ever believe anybody?"

"I believed what I saw when I first met you," R.J. said defensively. "It's just that I don't think we were told the whole truth about why we were put in jail. I think it was the story that was put out, but it doesn't make sense."

Sara was still trying to figure out what R.J. meant about first seeing her. She was told that he'd been on the elevator, the doors were about to close, and R.J. had said, "That one. I want *her.*" People said that he was trying to make a point, that you could choose some nobody clerk and elevate her to the glorious job of waiting on R.J. Brompton hand and foot, 24/7. But now R.J. was implying that there was more to it. "No, it doesn't make sense," she said.

"Right. Jail and dead bodies in the bathtub aren't going to make a person want to stay someplace."

Sara had to work to come out of her reverie. "They want to make sure we *don't* want to buy any property, don't they?"

"That's what I think. I think there's something here that someone wants to keep secret."

"I can't imagine what," Sara said. "Kidnapping, shipwrecks, you name it, it seems to be going on in this place."

"Not to mention murder." He looked at her. "What if we found a dead body in the bathtub, but later managed to get off the island without being found out?"

Sara nodded. "We wouldn't come back, would we?"

"No. And King's Isle would become our worst nightmare. We'd spend our lives reading the newspaper and searching the Internet to see if the body had been found yet."

"We'd live in terror that they'd come after us," she added. "And in the business world, word would get out that Charley Dunkirk had checked out this island and said it was a bad bet."

"That would mean that whoever didn't want outsiders here would have another few years to hide whatever he's hiding."

"Good thinking," Sara said.

"Come on, Johnson," R. J. said. "You can give me a better compliment than that."

"It's a good theory, but we don't know if it's true or not. Why did you hire *me?*" she blurted out. "There are a dozen women in your office who *can* type. Why didn't you hire one of them?"

"Your great memory."

"You didn't know anything about me when you hired me—except what was in a personnel file and that wasn't much."

"Think not?" he asked. "You think that story's true that I picked you out at random?"

Her eyes were wide. "Yes, I do . . . did.

But you—" She was interrupted by Gideon and the twins bursting into the room.

"Come see what we got!" he said excitedly.

R.J. and Sara went onto the porch. Before them was a large Radio Flyer wagon full of gear. On the top was a kit that had been put together by a shopping channel for emergencies. There were two flashlights, matches coated in wax, two space blankets in tiny pouches, packets of food, candles, water bottles, a first aid kit. Under the box were heavy hiking boots in size six and three pairs of women's cotton socks.

"Thought you might need these," Gideon said, holding up two flannel shirts, a man's large and a woman's small.

"We did good?" the little boy asked.

Sara swooped him into her arms and hugged him. "You did brilliantly. Wonderful. Fabulous." She buried her face in his neck and blew raspberries until he was screaming with laughter.

"Me! Me!" the girl yelled as Sara put the boy down and grabbed her. She raspberried and tickled the child until she too was squealing.

When she set the girl down, Sara turned to Gideon. "What are their names?"

"Beatrice and Bertie."

"Not what I'd call Nezbit names," Sara said.

"Yeah," Gideon said, "I've wondered if they're their real names."

"Knowing would make it easier to find their parents."

R.J. was going through the items in the wagon and shoving them into two nylon backpacks.

"Want to go with us?" Sara asked Gideon.

"I'm sure he has other things to do," R.J. said quickly, letting Sara know that he wanted the two of them to go alone. "But maybe you could draw us a map."

"Sure," Gideon said, though Sara thought he was disappointed at not being asked to go. As he and R.J. went into the cabin, the twins behind them, Sara looked at Gideon's strong, young back and thought how much somebody somewhere had lost in not seeing him grow up.

Bending, she rearranged the contents of the two backpacks, then pulled on a pair of socks and laced up the heavy boots. Holding Ariel's pretty sandals on her fingertips, she wondered how her cousin was doing. What had she thought when she awoke this morning and found a note from R.J.? What had the note said? Had it been nice, or had it been R.J.'s usual brusque style? *You two are worthless so Johnson and I are going on without you. Have a nice day. R.J.*

Sara hadn't had time to think about anything since she awoke on a cold, hard cushion this morning, but she'd been glad to hear that David and Ariel hadn't stayed cowering in Phyllis's house, scared and trembling. Instead, Ariel had found a way to earn money.

"And hear gossip," Sara said, standing up straight. R.J. had left them two hundred dollars, the money he always kept in his shoes. There was no need for Ariel to get a job, but she had. And not just any job. Ariel had set herself up as the person who every woman in town would want to visit. And talk to.

Sara looked up at the cabin and saw R.J. and Gideon inside, standing by the window and talking. From the arm gestures, R.J. was getting directions to the top of the center of the island. And what did he expect to find up there? A motive for murder? A reason that the people on this island didn't want them to be here? Sara agreed with R. J. that it was more likely that they'd been accused of a false crime to keep them away from King's Isle, not to make them like it. Even if the murder hadn't happened, even if on Monday the judge said the dog case was ridiculous and threw it out, they'd still never want to return to the island.

If she was sure that whoever was doing this only wanted to make them go away and never return, Sara would want to return to Phyllis's house and wait it out. But she wasn't sure what was going on. Young Gideon was the only person who would talk to them, so it wasn't as though they could go around town asking questions.

Like Ariel can, Sara thought, smiling.

R. J. came onto the porch and looked at her in question. Why was she smiling? She made a little gesture meant to say that she'd tell him later.

"I could leave the twins with Effie and the girls," Gideon was saying. "They won't like it, but I could do it."

"No," R. J. said. "We can do this by ourselves. Both Sara and I've had some experience climbing, so we'll be fine."

Sara's eyes widened. Experience climbing? Did that include getting on and off the Fifth Avenue bus? Turning away so Gideon wouldn't see her face, Sara slipped the lighter backpack on and tied the flannel shirt around her waist.

"You look funny," Beatrice said.

"I feel funny."

"Will you come back?"

"I certainly hope so," Sara said, adjusting the straps to fit her height.

"Sometimes they don't," Bertie said.

"Great," Sara said. "Thanks for telling me that. Would you guys mind not telling anyone about us?"

"We never tell what Gideon does. He has lots and lots of secrets, but we never tell them."

Sara didn't like what the twins were saying. R.J. and Gideon were still talking and there was a light across Gideon's handsome face that made him look older and sinister. She knelt down to eye level with the children. "Does Gideon ever hurt you?"

"No, silly," Beatrice said. "He's nice. He gives us candy when we're good."

Sara looked at Bertie. "Does anybody hurt you?"

His little face scrunched up into a fierce look. "If Effie tries to hit me I hit her back."

Sara laughed, then caught herself. "It's not nice to hit anyone, but—"

"Come on, Johnson," R.J. called. "You can adopt the kids later. We're burnin' daylight."

"Daniel Boone calls," she muttered, standing up.

"*Will* you adopt us?" Bertie asked, his eyes wide. "Gideon said that somebody would."

"I . . . I have to go," Sara said, glaring at R.J. when he smiled at her predicament.

When Gideon stepped forward, the children attached themselves to his legs. "Maybe she'll marry me and we'll all be a family," he said, smiling at Sara in a way that made her blush.

"Let's go!" R.J. said loudly.

"See ya!" Sara called as she followed R.J. past the cabin and into the woods. "See you when we get back."

"Which will be next week at this rate," R.J. mumbled.

"Jealous?" Sara asked.

"Of you and that boy?"

"Of me and that boy and David. Don't forget David."

"Wonder what he's doing while Little Miss Makeover is doing all the work?"

"Smiling at the women," Sara said. "Or taking his shirt off and letting them look at him. There are lots of things that David can do."

"Stop lusting after those kids and watch where you're going," R. J. said gruffly.

Sara laughed.

"Where you goin', Gideon?" Beatrice asked.

"After those two idiots," he said, lacing on a pair of heavy hiking boots. "They're our best chance of getting off this island so I'm not going to let them get killed."

"Da won't let us leave King's Isle," Bertie said.

"I've told you a thousand times that he's not your father, so stop calling him that."

At Gideon's tone, Beatrice began to cry.

"Hush, honey, I'm not mad."

"You were gonna take me fishin'," Bertie said. "In the boat."

"I can't today. Go down to the house and tell Effie she has to feed you."

"Won't," Beatrice said and the twins backed up against each other.

Gideon sighed. "Okay, then stay here in the cabin. Don't go more than a yard from it, you hear me? There are cold biscuits and bacon in the cabinet and apple juice in there too. Just stay here and play with your toys and don't get into trouble. You hear me?"

Both of the twins nodded, then watched in silence as Gideon strapped on an old backpack and slung his rifle over his shoulder. He put a box and a half of cartridges in the bottom of his pack. "No fighting, no hitting, don't get into anything that will hurt you, and stay as far away from the girls as possible."

"But you said—" Beatrice began.

"I know, I said to go to Effie, but I'm afraid you'll tell her too much."

"We don't tell," Bertie said.

"That's true, but this secret is bigger than the others." Gideon looked out the window. "I'm glad you don't know where we're going."

"Top of the mountain to the hot springs," Bertie said proudly.

Gideon groaned. "Too smart is what you are. Now stay here and color. I should be back before dark. I just want to make sure those city slickers don't get killed."

"Our ticket out," Bertie said, making Gideon laugh.

"Okay, that's all the TV you get. Now give me a hug and let me go. I'm going to have to doubletime it to get there before they do."

"Why do you have to get there first?" Beatrice asked.

"There are some things that I need to—"

"To win!" Bertie said.

"That's right. It's a race and I need to win. Now hugs," Gideon said.

Gideon was only a quarter mile up the trail when the twins decided to follow him. They'd had a lifetime of hiding to escape the notice of the Nezbit family, so they were good at being quiet. Gideon never heard so much as a footstep.

Chapter Sixteen

"Why were you smiling?" R.J. asked as soon as they were on the well-worn trail toward the center of the island.

"I was thinking about Ariel. She put herself in a position to hear all the gossip of the town."

R.J. gave her a sharp look.

"Didn't think of that, did you?"

"No, but that was smart of her," he said, smiling. "Maybe she *is* your cousin after all."

"Okay," Sara said, halting on the trail. "That does it. First you kiss me and now you've given me more than one compliment. Either the world is ending or you think you're going to die soon."

Reaching back, he took her hand. "I want

you on my side at the hearing on Monday. As for the kiss, a pretty girl and—"

"Spare me," she said, starting to walk again and dropping his hand. She was just one of many women. It was the big complaint of all the women who came weeping to her, saying that R. J. had broken it off with them.

As they walked, she looked at the back of him and wondered what the truth was. "Do you have a plan about all this?"

"None whatever. What about you?"

"None," she said cheerfully. "Are you sure Nezbit was dead? He wasn't planted in the bathtub and pretending to be dead, was he?"

"Very sure. His body was disgustingly cold."

"Do you think—?" she began but stopped when R. J. halted. She stopped beside him.

"Don't look back, but someone is following us," he said quickly. "And I think someone is ahead of us too. I think it's just possible there are a parade of people around us. See those rocks up there?" he asked. "Think you could walk along the edge of them?"

"Yes," Sara said, but she wasn't sure she

could. They seemed to go straight up and straight down.

"Come on then," he said. "Want me to carry your pack?"

"No. I put all the heavy stuff in yours so I'm fine."

She followed R. J. through tall grass until they emerged on a rocky surface. Above them were sheer rocks, looming high overhead. "I think we can go this way," R. J. whispered and held out his hand to help her up.

She couldn't find a foothold in the stone surface, so R. J. had to pull her up, and she scraped her knee on the rock.

"All right?" he whispered.

When she nodded, he turned and started climbing up until he was against the tall rocks, then he reached down for her. Sara was determined to make it on her own. She threw one leg up high, then used all her muscles to follow her leg with the rest of her body. She made it up, and R. J. caught her to him in his arms, his finger to his lips bidding her to be quiet.

They inched along the rock, their backs to it, feeling their way to the left. Twice R. J. paused and looked out at what they could see of the countryside. Both times Sara was silent, hating the height, hating not having a good foothold, but she said nothing. When R.J. nodded, she started inching along again.

"Look!" he whispered, but she couldn't see around him to what he was seeing.

With her breath held, she watched him remove his pack, then hand it to her. "Too many doughnuts," he whispered, then he turned sharply left and disappeared from her view. Holding on as best she could, her pack on her back, his on her front, she tried to turn enough so that she could see what had happened to him, but she could see nothing.

"In here," she heard R.J. whisper. "Can you hand me the packs?"

Sara shook her head. Taking off the packs would make her fall.

He must have been able to see her because he said, "Okay, then, I think you're skinny enough to come through with them on."

"I can't move," she whispered back to him.

In the next second, he grabbed her arm and pulled hard. Sara went flying back into what seemed to be solid rock. The front pack caught but R.J. kept pulling, and she finally slid through the narrow space into a passage about six feet wide. Ahead of them the space widened and she could see light.

She wanted to cover her fear. "We found Fenny's gold, didn't we? Tell me this is the cave where he disappeared and where no one could find him."

R.J. kicked something on the rock floor and Sara looked down. It was an old beer can. "I don't think we're the first ones to find this place."

They walked between the rocks for a few yards until they came out at a pool of water. Above it, the rocks formed a roof with a hole in it. "How beautiful," Sara breathed. "Breathtaking."

"Yet another thing that someone doesn't want to be found," R.J. said. "I'll bet this is the local skinny-dip pool." He gave her a look from under his lashes. "You wouldn't want to . . ."

She knew he was teasing her, as he always had, but suddenly Sara felt different. Instead of turning up her nose at him, she thought it might be nice to strip off and dive into the pool.

"Don't look at me like that," R. J. growled. "We have work to do. We have—"

Turning abruptly, he pulled her into his arms and held her. "I shouldn't have brought you here. I shouldn't have let you come with me, but I couldn't bear to think of you with that kid David, then with Gideon. Don't you understand that they're just *boys?*"

Sara felt anger well up inside her and she pushed him away. "I'm not going to be one of your women," she said. "I've seen what you do to them and I won't be one of them. I knew why you let me come with you, but it didn't matter as long as I got to go. I let you kiss me because . . . I don't know why I did it. It was the right moment and the right time, but now . . ."

She had to push away from him because she was afraid she'd fall against him and give herself to him. She'd worked hard in the last two days to control the fear that was coursing through her, and she'd been closer to R. J. than she ever had before. He was a sexy man. He wasn't handsome, but there was a charisma about him that drew women to him. But she wasn't going to be one of many!

"Sorry," he said, looking into her eyes. "I mistook what I was seeing. I thought—"

"You don't have to tell me what you thought. I know you, remember? You think all women are dying to jump into bed with you. But I'm not!"

The moment the words were out, Sara wished she hadn't said them. She knew she had given him a look that was suggestive. She'd thought about jumping in the pretty pond with him and her eyes had said that. But when he reacted, she'd attacked him. "This is my fault," she said under her breath. "Could we just go wherever it is we're going?"

R. J.'s face was cold. "Maybe you should go back to Gideon. Or to Ariel. Help her with her makeovers."

"No, I don't want to," she said more fiercely than she'd meant to. "Could we just go? Please?"

He nodded, then turned and started walking, and she could tell by the set of his shoulders that he was angry.

They managed to climb out of the big room, up the side of the rock, and Sara wished she hadn't been so adamant when R. J. put his arms around her, for his attitude had changed. Instead of laughing and teasing, flirting, he was now cool and distant, formal and polite. He held out his hand when she needed help, but he withdrew it quickly.

She followed him across the top of a ridge of rock and when she tripped, he stopped and looked back at her, but he didn't offer to help her up.

The first time they stopped to rest and drink water, she asked if she could see the map that Gideon had drawn. She studied it and saw that the trail Gideon had marked was below them. They were heading in the right direction, but they weren't on the trail that Gideon had marked.

"You don't trust him, do you?"

"I don't trust anyone on this island." R.J. took a deep drink of water. "I'm beginning to think that if I get out of here, I'll tell Charley to buy every inch of land and evict all these people. My gut feeling is that there are some very ugly things going on around here."

"Or we're being lied to," Sara said idly.

"Nezbit's dead body wasn't a lie."

"No, but in a way, murder is sort of normal, isn't it? Shipwrecks and children being brought home like puppies in a blanket are not normal."

R.J. was looking at her with his head cocked to one side. "Do you think we were sent up here to get rid of us? Get us out of the way until the hearing on Monday? Maybe the goal is to keep us quiet for a few days and what better way than to send us up to have a look at the old hot springs?"

Sara moved away from the rock she was leaning on and looked around her. It was afternoon now and she was hungry. "How about if we get to the hot springs, look at them, then get ourselves back to town as fast as possible?"

"I think you're right," R.J. said. "Or we could skip the hot springs altogether."

At that moment they heard a shot. It was a long way off, but it still echoed until it sounded as though there were a thousand people firing rifles. "Let's go," R.J. said, shoving the plastic water bottle in his pack and putting it on his back.

In the next second they felt the first warm drops of rain. Two seconds later a storm erupted. Fierce thunder and lightning split a downpour so thick that Sara could hardly see R.J. in front of her. Bending over, his

head down, he was running along the narrow, steep trail.

"You okay?" he yelled back at her. She
shouted yes, but she wasn't sure he heard
her. They had ponchos in their packs, but
there was nowhere to stop to put them on.

Around them were tall trees, and the lightning seemed to be cracking right above
them. In one particularly loud flash, with the
thunder coming instantly and so loud that it
was deafening, Sara screamed. In the next
second, R. J. was beside her, his arm across
her shoulders protectively.

"I think I saw shelter," he yelled. "Come
with me."

She kept her head down, hiding under his
arm, trying to keep the rain from lashing at
her face. Twice, she tried to look up, but
R. J. pushed her face back down. Around
them the lightning came fast and brilliant,
and she heard what sounded like trees
breaking. "Can we go back?" she yelled up
at him and thought she heard the word
"no."

She twisted around to look at the trail behind them. A flash of lightning exposed a
blurry image. Had a tree fallen across the
trail?

As she looked out from under his protective arm, a flash of lightning came and for a split second she saw Gideon standing about a hundred yards behind them. He was clearly outlined in the light, a pack on his back, a rifle in his hands. For all that the rain was coming down hard, he had his head up, his eyes straight ahead, watching them. He looked like a mountain man of old, as though he belonged there on that rocky surface, with the trees all around him. And he looked as though he was hunting bear— but his eyes were on *them.*

Twisting around again, Sara got as close to R.J.'s ear as she could and said, "I saw Gideon. He's behind us."

"Yes," R.J. said, then he started walking faster.

When she tripped over the rough ground, his grip on her tightened until he was nearly carrying her. She wanted to ask where they were going, but she was sure he didn't know. Or did he? Had he asked Gideon for a map to test him? R.J. said he'd studied King's Isle for weeks before they came here. Had he studied maps also? For all she knew, R.J. had called in engineers to report on the place. Had R.J. seen that Gideon's map wasn't correct and he'd gone the way that he knew to be correct? But correct to get them where?

"Here!" R.J. shouted, then he turned left abruptly. Again, she looked under his arm and waited for the lightning to flash. She saw no one, just an empty trail and the hard-driving rain. When a second flash came, she saw what looked to be a pile of stones where R.J. had turned left.

In the next second, everything happened at once. Lighting flashed beside them, a huge tree cracked, R.J. tightened his grip on Sara and made a leap. When they hit the ground, Sara started to take another step, but R.J. pulled her back.

There was no other step. They were on the edge of a precipice.

With the tree crashing down above them, they dropped to the ground, clinging to each other tightly, R.J.'s arms over Sara's head. The tree came down all around them, but none of the heavy branches hit them. When the tree stopped coming down, and the earth stopped vibrating, they looked at each other and smiled. They had made it!

But then the ground under them broke away and they fell down. Wrapped into one being, they fell down and down, to land hard on the floor below.

"Sara?" R.J. whispered after the dirt settled. His arms were still around her. He'd managed to twist so he came down on the bottom. "Are you all right?"

When she didn't answer, he disentangled their bodies and tried to look at her. There was little light. About fifty feet above them he could see the hole that they'd come through. The branches of the fallen tree covered the opening, blocking out the dim light that got through the storm.

As his eyes adjusted, R.J. looked at Sara. She was limp in his arms, and for a horrible moment he thought she might be dead. But he could feel her breathing. Slowly, he ran his hands over her body. He began to breathe again when he found no blood on her head, nor even any lumps that showed she'd hit her skull. When he felt her ribs, she didn't gasp so he didn't think she'd broken any ribs. It was when he reached her leg that he realized her right leg was broken. He could feel the break in the shinbone, but was glad it wasn't protruding from her skin.

Carefully, he laid her down on the ground, then got his backpack and pulled out the flashlight. The first thing he did was make a quick inspection of where they were. It was a round cave that seemed to open only at the top, a lot like the one they'd seen with the pool, except much smaller. As far as he could tell, there were no signs that any other human had ever been in the cave. He was glad to see that no resident of King's Isle was lurking in the corners.

He ran the light over Sara, making another inspection of her body. Pulling out a big knife from a front pocket of his pack, he cut her trousers up to the knee. Broken but not bad, he thought, and he was glad she'd passed out in the fall. He needed to bind her leg to keep it from moving. He would have to carry her out of here and he didn't want the jarring to dislodge her broken bone.

He used two broken tree branches as stabilizers, then he cut long strips from one of the flannel shirts and wrapped her leg from knee to ankle. When he'd finished, she began to move her head and groan. He grabbed a bottle of water and pulled her head onto his lap as he gave her something to drink.

She choked a bit, coughed, then opened

her eyes. "What happened?" she asked, then the pain hit her.

"Sssssh," R.J. said softly, stroking her cheek. "We fell into one of those holes. I think there must have been a volcano here at one time. You broke your leg and I tied it up."

Sara tried to sit up, but the pain was too much for her. She bit her lip to keep from crying.

"You don't have to be tough," R.J. said. "Go ahead and cry. Yell. Scream at me for being a fool to bring you here and getting you into this mess."

"I did it," she said, gasping out the words. Above them the storm had quietened to just rain. The thick covering of the fallen pine tree kept out most of the rain, but little patches dripped through onto the floor. "I agreed with Ariel and she made Mr. Dunkirk's wife get him to—"

"I know," R.J. said. "But I only agreed to go because Arundel is your hometown."

"My—?" she began, then waited as a wave of pain went through her. "That's not on any application I ever filled out. How did you know that?"

"I know a lot about you, Sara Jane Johnson," he said softly, stroking her hair. "Haven't you realized that yet?"

"No," she said flatly, then turned her head to look at where they were. The flashlight was beside R. J. and he lifted it to shine it on the walls. Rock walls that oozed little trickles of water were around and above them. Beneath them was a thick padding of dirt and rotten wood.

He pointed the flashlight up to the tree above them. "We didn't make that big of a hole. I think we were on the edge of it and . . . see? It broke there. We just missed being hit by the tree. I think that over the centuries lots of trees have fallen across the hole and have rotted. Lucky for us or we would have hit rock."

"I don't feel very lucky right now," Sara said.

He moved her head out of his lap and carefully put it on the second flannel shirt. "I'm going to see if I can find anything we can burn. It's going to get cold tonight."

"What about—?" She broke off.

"About Gideon?"

"Yes. I know I saw him just before you turned. You seemed to be heading toward something, as though you knew where you were going."

"I'd seen some maps on the Internet," he said, but didn't explain more. He was looking inside his pack and withdrew a small bottle of Amaretto di Saronno, an almond-flavored liqueur. "I want you to drink this."

"Where did you get that?" Sara asked, again trying to sit up.

Without a word, R.J. bent and picked her up, then deposited her in the farthest, driest corner of the cave. "While you were drooling over the kids, I found it in Gideon's cabin and put it in my pack. I had hoped for a romantic moment and—" The look she gave him made him smile. "Can't blame a man for trying."

"Sure you can," Sara said, panting, her face breaking out in a sweat from the pain. She wanted to yell at R.J. She wanted to yell at anyone right now, about anything. Maybe rage would take her mind off the reality of the situation. How were they going to get out of here? Was Gideon, that nice-seeming young man, above them with a rifle? Was he planning to shoot them like fish in a barrel? Her thoughts showed on her face.

"None of that now," R.J. said, his hand caressing her cheek. "It's going to be all right."

"You don't know that, do you? We're strangers on this island and no one knows where we are. You left a note to Ariel and David saying heaven only knows what, so they'll be angry and won't look for us. As for the rest of these people, they hate us. And they don't even know that they're going to think we killed someone."

Standing up, R.J. handed her the bottle of liqueur. "I want you to drink all of it. Maybe it'll give you a better outlook on life."

"Life," Sara said, taking a swig from the bottle. "That's what I'm trying to hold onto. I still can't understand why I let Ariel talk me into that ridiculous switch."

"Which didn't work for even five minutes," R.J. said as he examined the cave with the flashlight.

"I think it did. David said—"

"What does he know? He's so in love with Ariel that he can't think about anything else. 'David, dear,' " R.J. said in a falsetto voice, " 'please go outside and shoot yourself, but be sure and do it in a field somewhere as I wouldn't want the mess to soil my pretty house.' "

"David isn't like that. He wants to be—"

"Yeah, I know. President." R.J. was trying to climb up one part of the wall that was less steep, but his feet kept slipping. Leaning against the wall, he removed his shoes and socks to try again. "I think Ariel would make a great first lady. She could wear pretty clothes that the government didn't pay for and she'd love having her picture taken."

"She's not as bad as you think. There are things in her life that you don't know about. Ariel and I've exchanged letters for years, so we know about each other. She told me that when she was nine years old her mother took her to a psychiatrist in New York because Ariel kept making plans for her funeral."

"Her funeral? Was she suicidal?"

"No. Ariel told the psychiatrist that since her mother had planned her wedding down to the color of the bridesmaids' dresses, the only thing left for Ariel to plan was her funeral. What was so funny about it all was that when the psychiatrist asked Ariel's mother if it was true, she said 'of course.'

Then he asked her mother if she had the groom picked out too, and Ariel's mother thought the man was crazy. She said, 'How can you have a wedding without a groom? Of course he's been chosen.' Ariel told me that when the doctor said he wanted to see her mother next time and not Ariel, she left his office in anger and they went home to Arundel the next day."

R.J. gave a one-sided smile. "I can believe that story. I met the old bat. She threatened me with a lawsuit just for looking at her daughter. But if you ask me, Ariel is in danger of being just like her. Unless she can find a man who'll stand up to her, that is, and from what I've seen, that's not David the wimp."

"He . . ." Sara started to say that David wasn't a wimp, but she took another drink instead. Under the current circumstances, it didn't seem to matter what David Tredwell was or wasn't. "They won't come after us," Sara said quietly, looking up at the tree that covered the roof opening. It was still daylight, but it would be dark soon. Then what would happen? "We didn't find out anything, did we?" she said, and wasn't fully successful in keeping the tears out of her voice.

"I beg to differ," R.J. said, rubbing his knee where he'd hit it on the rock. He couldn't get up the wall; it was too slippery, too wet. "We found out pretty much all that we need to know."

Sara took another swig of liqueur. "So tell me, professor, what have we found out?"

"That lots of people hated the victim and had a motive to murder him. I don't think any court is going to believe that any of us killed a man over a dead dog. You know, don't you, that I have a photo of the dog?"

"You what?"

R.J. stepped back from the wall and dug into the tiny watch pocket in the front of his trousers and withdrew a little disk for a digital camera. "There was a full fifteen seconds between when the police appeared and the handcuffs were placed on me. I took the disk out of the camera and put it in my pocket. I haven't seen what's on there, but I know you took—"

"Several photos of the dog lying in the street." She was looking at him in wonder and admiration. He was certainly able to think quickly in an emergency.

"No," R.J. said, "you took half a dozen photos of your precious David, but I think the dog is probably in there too."

Sara was feeling the effects of the booze, so she didn't protest what R.J. was saying. Besides, it was true. Most of the time she was taking photos, she'd been in the car, but when David was looking at the dog, she'd snapped away. It seemed like years ago now, but she seemed to remember that she was thinking that someday he could use the photos in his political campaigns. When he was a young man he'd been concerned about animal rights, that sort of thing.

"So you have photos showing that the dog was emaciated," Sara said. "That doesn't prove that we didn't hit it."

"True, but it would have proven that Nezbit was a liar."

"But now Nezbit is dead. In *our* bathtub."

"In Phyllis Vancurren's bathtub," R.J. corrected. He was pulling on some weeds that were hanging down from the top of the hole, but they fell away in his hands. "The people on this island have changed their fates," he said. "If none of this had happened, I would have gone back to Charley and recommended that he not buy an inch of this place, but now I might buy it myself."

"And bulldoze it?"

"No," he said, looking at her in surprise. "I'm going to send in a team of geologists and spelunkers to explore every inch of this place. I'm going to find out what it is that ol' Fenny Nezbit found, how he disappeared, and what he was killed for. I think the middle of this island is riddled with these little bowling ball caves, and I plan to get a report on every one of them. If tourists come here, we can't have them falling through the center of the island."

"And breaking their legs," Sara said. "And having trees cover the top so they can't get out. And you'd better tell the natives to stop shooting at strangers. And kidnapping their children. And . . ." She took another swig of liqueur and stopped talking. Thinking about the future and what they were going to do didn't help the present. "If we yell, do you think anyone will hear us? And if they do hear us, will they come to help or to shoot us?"

"You really are a glass-half-empty type of person, aren't you?"

"It helps when you have a boss like mine," she said, then looked at him. "Sorry."

"Okay, answer me this." He was trying to move a rock that was against the wall to the center so he could stand on it. "If I didn't make up things for you to do for me, how else was I going to keep you near me?"

"I think I'm drunk. Why would you want me near you?"

R.J. gave a little snort. "Can't imagine. How's your leg?"

"Most of me is numb. I've never been much of a drinker. Imagine having a father like mine and not having a capacity for booze. Where are genetics when you need them?"

"My old man was a drunk too."

"I know. All the girls at the office talked about you endlessly. Sometimes I listened."

"What else did . . . they . . . say about . . . me?" He was pushing against the rock so hard that he could hardly talk.

"Just that you were rich and unmarried and that they wanted you."

"But you didn't."

"No," Sara said. "I want . . ." She trailed off. At the moment, she couldn't think what it was that she wanted in life.

"To be a great actress?" he asked, standing and staring at the rock. "You have talent."

"How do you know that?"

"I saw your play three times, remember?"

"Oh, yeah," she said, smiling. "You told that to Ariel."

"I told it to *you,* and I knew it was you." He was looking up at the tree lying across the opening. "Too bad your leg is busted or I could hoist you onto my shoulders and maybe you could grab a branch."

"If I drink any more of this, I'll be able to do it on one leg. Did you really think I was good on the stage?"

"Excellent, but then I'm prejudiced. The question is whether or not you liked being up there onstage. Did you? Or did you like being your cousin more?"

Sara closed her eyes for a moment. The pain was a dull ache and she thought that if she didn't ever move again she'd be able to stand it. "I wasn't Ariel long enough to know. I think I want . . ."

"What?" R. J. asked, looking through both their packs and seeing what he could use.

"I don't know. Or maybe I do. I think I want what everyone wants: a home, a family."

"With a jock like David," R.J. said flatly. "Look, if you'll stop talking about him right now, when we get out of here, I'll get him for you. I'll get him a job and you can work with him. Once he spends time with you, he'll forget all about Ariel."

"I must be very drunk," she said, her head lolling back against the rock, "because I keep hearing you say good things about me. That couldn't be."

R.J. stopped searching the bags and looked at her as her head fell forward onto her chest in sleep. Good things about you, he thought. Was being in love with her from the first moment he saw her a "good thing"?

At the moment, his objective was to keep her from seeing how really frightened he was. He too had seen young Gideon following them. Was the boy skulking about in an attempt to protect them? Or was there something else? When Nezbit's body was found, someone was going to take the fall for it. Was Gideon making sure that it was the tourists who were blamed?

In the next second a light shone into the cave. Looking up, R.J. saw Gideon hanging over the edge, a flashlight in one hand and a rifle in the other.

Chapter Seventeen

"I hate that man," Ariel said under her breath. "Deeply and truly *hate* him. He has kidnapped my cousin and left us here alone."

It wasn't even daylight, Saturday morning, and she was holding the note R. J. had left behind. David turned away to hide his smile. The note was curt and to the point, saying that he, Brompton, *and Sara* wouldn't be returning to the house. He told Ariel and David to stay in Phyllis Vancurren's house and wait for their return.

"Wait for him?" Ariel said. "Should I knit while I wait? Or would he rather I just take some laudanum and prostrate myself on the bed? I thought Sara was exaggerating about him, but I can see that she wasn't."

David was stretched out on the couch and pretending to yawn. In spite of the fact that last night had been harrowing, he was very pleased by Ariel's reaction to R.J. He'd never believed she was in love with him, but oh! the satisfaction of hearing her say she *hated* him.

Last night he and Ariel had taken one of Sara's dummies through the outskirts of town, having no idea where they were going or what they were supposed to do with the fake body. Brompton had said, "Dispose of it so no one can find it," then left them. He was too eager to get back to Sara to say anything else.

It was after David and Ariel were outside alone that he again began to wonder who had put Brompton in charge. Was it his age? Or his self-made status? Whatever he thought it was, Brompton had taken over and David didn't like it at all.

When Brompton had disappeared with Sara and their dummy into the woods, David realized that the old man knew a great deal more about the layout of King's Isle than he'd let on. He has secrets, David thought. Yeah, well, David had a few of his own, secrets that not even Ariel knew. David had spent a month on King's Isle when he was nine years old. That had been a difficult summer for his mother, and, as always, she'd dumped all her troubles onto her son. Never mind that he was just a child, his mother expected David to fix whatever was ailing her. That summer, her problem had been loneliness, so she'd taken a cruise—and David had been sent to a camp on King's Isle. The camp had been a bust, run by a hippie couple that just wanted to sit around and smoke grass. The good part was that the children in their care had been left on their own, so David had done some exploring—and some thinking. Even though he was only nine, he knew he needed to figure out his life. His mother had no husband to speak of. She had one on paper, but on their honeymoon they'd found out two things about each other. One was that he'd married her for her money, and two, that her money was tied up so he couldn't touch it unless she said so—and she rarely said so. When it came to money, Inez Tredwell resembled her father, which was why David had been sent to a very inexpensive camp. After a year of hell, David's parents came to an agreement. If he'd give her a baby, she'd pay him to live elsewhere. It had worked perfectly.

Inez had often said that what saved her sanity was Ariel's mother. To the rest of the world, Pomberton Weatherly was a snob without equal, but to Inez Tredwell, she was kind and loving. They were two women alone, raising children alone, fighting the snickers of a gossipy small town by themselves. Whereas Miss Pommy was a bulwark of strength, Inez Tredwell seemed to be a portrait of feminine helplessness. Of course no one knew about her rule of the purse strings, or how she'd stood up to her bully of a husband and the deal she'd made with him. To the outside world, Inez seemed to be the neediest, weepiest woman on earth. She certainly used her tears often enough on her son.

On the day David entered first grade, his mother told him that he was now the man in her life—and from that day on, she'd treated him as such. She told him all about her life, cried on his shoulder about anything that upset her, and expected him to handle problems. By the time he was eight, David was dealing with tradesmen and the servants who ran the big house that had been in his father's family for generations.

When his mother told David he was to marry Miss Pommy's daughter, on principle, he'd wanted to refuse, but he couldn't bear his mother's crying fits that could go on for days—or however long it took before she got what she wanted. But then, David had known Ariel and her mother all his life, and to him, their house was a haven of sanity. Yes, Miss Pommy wanted everything around her under her control, but she gave warning before she attacked. She told people under her charge what she wanted and if they didn't do it, there were consequences. David had never once seen her cry, and a lack of tears was a relief to him.

To David, Ariel was just like her mother. In all their years together, he'd never seen Ariel cry. She made up her mind about what she wanted, then went after it.

But the problem was that Ariel had decided she wanted an old man, R. J. Brompton. David had disliked him from the moment he'd seen him. Brompton was a man experienced in the world and in the ways of women—all the things that David wasn't, and all the things he despised. David had only seen his father six times in his life, but Brompton reminded him of the man. Ruthless, experienced, without conscience. Not wanting to be like his father had been a driving force in David's life.

The other force in his life had been the love he bore for Ariel. In school, David had been president of every class since he was in the fifth grade. He was always on the honor role. He was the captain of the football team. At graduation, he was voted both "best looking" and "most likely to succeed." Since he was a child, he'd been confident and self-assured. "My little man," his mother called him.

But when he got around Ariel, he was a blithering idiot. She was like a princess living in her richly decorated house with her elegant mother, never going to school with the other children, never wearing clothes that had been made for anyone but her. Ariel had never owned a pair of jeans.

His friend Wesley said David loved Ariel because she was unobtainable. "All the other girls are writing their phone numbers on your arm, but Ariel says, 'Are *you* here again?' You love it."

Maybe so, David thought. But whatever it

was, he'd been her slave since they were kids—and Ariel had treated him as such. When they were children she'd give him a list of what she needed, things such as one-inch-diameter wheels, transparent fabric, and glitter. He'd swallow his embarrassment and get what she wanted, then he'd sit in silence as she used the set of miniature tools he'd bought her and create little houses for fairies to live in. She never played with him, but she would grant him the honor of allowing him to watch her play.

When he got older, he heard Miss Pommy referred to as "the Queen of Arundel" and Ariel as the princess. "Waiting for the queen to die," someone would say, then everyone would laugh. Ariel's family wasn't the richest in a rich town, but it held the most prestige and the longest lineage.

Sometimes he'd take her to a movie. The other girls would be wearing cheap tank tops that showed their belly buttons, while Ariel would have on a suit that buttoned up to her neck. Her idea of casual was a thousand-dollar pair of slacks and a pristine white shirt. "I just want the best," David learned to say to Wes and to anyone else who made a comment about Ariel.

It had seemed natural to David to go from being in love with Ariel to wanting a political career. With his ability to persuade people and his belief in the fundamental goodness of mankind, he thought he could do some good in the world. And with Ariel's beauty and style, and her knowledge of manners and etiquette, he could imagine the two of them in the White House together.

Until recently, David thought that it had come to the point that Ariel was going to give in to her mother and marry him. He knew that if he could get her past that hurdle of the actual ceremony, she'd be his. Ariel was a sensual person, a virgin at twenty-four, and he longed to make love to her. He was sure that underneath her protests, she loved him. She didn't know it, but he did.

But then she told him she'd seen R. J. Brompton and was in love with him. In love with a man she'd just met? After David first heard of her intentions toward Brompton (and he'd worked hard not to go berserk), he'd researched the man and seen what it was that Ariel wanted. She wanted someone she believed could stand up to her mother. That David had charmed Miss Pommy for all his life seemed to make no difference to Ariel.

Unless he wanted to make his love for her known—and risk permanent rejection— David had to go along with whatever Ariel wanted. He'd helped her with her asinine scheme to trade places with her cousin, and had agreed to go to King's Isle with them. It had been his help that had enabled her to get to Brompton. Did that mean it was David's fault that they were in the situation they were in now?

But David was a man who believed in looking at the situation as it was, then trying to fix it. He had to work to keep from smiling at what Ariel was saying about hating Brompton, but he knew from experience not to take her side. Ariel liked something to fight against.

"I'm sure he meant well," David said. "After all, he's had experience in situations like this."

"How can anyone have had experience in a situation like *this?*" she asked. "Unless he's in the Mafia. Are you trying to tell me that the business world in New York is so cutthroat that bodies in the bathtub are routine?"

"I'm not telling you anything, but I think he's right about our staying here in this house. We should guard the body. If Phyllis wants to get something out of the freezer for dinner, we need to be here to stop her."

Ariel whirled on him. "Are you saying that we should stay here in this house all day and just *wait?*"

"Isn't that what R.J. said to do? He is—"

"A businessman from New York," Ariel said. "What does he know?" She held up the two one-hundred-dollar bills R.J. had left with the note. "Do you think this was all the money he had? Did he give us all of it and keep none for himself?"

David made himself more comfortable on the couch, as though he meant to spend the day there. "I guess he thinks he can earn money anywhere, so he doesn't need what he had secreted away. Remember that he and Sara are workers. You and I are . . ." He shrugged as though there was no description for them.

"Worthless. Are you saying that you and I are *worthless?*"

"Not at all. I'm sure that if anyone wanted to host a party, you'd be very valuable. But the fact that everyone on this island seems to hate us—"

"Do they? Or have they been told to stay away from us?"

"Same difference."

Ariel sat down on the end of the couch. The tips of David's feet were under her thigh, but he didn't move. He'd never seen her so upset. "Money!" she said in disgust. "Do you realize that money is the cause of all my problems?"

David frowned. "Do you and Miss Pommy have money problems?"

"Yes!" Ariel said. "She has it all and I have none. If I just had my own money, I could live my own life." She stood up and David wiggled his toes. "She's raised me to be as helpless as a foot-bound woman. My education, such as it is, has carefully prepared me for nothing whatever. I can set a table with twelve pieces of silverware by each plate. Did you know that I have never eaten a banana out of its peel in my life? Knife and fork only. Usually all fruit is cut up for me."

David was looking at her with interest. He didn't know Ariel knew there was another way to eat a banana—or knew there was another way of life other than her own.

"What can I do in life except marry some man and plan his dinner parties?"

"I think there should be more of that in the world," David said softly.

"Oh, do shut up! You're always thinking about your own future and what *you* want from a woman. Perfect wife; perfect parties. David, you are the most *perfect* person I've ever met."

"Me?" he said in disbelief. "You're so perfect—"

Ariel cut him off. "I want to *do* something. *Be* someone."

He sat up on the couch. "Excuse me for being stupid, but how does marrying R. J. Brompton achieve that?"

"He's strong. He's independent. He'd tell my mother to get off my back, then he'd go to work and let me do what I want to do in my own life."

"Which is?" David asked with interest.

Ariel sat back down on the couch. "That's just it. I have no idea what I want to do."

"You could always earn some money for the next two days, so when you see Brompton next time you could throw his bills in his face. Unless we're arrested for murder," he added as an afterthought.

"All my life I've lived in fear of my mother. She controls what I wear, what I eat, even who I marry, but right now, when I think of that body in the freezer, I wish she'd show up here. I think I'd run to her and throw my arms around her."

"And what do you think Miss Pommy would do when your mascara messed up her outfit? She'd be furious if she couldn't get the makeup off her clothes."

"Makeup? Are you kidding? I don't have any makeup on."

"Could have fooled me, but then you always look great." David touched her forearm, his fingers beginning to climb upward.

Suddenly, Ariel stood up. "Remember when we were in the pub? Remember that I told Sara I was going to make old Phyllis dress her age?"

"I think she does dress her mental age."

Putting her hands on her hips, Ariel looked down at him. "That woman wants a man."

"I think she has a few of them."

"No, not like that. Think with something besides your lower extremities. She wants a husband, but what kind of 'husband' is she going to get wearing what she does?"

"Bikers. Teenage boys."

"Right. Exactly."

David smiled. "I saw half a dozen women looking at you since we've been here."

"No, not me, at Sara. She has on the good clothes." She looked down at her simple cotton slacks and cotton knit shirt. "These are reproductions of Sara's clothes, but still . . ."

"The clothes don't matter. It's you they were looking at. Ariel, you don't realize what a presence you have, what style, how different you are from other women."

"Really?" she asked softly. "I've not been to places that other women have. I've always been cooped up with Mother."

"And who is more stylish than Miss Pommy?"

"No one," Ariel said. She looked at David. "Do you think that what I know is worth something?"

"I think you could run a modeling agency in New York City. Or be editor in chief at *Vogue.*"

She smiled. "What about on King's Isle, North Carolina?"

"I think the lines would be out the door. Just imagine the gossip you'd hear!" David had meant the comment as a joke, but the minute he said it, they looked at each other.

"What do you think I could find out?" she whispered.

"Anything. Everything. You could get the women to tell you what's really going on." He'd gone from laughing to serious. "Ariel, honey, exactly what can you do? Could you do one of those drugstore makeovers?"

"I don't know. I never thought about it before, but a lot of times when I see a woman I think about what she could wear or how she could do her hair to make her look better. Take Britney, for instance."

"Who?"

"Britney. The woman you love. The one you stayed in Arundel for, remember?"

David gave a little laugh. "Yeah, love of my life. Britney. What about her?"

"She could be pretty if she tied her hair back and quit drawing that black liner on a quarter inch outside her eyes. And her mascara clumps too much. If she—"

Ariel stopped talking because David put his hand to the back of her head and pulled her mouth to his. It was the first time he'd kissed her in any way except brotherly. It was a hard, firm kiss that let her know that he wasn't her brother.

When he broke off, he stood up, his back to her, and stretched. "I think I'll take a shower, and when I get out, we're going to see about getting this started." He didn't glance back at her until he was at the bathroom door. When he saw that Ariel was still sitting there, a shocked look on her face, he smiled. Sink or swim, he had decided to let her know how he felt about her.

Chapter Eighteen

"You promise, right?" Phyllis said, looking at herself in the mirror. She had on half the makeup she usually wore, and was wearing a man's shirt and trousers that, to her mind, looked too big. But she had to admit that she looked . . . different. Classy, almost.

"I swear it," Ariel said. "R. J. Brompton will put you up in New York for one week and he'll introduce you to at least four eligible men. What happens after that is up to you."

"And Saks?"

"A five-thousand-dollar shopping spree."

"With a stylist," Phyllis said.

Behind her, Ariel made her hands into claws, but smiled and nodded when Phyllis looked at her again.

"I don't know . . ." Phyllis said, looking back at the mirror. "I'm not sure how people would take it if I helped you."

"I understand," Ariel said, straightening Phyllis's cosmetics. She'd had to pound on the bedroom door to waken the woman from her drunken sleep, and Phyllis hadn't understood a word Ariel was saying to her. "You want to do what to me?" Phyllis had asked. In the end, David had had to pull the woman from the bed and set her in front of her mirrored dressing table.

"He is gorgeous," Phyllis whispered to Ariel as she was putting brown eyeshadow on her. "Is *all* of him beautiful?"

Ariel glanced up at David and for the first time in her life, she felt jealousy. How many women had he been to bed with? she wondered, then shook her head, annoyed with herself. "I have no idea," Ariel answered, trying to concentrate on the eyeshadow. Only once before had she applied makeup on a person and that had been a maid who was going out to dinner with her boyfriend of three years. When she returned with an engagement ring, Ariel felt as if she'd helped.

"You've never torn his clothes off?" Phyllis asked.

Ariel wanted to set the woman on her ear, to give her a look that said she should keep her lusting to herself, but she knew she was going to have to swallow her pride if she wanted to find out anything. "If a woman tried that, David would fight her." Ariel had meant that David was a man of honor, but it didn't sound like that.

"You mean he's gay?"

Ariel smiled. "As pink tea roses."

"Maybe I could change him."

"Believe me, a lot of women have tried. You should talk to Britney. She's tried for years, but . . ."

"Failed?"

"Completely." David is going to kill me, Ariel thought, but she was smiling. However, without the promise of David's "services," so to speak, she'd had to think up something else to get Phyllis Vancurren to help them. Ariel had made one promise after another.

"So you'll call them?" Ariel asked as she was applying a heated curling iron to Phyllis's overpermed, overdyed hair.

"No telephones," Phyllis said, holding up a hand mirror and examining the makeup Ariel had applied. "Cable cut, remember?"

"I forgot for a moment. But you do have a way to get information around town, don't you?"

"You're trying to get me to tell you things, aren't you?"

"I'm trying to earn enough money to feed David and me," Ariel said, her lips clenched. "He won't say so, but he's scared out of his mind, and *I* have to do something. I can't tell you how glad I'll be to turn him over to his mother as soon as we get back to Arundel. That woman pampers him to no end. She never lets him do anything at all." Forgive me, she thought, making a silent apology to David. If there was any person who wasn't pampered, it was David. All her life, Ariel had seen David doing things for his mother that only grown-ups did. He paid the house-hold bills and she'd often seen him in the bank talking to the manager about his mother's great masses of money.

"Did you hear me?" Phyllis asked.

"No, sorry. I was lost in thought. There, that looks good." She had taken about four inches of height from Phyllis's hair.

"You don't think this makes me look older?"

Ariel almost said, You *are* older, but she

didn't. "I think it makes you look more intelligent. Looking like this will attract a better
class of man than you would have before."
It was an honest statement and Phyllis
heard it that way.

"So can you set it up?" Ariel asked, trying
not to sound desperate. "I really do need to
try to earn some money for David and me."

"What about R. J. and that girl? What was
her name?"

"Sara. They went off somewhere else."

Phyllis turned quickly to look at Ariel.
"They'd better not leave the island!"

"How can they?" Ariel asked calmly, but
her heart was beating fast. What if R. J. and
Sara found a way off the island? "What
would happen to them if they did leave?"

"Nothing good," Phyllis said, turning back
and seeming to decide that she'd said too
much. "I can help you get information out.
The kids around town can take messages."

"Can they put a flyer in the mailboxes? I
mean, if I can persuade the shops in town to
participate, that is."

"You don't have to worry about that. Business around here is so bad that most people will do anything to make a buck."

"They should find treasure like Mr. Nezbit

did," Ariel said, then waited to see what Phyllis would say.

"Fenny's gold," Phyllis said, smiling into the mirror. "It's what everybody here talks about after they've had a couple of beers."

"But no one's found it?"

"Not even close. Except . . ."

"Except what?"

"I think Gideon knows more than he's telling. Even I couldn't get it out of him."

"And you've tried?"

Phyllis laughed. "Honey, that boy and I have rocked that old bed of mine so many times. . . . Let's just say that he keeps what he knows to himself."

"Who is Gideon?"

"Fenny's son. Or maybe he is. Gideon says he isn't. But Fenny and Eula say he is. I never saw her pregnant, but she said she didn't show all that much and she had a home birth." This made Phyllis laugh hard, but Ariel couldn't tell what the joke was.

"So David can use your computer, print out flyers, and someone will deliver them around town?"

"Sure," Phyllis said, patting her hair.

"But won't they get angry?"

"Who?"

"Whoever is in charge of this town?"

Phyllis looked in the mirror at Ariel. "Don't worry about the hearing on Monday. Brompton can afford what he'll be charged."

"I'm sure he can," Ariel said softly as she backed away. "I'd better go tell David that . . . about this." Tell him he's gay, she thought, and she couldn't help smiling.

"Let me do this," Ariel said. "Please."

David narrowed his eyes at her. "And what are you going to tell them? That I'll be your wash girl?"

"Maybe you could help find matching accessories."

"You keep on laughing and I'll tell them you live in a trailer out on seventeen."

"Next door to Britney?"

"With Brit. As her lover."

Ariel laughed. "I had no idea you had a cruel streak in you."

"That's because you don't know anything about me. I think I'll go over to the hardware store and see if the men know about something other than chain saws."

"I bet they'd love to hear you pontificate on saving the wetlands."

David gave a reluctant smile. "Maybe I'll

wait on that. So what am I supposed to do to help you make these women into beauty queens?"

"Not beautiful, just to be the best they can be, remember?"

"Yeah, I wrote the flyer."

"You really think I can do this?" Ariel whispered.

He smiled at her. "Yes, you can. No more doubts now."

It wasn't easy for him to stand behind Ariel as she gently knocked on the door of the house of the woman who owned the only dress shop on King's Isle. The dress store was next door to the beauty shop, which was owned by her sister, and both shops didn't open until 10:00 A.M. It wasn't even eight o'clock yet.

When no one answered, Ariel stepped back. "Maybe they're not up yet. Maybe we should come back later."

David reached over her head and knocked on the door loud enough to wake the neighbors. Minutes later, a middle-aged woman wearing an old bathrobe opened the door and squinted against the daylight. "Yeah?" she said.

David started to speak, but then closed

his mouth and gave Ariel a little shove forward. She didn't have much experience talking to people she hadn't known all her life. Or been introduced to properly.

"I'd like to talk to you about a business arrangement," Ariel said cautiously.

"We can't help you," the woman said, and started to shut the door.

Ariel put her foot in the doorway, then looked at the woman. "I just redid Phyllis Vancurren's face and hair. She looks her age now and elegant enough to find herself a husband off the island."

The woman blinked at her a few times. "You're either a magician or a liar."

"No," Ariel said, "I just have my clothes made in New York and I've had enough makeup sessions I could work at the Estée Lauder counter. We need money and I'd like to offer makeovers to the women of this town. Clothes, shoes, cosmetics, and hair. I'd get twenty percent of everything they buy."

Behind her, David smiled—and was impressed.

"I'll get in trouble for this, but come in."

"If we aren't put in jail for life I'm going to kill you," David said so just Ariel could hear.

"Do you have any idea what these women are doing to me?"

Ariel knew, since the women had delighted in telling her everything. "If he can stand *that,*" they said, "then he *is* gay." Ariel was split between laughing and leaving the dye on too long. As it was, she was too busy to do much of anything other than try to keep up.

There were double doors between the beauty salon and the dress shop and they'd been thrown open so the women could go from one room to the next. Ariel had been in the middle of them, for the most part saying no. "That's not for you. Try the blue one. No, no, no! Not that belt!" At first she'd been almost timid, and she'd worked hard to be diplomatic. But by eleven o'clock, she'd stopped being polite. The women weren't being courteous, so why should she be? They were shoving and grabbing and pushing ahead of one another in the queue, and in general acting like what they were: starving for fashion and beauty.

To accommodate so many, Ariel stopped doing things herself. She'd started applying the cosmetics herself, and had even done the foil highlights on one woman's hair, but after an hour, she began directing and the women hurried to obey. Cosmetics, hair, clothes were all being done at once, while Ariel barked orders. "She doesn't need more blonde! Her hair's been bleached white as it is. And look at her eyebrows! Somebody get me a weed whacker!" Instead of being insulted, the women laughed and pushed harder to get closer to Ariel. "I brought all sixty-one of my handbags and I thought you could tell me which ones I should keep." Ariel looked into a black plastic bag full of purses that were stiff with age and gray with mildew, but she recognized gems from the forties and fifties. "Get some saddle soap and some colorless shoe polish," Ariel said, "then sit in that corner and clean those bags up. When you're done, put them on that table and I'll sell them for you. I get twenty-five percent." The woman blinked a couple of times, then ran out the door to go to the hardware store to get the supplies.

David had helped her for a while, but the women got to be too much for him. They were fascinated by his good looks and by what Phyllis Vancurren had conspiratorially told them.

At about one o'clock, she overhead a woman who had severely sun-damaged skin say the word "Gideon." Ariel went to the girl who was slapping on bright blue eye shadow and took away the brush from her. "I'll handle this one," Ariel said and the girl looked at her gratefully.

"You need laser treatments on your skin," Ariel said flatly.

"Don't I know it. All those years on Fenny's boat."

Ariel had to pause to keep her hand from shaking. Fenny Nezbit. The dead man in the bathtub. The man who was suing them.

"It's okay," the woman said softly. "I won't let Fenny hurt you on Monday. It's just a game he plays. He don't mean no harm in it. He knew that man was rich."

"R.J."

"Yeah, the older one. He sure is in love with that girl, ain't he?"

Again, Ariel paused. "With Sara? She works for him, but I don't think they're in love."

"Hmph!" the woman said. "You should have seen them this mornin'. I was comin' here and I guess he thought I was gonna run him over with my truck because he threw her in a ditch and covered her up. If anybody was gonna get hurt, it was him. I can tell you that Fenny ain't never done that with me." She leaned toward Ariel. "I bet that young man of yours would do that for you."

Ariel glanced at David. Some woman was asking him if the blouse she had on was too low cut. "David is—"

"Don't tell me that lie. I know a lie when I hear one. I live with Fenny and that's all the lyin' I can take. That boy ain't no homosexual."

"I wonder if I could talk to Mr. Nezbit," Ariel said. "Maybe tonight I could see him."

"He's gone and I don't know when he'll be back. Probably not till Monday when he sees the judge."

"Did he leave the island?" Ariel was putting shadow on the woman's lids, but the wrinkles were making it difficult not to cake it.

"Naw. He's just gone up to sleep with his gold."

"Sleep with his gold," Ariel said.

"Surely you've heard about Fenny's gold."

"Phyllis—"

"Don't say that woman's name to me! Her and Gideon—"

"Who is Gideon?"

"The devil's spawn, if you ask me. Evil little bastard."

"He's your son, isn't he?"

She looked at Ariel in the mirror and her
eyes began to sparkle. "If you say so."

Ariel was trying to calm her rapidly beating heart. "When you saw R.J. and Sara,
where were they going?"

"To my house. I told 'em to take care of
my kids."

Ariel started to smile at the idea of R.J.
being stuck baby-sitting, but then she
thought of the kid Gideon and of her cousin
Sara. "Tell me more about Gideon."

"The meanest, most underhanded devil
on this island. I'm Eula, by the way. You
have kids?"

"No," Ariel said.

"Good thing. Now my girls are just lovely,
but Gideon is and always has been out for
what he can get. I just hope those friends of
yours don't meet him. They might be taken
in by his good looks. He gets that from my
side of the family."

Ariel couldn't help pausing at that, and
Eula cackled. "You wouldn't believe it now,
but I used to be a real looker. Too much of

bein' on this godforsaken island and my beauty is gone."

"If your husband has gold, then why don't you leave here?"

"You think he'd give me any of it? He doles it out by the penny. He gets it from somewhere on the island, then takes it to the mainland and sells it for cash."

She's lying, Ariel thought, watching the way the woman moved her eyes to the side when she spoke. But what was she lying about?

Ariel didn't get the time to find out. The door opened and in came a woman who was as round as she was tall, and from the hush that spread, she was someone important. Ariel quickly learned she was the wife of the mayor of King's Isle and Ariel had to leave Eula Nezbit to tend to her.

It wasn't until 5:00 that evening that Ariel was able to speak to David. "Where have you been?" she hissed at him. The sisters who owned the stores were locking the doors. There wasn't much merchandise left in the dress shop and the beauty shop was out of hair dye and most everything else. Everyone except Ariel looked exhausted.

"Could we get something to eat?" David asked, cutting his eyes at the two women.

"As soon as we divvy up the proceeds," Ariel said. "I've kept a running total in my head so I have an idea what I'm owed. This shouldn't take too long."

One of the sisters looked at David as though to say "what a shame," then went to the cash register and began punching keys. Ten minutes later, she handed Ariel some bills.

Before Ariel could say anything, David pushed her out the back door.

"Two hundred and thirty dollars?" Ariel said. "Is that all I get? I cleaned out that place."

"They sold about twenty-three grand of merchandise; cut that in half for what they paid for it, so twenty percent of the profit comes to two-thirty," he said.

Ariel folded the bills and stuffed them inside her bra. "There must be ways to increase the profit," she said, then smiled. "But I've never had so much fun in my life. Do you think I could open a dress shop in Arundel?"

"If you want to kill your mother instantly."

"I'd want her to work in it."

David started to express his horror, then

saw that Ariel was teasing. "Come on, rich girl, and buy me dinner. I want to hear every word of what you found out."

Twenty minutes later they were in the pub and the atmosphere couldn't have been more different than it had been the first time they'd been there. Nearly every female who came in waved to Ariel and asked how she looked. Throughout the greetings, Ariel kept discreetly telling them what to do: soften their lipstick, flatten their hair, cover their belly buttons.

"So you didn't find out anything?" David asked.

"Just that this kid Gideon is a sick person. The local mass murderer in the making. Everyone on the island stays away from him." She leaned toward him. "He takes care of two little kids that Eula said are his. The town thinks that they're hers, but they aren't."

"So who's the mother?"

Ariel leaned back. "She wouldn't tell me, but I think it's Phyllis Vancurren. If she had her children taken away by Nezbit, maybe that's why she drinks."

"This whole island makes me sick," David said.

"I don't think we'll have any problems on Monday. I think R. J. will be fined something and the case dismissed."

"Then what?" David asked. "The ferry comes for us and we leave the island? Don't you think that they'll come after us when they open the freezer?"

"Or they'll go after Phyllis," Ariel said, looking down at her plate of broiled scallops.

"I thought you hated her, that you didn't trust her."

"I don't, but I don't think she's a murderer. If the body is found in her freezer and what with all the evidence you and R. J. put on it, I think Phyllis may be accused. I don't think she knows anything."

"So who does? By now you know the whole town, so who's guilty?"

"I think somebody wanted Fenny's gold and when he wouldn't give it to them, they killed him. I wouldn't be surprised to hear that it was their idea of a joke to put the body in our bathtub."

David looked at her for a moment. "I bet if you went to a woman whose husband is a fisherman, she could get him to take you off this island."

"I thought of that. In fact, I almost asked

one of them to do it. After all, R.J. is the only one who has anything pending against him. The rest of us . . ." She shrugged.

"Ariel," David said softly, "did you hear anything that you're not telling me?"

She kept her eyes on her plate. "Why did you kiss me this morning?"

"Don't change the subject."

"The subject being that I must tell you everything I heard or thought? What about you? Where did you go this afternoon? You were gone for nearly three hours."

"Never mind that. I think you should leave this island."

"You're up to something, aren't you?"

"Nothing," David said, his eyes wide.

"You are the worst liar in the world. I think we should try to find Sara and R.J."

"I thought you hated him."

"Maybe. Tomorrow's Sunday so I think we should—"

"I have something to do tomorrow, so I want you to stay at Phyllis's house and rest."

Ariel looked like she was going to say something, but then she smiled. "David, you are the kindest person in the world. It's as though you read my mind. There's nothing I want to do more than stay in one spot and rest. Working has worn me out."

David looked at her hard, but she yawned and her eyes seemed to droop at the corners. "Come on, sweetheart, let me take you home."

"Home. What a nice thought. Do you think my mother is worried about me?"

"Frantic. You didn't by chance tell her where you were going, did you?"

"I was Sara, remember?" Ariel said, allowing David to help her out of the booth. He liked it when she leaned on him. Smiling to himself, he led her back to Phyllis's house.

While Ariel got ready for bed, David rummaged in the attic alcoves, searching for all that he'd need in the morning. He felt bad about leaving Ariel behind, but it was just for a few hours, then he'd be back for her. Today, while the women were making passes at him, he'd remembered something from when he'd explored King's Isle. He'd never found the source of the hot springs as the other children had, but there were some other things he'd found.

Chapter Nineteen

"David?" Ariel whispered. She was standing in the bedroom doorway wearing a too-big nightgown that Phyllis had lent her. "Are you awake?"

On their way back from the pub, the skies had opened and they'd been caught in a sudden storm. Cold and wet, Ariel had gloried in curling up with a cozy old quilt and a hot water bottle. She'd heard David rummaging about in the spaces under the eaves and wondered what he was doing. She'd also wondered what R.J. and Sara were doing. Was it true what Fenny Nezbit's widow said, that R.J. was in love with Sara?

Ariel tried to remember all that Sara had written about her boss. He had been her major topic of conversation. What he did, who he saw, whose heart he had broken. "The women make such fools of themselves," she'd written. "If they'd just realize that he likes to work for what he gets." Had all Sara's protest been a cover for her true feelings? Ariel smiled. If protests and talking endlessly meant love, then Ariel *was* in love with David.

In love with David? What an absurd thought! David was the dullest, most boring—

Ariel sighed, remembering how he used to climb the big old apple tree on his family's farm and toss down the largest, ripest apples to her. She sighed again, remembering all the times he'd listened to her complain about her mother—and would then fix the problem for her. He could sweet-talk her mother in a way that nobody else could.

When she was fifteen, David had asked her what she wanted for her upcoming birthday. Ariel had grimaced. Her mother would give her something useful and practical, or something expensive and ornamental that she wasn't allowed to touch.

When David asked her what she wanted, she'd come up with the wildest thing she could think of. "I'd like to ride a motorcycle with a man wearing black leather."

When David said, "I'll ask your mother about that," she'd tossed a pillow at him.

But then came the morning of her sixteenth birthday. Her mother received an emergency call from someone Ariel had never heard of and she'd left for the day. "When I return this evening, we'll have a cake," her mother said, pulling on her gloves. "And there will, of course, be a gift."

"Yes, ma'am," Ariel said. When her mother turned her head, she'd stuck her tongue out. One of the maids saw and had to run from the room to keep from laughing.

An hour later, David called and said, "Put on your cheapest clothes and wait for me," then hung up. Ariel didn't want to be bossed around by him or her mother, but his manner was so odd, she'd obeyed. When he showed up, she had on cotton trousers, a cotton shirt, and her tennis shoes.

David walked into the small sitting room wearing black motorcycle leathers and carrying two helmets under his arms. "Are you ready?" he asked.

"For what?"

He nodded toward the window. Under the

porte cochere was a huge black-and-silver motorcycle.

Now, curled up in the quilt, Ariel remembered that perfect day when she and David had spent the day riding the motorcycle. He'd packed the saddlebags with sandwiches, fruit, colas, and a tiny bottle of peach wine. "I shouldn't," she said, laughing.

"I didn't know you could ride a motorcycle," she'd said, her arms around his waist.

David had just laughed.

Until today when she'd been a businesswoman, her sixteenth birthday had been the most exciting day of her life. Riding across the bridge, her hair flying from under the helmet, holding onto David, the feel of leather on her cheek.

Still standing in the bedroom doorway, Ariel cleared her throat. She stood there, silently, wearing the cotton nightgown and robe set Phyllis had lent her. David was reading a two-day-old newspaper in bed and paid no attention to her. She looked around to see what he'd been doing in the little closets, but there was no sign of anything having been moved.

"You were great today," she said.

David didn't look up. "Thanks. So were you."

"Sorry about telling them you were gay."

"That's okay." He still didn't look up. "It kept some of the women off me."

She looked at him, at his perfect profile. He'd taken a shower and his hair was still damp. He had on jeans and a clean white T-shirt the owner of the dress shop had given him. "Do women usually get on you?" she asked softly.

His eyes still on the paper, he grinned. "Sure. A real nuisance. All over me all the time. Why?"

She didn't answer his question because she didn't know how. "I'm going to bed," she said, then waited for him to say something. But what? she wondered. Please stay?

David said, "Good night. See you in the morning," as he turned a page.

When she was out of the room, David went to the bathroom, turned the shower on cold and held his head under it. Being alone in an apartment with a ready-for-bed Ariel was more than he could take. He hadn't dared look at her for fear he'd leap on her.

The day spent around half-dressed women had nearly pushed him over the edge.

When he left the bathroom, a towel draped around his neck, he looked at her bedroom door. It was slightly open and her light was on. If it had been any other woman on earth, he would have seen that as an invitation.

But not Ariel, he thought with a sigh. Three times today he'd thought he should give up on her. Over twenty years of unrequited love was more than enough for any man. He should get a girl who looked at him as Sara did.

Even as he thought it, David smiled. Sara was the kind of woman who'd say, "Whatever you want to do is okay with me." David knew himself well enough to know that with a wife like that, he'd achieve nothing in life. He wasn't like R. J. Brompton, a man who was a force against nature. David had been given too much in his life and his mother's tears and calls of "don't leave me" tended to make him stay in one place. But with Ariel . . .

David smiled at the thought. There'd be no ambition in the world too big for Ariel. President? Sure. King? Even better.

He shook his head to clear it. Now was not the time to think of his ambitions. He hadn't told Ariel, but today he'd encouraged the women to talk as much as possible. They were sickened and angered by the way the local government frequently arrested their few tourists, but they had the attitude that there was nothing they could do about it. Judge Proctor owned many of the fishing boats, as well as holding mortgages on many houses. People who went against him found themselves on the streets, with no job and no house.

"One of you must be rich," one of the women said today, then hiccuped. David had persuaded the owner of the dress shop to serve wine to the women who were waiting their turn with Ariel.

David had just smiled, but he realized that all of them, except Sara, were rich. And Sara was too, but she didn't know it. For all that her grandfather had disowned his daughter when she'd married the redneck Johnson, he didn't disown his grandchild. Braddon Granville was David's mother's attorney and he also managed the estate of Sara's mother. David had helped Miss Pommy with her accounts many times, so he knew that when Sara turned thirty, she would inherit millions.

How many others knew that? David wondered. He thought back to their lunch at the restaurant by the ferry dock. The waitress, seeming to be friendly and curious, had quizzed them hard about who they were. Anyone who knew anything about Arundel would recognize David's and Ariel's last names. A quick check of the Internet would tell about R.J., and even Sara, since she'd been on Broadway.

Though Brompton had left them a curt note and run off without them, and despite the fact that three women said they'd seen R.J. and Sara early in the morning, David was still worried about them. The storm, the stories he'd heard about some kid named Gideon, were preying on his mind. Were they all right? Why hadn't Sara and R.J. made an attempt to communicate with them?

By the end of the day, David decided that in the morning he would set out to find them. While Ariel soaked in the tub he'd filled a backpack he'd found in Phyllis's basement. While he was down there, he'd made himself check inside the freezer, and, yes, Nezbit's body was still there.

The full pack was now hidden in the closet nearest the door. His plan was to leave about 4:00 A.M. He had an idea what had been in Brompton's head and where he wanted to go. What no one knew—or did they?—was that David knew a great deal more than they thought he did.

He went to bed, but he couldn't sleep. He kept trying to remember a story he'd written when he was in the fifth grade: "What I Did This Summer." An ordinary assignment, but David had made an extraordinary story out of it. His teacher had liked it so much that she'd entered it in a state essay contest and David had won second place. His mother had been so proud of him that when she got a computer a few years later, she had it posted on the Web. On the Tredwell genealogy site, when one clicked twice on David's name, up came photos of him and the essay that had won a prize.

For the last twenty-four hours, David had begun to wonder if that essay was why John Fenwick Nezbit had been killed. The man had been safe as long as he alone knew where his treasure was. But if someone else knew, then Nezbit would become redundant, unnecessary. Maybe the someone else who knew where his gold was was David.

"David," he heard Ariel whisper. "Are you asleep?"

He looked at the clock: 1:23 A.M. He needed to get up in just two and a half hours. He was tempted not to answer, but he couldn't. "I'm awake. The storm scare you?"

"No," she said, then to David's disbelief, she came into the room, pulled back his blanket, and got in bed with him. "Ariel, you can't do this," he said, moving as far away as he could get from her. If the bed weren't up against the wall, he would have gotten out. But what was he to do? Climb over her?

"I was good today, wasn't I?" she asked softly.

Her arms were behind her head and she was staring at the ceiling. Light came in from the hallway and made her face look like that of an angel's. "Ariel . . ."

"Yes, David?" she said, turning and looking at him.

David's back was slammed against the

wall. There was about two inches of space between their bodies. "Exactly what are you playing at?"

She turned over on her back again. "Remember the day you took me out on the motorcycle?"

"Yeah. Could you move that way a bit and give me some room?"

Ariel didn't move. "Why didn't you kiss me that day? We were sixteen and alone and—"

"Untouchable," David said, beginning to become annoyed. "You were and are the ice princess. No one dares touch you."

She turned her head to look at him. "My mother is the ice queen so that makes me the ice princess?"

"Ariel, you may think I'm just your boy companion, but I can assure you that I'm a man."

"I know," she said softly. "I am at last beginning to realize that."

"Ariel . . ." David said as he reached out his hand and touched her cheek.

In a second, she was in his arms.

David held back. He looked into her eyes and said, "Are you sure?"

"Totally," she said. "Completely."

Smiling, he kissed her lips gently, knowing how innocent she was, how completely untouched she was.

Ariel drew back. "Is this how you feel about me? Is this all there is?"

"Ariel," David said softly, "you're a virgin. You're—"

Frowning, she sat up in bed, then grabbed the front of the nightgown with both hands and pulled. Fabric tore; buttons went flying. "I'm a woman!" she said.

Laughing, David grabbed her. "Yeah? Are you?" He put his hand behind her head and pulled her down on the bed. When his mouth came down on top of hers, all Ariel could do was murmur yes.

Chapter Twenty

Stretching, Ariel opened her eyes slowly. So that was what it was all about, she thought. "And well worth all the fanfare," she said aloud, smiling. She turned to share the joke with David, but he wasn't there. Still smiling, she listened for the shower, but heard nothing.

During the night they'd moved from his narrow bed to the two beds in the other bedroom. In between, they'd made love on the two couches and the rug in the sitting room. At 3:30, they took a shower together, soaping each other's bodies, Ariel's hands exploring every growing inch of David's anatomy. They'd made love for the fourth time in the tub.

At 4:30, David said he couldn't do any more and had begged for sleep. Ariel had called him a wimp, but she'd happily nestled in his arms and fallen asleep. "I didn't know we fit together so well," she said.

"I did," David whispered. "I always knew."

Smiling, more content than she'd ever been in her life, Ariel fell asleep.

Now, awakening slowly, she listened for David. No sounds. She looked at the clock: 7:14. It was still early yet, the stores were closed today, so maybe they could. . . . Dreamily, she thought of their night. "Make love all day long," she whispered.

She waited for David to return, but she still heard no sounds. Did he go downstairs to make breakfast to serve it to her in bed? A fitting ending—or beginning, she thought.

She waited another fifteen minutes, then got up. David wasn't in the apartment. Good, she thought. She'd have time to make herself pretty. Yesterday she'd asked for and received a whole new, clean outfit, plus cosmetics. With forty-five minutes and a good hair dryer, she knew she could look like herself again.

An hour later she was clean, dressed, made-up, and her hair was as good as she could get it since her styling brush was at home. But David still hadn't returned to the apartment.

Frowning, she went downstairs. Phyllis was standing in front of the coffeepot. "Where is he?" Ariel asked.

"David?" Phyllis had on an ancient chenille bathrobe, a guarantee that no man was within three miles of her.

"Yes, David," Ariel said, her hands gripping the back of a chair. If she's touched him, I'll murder her, she thought.

"I heard him leave about five," Phyllis said.

"Five? This morning?"

"It wasn't last night, was it? Not from what I heard upstairs. David may have come, but he didn't go."

"There's no need for vulgarity," Ariel said haughtily. "What David Tredwell and I do is—Bugger it!" she said and dropped the attitude. "Where'd he go, and if you tell me you don't know I'll tell you the truth of what's going on, then you'll be an accessory."

"Eula Nezbit," Phyllis said quickly.

"Nezbit," Ariel said, blinking. She knew without a doubt that David had gone to help R.J. and Sara. Without me! she thought.

"What did he take with him? And don't you dare tell me you didn't spy on him. If you were sober enough to eavesdrop on us, and you were awake enough to hear him leave, then I know you spied on him."

"Yesterday, I liked you," Phyllis muttered. "He had on an old backpack he stole out of my basement. I wonder what else you people have stolen? I'm going down there and—"

"Don't," Ariel said quietly as Phyllis started toward the door to the basement.

Turning, she looked into Ariel's eyes, then sat down at the table. "Something awful has happened, hasn't it? I knew it would. When Larry came to me and said he and Fenny were going to do it again and I had to take you in, I begged him not to."

"Why do they do it?"

She shrugged. "Larry needs the money. Fenny enjoys making people miserable, and the judge likes the power. It's just a game."

"Not to us it wasn't and it's not a game anymore."

"What's happened?" Phyllis asked, then raised her hand. "No, don't tell me. What do you want from me?"

"Do you have another backpack?"

"Yeah. A cute little thing, but not very sturdy."

"I need it."

"For what?"

"I have no idea," Ariel said and for a moment she almost lost her resolve. Damn all of them, she thought. Damn all three of them. R. J. and Sara went off together, leaving her behind, then David left her. Obviously none of them thought Ariel could help do anything.

"So what should I put in it?" Phyllis asked.

"Water, sandwiches, and . . . and . . ."

"Nail polish?" The look Ariel gave her made her say, "Sorry."

"You pack it while I change shoes. Where can I get some hiking boots in size six?"

"I'll call Helen Graber. Her daughter—" Phyllis closed her mouth.

"The telephone cable wasn't cut, was it?"

Phyllis shook her head. "Does this mean that I don't get the trip to New York at R. J.'s expense?"

"I don't want to think about what he's going to do to this island when he finds out the extent of what's been done to him."

"Maybe he'll throw enough gold at it that it sinks."

"You wish. I'm going after my friends and I want a rescue helicopter here as soon as it can get here. If you don't do this, the consequences will be catastrophic. Do I make myself clear?"

"Yeah, sure," Phyllis said. "All of you snobs from Arundel make yourselves clear. You think you can order everyone around. You think—"

Striding across the room, Ariel flung open the basement door. "Shall I show you how we snobs 'control' things?"

Phyllis shook her head. "It was just a way to get money. We never meant to hurt anyone."

"You have. You did. I need the pack and I need the shoes. And keep your mouth shut about everything!" With her head high, Ariel turned and left the room, then went outside onto the porch. She didn't trust anyone enough to believe they wouldn't lock her in the prison apartment upstairs.

She sat down on a chair and wondered who she should be angry at. David? The residents of King's Isle? Her mother?

It took only twenty minutes before Phyllis handed her a filled backpack and a pair of shoes, then she gave her a ride to the Nezbit house.

"Where does this Gideon live?" Ariel asked, looking out the car window when Phyllis stopped the car.

"Somewhere back there. I don't know," Phyllis said, anxious to get away from Ariel.

"I want you to answer a question honestly. Are you the mother of Gideon's children?"

"Am I—?" Phyllis began, astonished, then she smiled. "Eula is a lying snake. The whole town has heard her husband say she should be pretty like me, or like any woman. That man makes his whole family crazy. As for me and Gideon, yeah, I got drunk once and ended up in bed with him. Once. As for being the mother of his kids, he's sixteen and the kids are four. Do the math. Any more questions?"

"No," Ariel said. "But I'm warning you that you'd better help us now. When the police get involved in this, you're going to need evidence to make the jury believe you weren't a ringleader."

"Right. Helicopters and police."

Ariel got out of the car and adjusted the

pack on her back. She didn't know if she believed Phyllis or not.

"Go to the left and stay in the woods," Phyllis said. "Eula has three daughters who look just like her and are as mean as she is."

Ariel nodded before Phyllis sped off, gravel flying.

Alone, Ariel looked around her at the country road. There was nothing but trees and fields. To her right was a mailbox and a dirt road that disappeared down a hill. Between the trees, in the distance, she could see the water.

Ignoring the two roads, she headed to the left of what she assumed was the driveway. She had to climb over two fences and walk around what looked like poison ivy growing in a puddle at the base of three trees.

When she wasn't far from the water, she saw a path and cautiously followed it. Turning a corner, she saw a cabin—and on the porch was a man's body. At first she thought it was David, but as she ran, she saw he was younger and he appeared to be unconscious.

She ran up the porch steps and bent over him. He was still breathing. Cautiously, she touched his face—and her hand came away bloody. She dropped her pack on the floor, then ran inside to get a towel and water. As she ran, she looked about the cabin but saw no one.

She threw a big towel in the sink, wet it with cold water, then ran outside to the young man. She put the sopping wet towel on the top of his head.

Groaning, he turned his head and opened his eyes. There was an ugly cut on the side of his forehead. Blood was caked down the right side of his face; it had soaked his hair and shirt.

"Help me up," he gasped.

Ariel put her body under his arm and helped him to a chair. She put the towel around his neck, then used the edge of it to dab at the gash.

"How did you get out?" he whispered.

For a moment she thought he meant Phyllis's house, but then she realized he thought she was Sara. Maybe she could trick him into revealing something. "I found a way out," she said. "After what you did to me, it's a wonder I'm not dead."

He took the towel from her. "I don't know what the hell you're talking about. You must be the other one. I heard there were two of you." He tried to push himself out of the chair, but fell back down again. "I *have* to go! I have to find the twins."

"I don't think you can walk. I'm assuming you're Gideon."

"Yeah. And what have you been told about *me?*"

Ariel couldn't answer, but just stood there looking at him. Was he a friend or a foe? Eula said the boy was "evil," but then she'd said the children were— Right now Ariel didn't have the luxury of taking time to decide whether someone's character was good or bad. He didn't make her skin crawl and his main concern was lost children. That was good enough for her. "Where are the children?"

Tears came to Gideon's eyes and again he tried to stand. "I have to go get them," he whispered. "They followed me. They've been out there all night."

"Where are R. J. and Sara?"

"Trapped in one of those damned holes. I told them not to go, but R. J. thought he could find Fenny's killer."

"They told you about that?"

"Yes. But that doesn't matter now. I have

to go find the twins. I saw them. Lightning came and I saw them."

"I'll find them," Ariel said. "I'll—"

"You?" In spite of his pain, his expression was one of contempt. "Is that pack Gucci?"

"And my earrings are real diamonds," Ariel snapped. "If you can get up and go with me, do so. If not, then sit there and wallow in your own superiority." She grabbed her pack and headed down the path to the left, hoping it was one that led to wherever R. J. and Sara and the children were.

She expected the boy to follow her, and hoped he would, but she walked for nearly thirty minutes alone. When he did show up, it was abruptly. He had a bandage on his head that was already spotted with blood, a pack on his back, and a rifle in his hand.

"Sorry about what I said. We King's Islanders are a bit standoffish with outsiders."

"Don't get me started," Ariel said. "I'm going to recommend this place for atomic bomb testing."

"We're not that bad," he said. He was trying to keep up with her but with every step he was wincing in pain.

"Are those children yours? Phyllis said they aren't, but—"

"You've been talking to Eula."

"Your mother."

"I don't think so. I think she—"

Ariel held up her hand. "The less I hear about the people on this island, the better I like it. Tell me about R. J. and Sara."

"Her leg is broken. She's okay, but she's in pain. They went off by themselves yesterday but I followed them. The twins must have followed me. A tree came down in the storm and I thought it had hit them, but by the time I got to them they'd fallen into a hole. This area is pocketed with them. I climbed over the tree to get to them, but then the lightning flashed and I saw the kids. I also saw a person behind them. R. J. and Sara seemed to be okay, so I went after the kids. It was raining hard and I couldn't see much, couldn't hear anything. I climbed all over the mountain. I went to the springs, and I—"

"The hot springs?"

"What used to be hot springs."

"Did you see the children?"

"Yes. I saw them twice and each time I thought I saw someone with them."

"Old? Young? Man or woman?" asked Ariel.

"It was too dark to see."

"How did you hurt your head?"

"There was a sound. It was like a shot, but it could have been lightning striking a tree. I don't know. One minute I was standing, then the next I was falling. I tried to catch myself, but it was all loose gravel. I thought I'd fallen into one of the pits, but it must have been down a hillside. I think I was knocked unconscious."

"How did you get back to the cabin?"

"I don't know. I was lying on gravel, rain was hitting me in the face, my head hurt, then the next thing I knew I was on my own porch and an angel hit me in the face with a wet towel."

Ariel didn't smile. "David must have found you."

"Who is David?"

"Did you see a man, tall, blond, handsome. Beautiful, really. He left Phyllis's house early this morning."

"I saw no beautiful men," Gideon said. "And no beautiful twins." Again, there were tears in his voice.

"We'll find them. I think that first we should—"

"Get R.J. and Sara out. What took me so long to get here was that I got a winch and some rope. The tree fell across the hole. I'll tie the winch onto the tree and haul them up. You can stay with Sara while R.J. and I look for the twins."

"You're injured, so *you* stay with Sara."

Gideon gave her a sideways look. "I bet you rule your household, don't you?"

"I don't have a household. I live with my mother and she rules everybody."

"Rules *you?*" Gideon asked, then before she could answer, he said, "There it is," and began to hurry forward.

Following him, Ariel saw that he was limping, skipping now and then to stay off an injured ankle and foot. There was dried blood on his neck and his shirt, and a long tear in the back of his shirt, covered in more dried blood. She had an idea that he had many more injuries than could be seen. He should be in a hospital, she thought.

Minutes later, she saw him stretched out on the ground, most of his body covered by the branches of a big pine tree. When she reached him, she looked down to see R.J. standing about twenty feet below.

"Ariel!" he said. "What are *you* doing here?"

She was disgusted at yet again hearing

that tone that said *she* could be of no help. "I heard there was a rare form of lizard up here and I need some new belts."

R. J. looked at her in silence, as though he didn't know if she was serious or not.

"I came to save the lot of you," she said. "How is Sara?"

"I'm fine," Sara called from the corner. "I just have a broken leg and a great need of painkillers. Opium, I need you!"

"Have you seen the children?" Ariel called down.

When R. J. and Sara were silent, Ariel looked at Gideon.

"They had enough to worry about, so I didn't tell them the kids were missing."

"The twins!" Sara said to R. J., then looked up at Ariel. "Get R. J. out and you three go looking for them. I'm safe here. Please hurry. How long have they been missing?"

"Too many hours," Gideon said. When he tried to get up, he stumbled and nearly fell into the pit, but Ariel put her body in front of his and steadied him.

"What happened to you?" R. J. called up.

"He fell down some rocks," Ariel said. "I think David may have carried him back to his cabin."

"Where is David now?" R.J. asked.

"I don't know," Ariel said, pushing on Gideon to get him away from the edge. "How do we get them out?"

Gideon pulled a big metal winch from his pack and a heavy nylon rope. "I'll tie this onto the middle of the tree, put a rope through here, then I'll pull R.J. up."

Ariel looked at the tree. Standing upright, she was sure it would look enormous, but lying down across an open hole it looked like a tightrope with branches. "You'll fall," she said.

"That's a chance I'll have to take."

She put her hand on his forearm. "The only knot I know how to tie is a shoelace. Show me what to do and *I* will do it." When he started to protest, she said, "If you do fall, it'll be just me here to get all of you out and to go find the twins. If I fall, there'll still be you and R.J. to look for them."

Gideon didn't argue, just demonstrated a solid knot to use to tie the winch to the tree. "Keep your eyes on the tree," he said as he tied a rope onto her waist.

Ariel kept twisting about to look at the narrow tree. Could she do it? The more she looked, the weaker her knees felt.

"So who's this beautiful man you're searching for?" Gideon asked.

"You're too young to know and it doesn't matter anyway because I'm going to kill him the minute I see him."

"Oh, yeah?" Gideon said. His face was inches from hers and his arms around her as he tied the rope about her waist. "I could think of worse ways to go than to be killed by you."

"I am *not* Phyllis," she said coldly as she moved away from him and toward the tree.

"Indeed you aren't," Gideon said, unperturbed by her coolness.

Ariel didn't like his insinuations, didn't like his flirting, and didn't like his levity in the face of the situation. She was so angry at him that she was halfway to the center of the tree before she realized it. When she looked down and saw R. J. and Sara far below her, she froze.

She looked back over her shoulder at Gideon.

"In those pants you look as cute as Phyllis," Gideon said, leering at her. "Are you sure you didn't grow up on King's Isle?"

"I'm from Arundel, North Carolina," Ariel

said and there was so much pride in her voice that R. J. laughed.

"That's right, honey," R. J. called up to her. "You tell him."

Ariel reached the center of the tree and looked back at Gideon in triumph. He was rubbing the side of his head but he was smiling at her.

"Okay, baby," Gideon said, "now straddle the tree like a man and tie him into a knot."

Ariel sat down on the tree, looked down at R. J., and said, "Who *is* this child?"

"I don't know, but I plan to find out," he said softly.

Ariel concentrated as she tied the winch onto the tree, then threaded the rope through the pulley as Gideon had shown her. Cautiously, she made her way back to the young man, then helped him pull the rope with R. J. on it up to the top of the hole.

When R. J. stepped onto land he grabbed Ariel's shoulders and kissed her hard on the mouth.

"Hey! I saw that!" Sara called from below. "He's mine, cousin."

"Oh?" Ariel asked, looking at R. J.

"We talked about some things," R. J. said sheepishly.

"Talked?" Ariel asked. "Your shirt is on inside out."

"Ah. Well . . . there are a lot of ways to communicate."

Gideon, coiling the rope around his arm, came to them. There was no more laughter on his face. "R.J., you and I are going to have to separate. Ariel, I want you to go back to town and organize a search party. Get every person you can find and get back up here as fast as possible."

Ariel didn't argue with him, just grabbed her pack and started back down the trail they'd come on. She was cursing Phyllis and all the residents of King's Isle with each step she took. She no longer cared who killed Fenny Nezbit. Obviously, he'd been killed out of greed. Someone wanted his gold.

She was just a short distance from Gideon's cabin when something bright pink on the ground caught her eye. Picking it up, she saw it was a tiny plastic high-heeled shoe. A shoe for a fashion doll.

She cut off the trail into the woods. She walked slowly, on the lookout for snakes, but also searching for any bright colors. The grasses seemed to have been trampled recently, but she wasn't sure.

When she saw a broken branch, her heart sped up. Fifty feet away was another tiny shoe. Holding it, she thought, Now what do I do? Did she stop there and go back to find the men? That would take at least an hour, and an hour lost looking for small children could mean life or death.

Also there was the surprise element. What if Gideon was right and there had been someone with the twins? There was a murderer on King's Isle. What if he—

She didn't think anymore. She put the shoes in her pocket, then started walking slowly and quietly—much quieter than three people could walk, she told herself.

Every seventy-five feet or so, she found another piece: sunglasses, Capri pants, a cute little peasant blouse. Tiny earrings had been placed on a rock.

When Ariel found the first body part, she wanted to sit down and cry. Poor little girl, having to disassemble her doll.

There were legs and arms, but after the torso, there was nothing. Ariel walked across what looked to be crushed grass, but even after a hundred yards, she saw nothing more. There were no broken branches, no doll parts, nothing.

She was about to turn back when something made her go right. It wasn't a sound, but a smell. A fragrance she knew as well as she knew her own body. David.

For a moment, she closed her eyes, then turned around in a circle, breathing deeply. When she stopped, she opened her eyes and smiled, then walked straight ahead, over rocks, through leaves, across a fallen tree. There, lying on the ground, under a ledge of rock, their hands bound together, their mouths gagged, were two beautiful little children.

As much as Ariel wanted to run to them, she crouched down behind a rock and waited and listened. She heard and saw nothing. Cautiously, she stepped into the open. When no one leaped out at her, she went to the children and untied them.

They clung to her, but they didn't cry, and when they called her Sara, she didn't correct them. She pulled them back under the rock with her, one on each side, and asked them their names. "Tell me every word of what happened."

"We followed Gideon," Bertie said.

"But we got lost."

"And it rained on us."

"Who tied you up?" Ariel asked.

"Mr. Larry."

"Larry Lassiter," Ariel said, unsurprised. "Was there another man here?"

"David," Beatrice said with a little flutter of her lashes. "He saved us."

"But Mr. Larry said he'd kill us unless David went with him, so he went."

"Why did he want David?" Ariel asked.

"He knows where the gold is."

"David knows where the gold is?!" Ariel said. "Are you sure of that?"

Bertie moved away from Ariel and out from under the overhang. He held an imaginary gun on Beatrice. " 'You know what I want, don't you, kid?' "

" 'Yeah, I know,' " Beatrice said in a voice that sounded remarkably like David's. " 'How did you find out?' "

" 'I looked you up on the Internet and read your paper. "The Weird Man's Hideout." Was that the title?' "

" 'More or less,' " Beatrice said. " 'Let me take the kids back to safety, then I'll go with you.' "

" 'Naw. They're fine here,' " Bertie said, waving his finger around like Ariel had seen Lassiter do. " 'Somebody'll find them.' "

" 'You can't leave them here! They'll die of exposure.' "

" 'They're tough little brats. They're used to hiding to get away from their mother. Ain't you, kids?' "

The twins stopped talking and looked at Ariel.

"Where did they go?" Ariel asked.

The children shrugged. How could they know when they'd been tied up?

Ariel had an idea. "Do you know where the hot springs are?"

"Sure," Bertie said. "We go there with Gideon all the time. It's how he gives us a bath."

Ariel smiled. "Can you lead me there?"

"Sure."

She turned to look at Beatrice and saw that in her hand was the head of her doll. Ariel reached into her pocket and pulled out doll pieces and clothes. "As we walk, I bet I can put her back together."

For the first time, she saw tears in the child's eyes. No child should be this tough, she thought.

"Can you?" Beatrice asked.

"I'm sure of it," Ariel said.

Chapter Twenty-one

Ariel didn't want the children with her when she found David. If that horrible man Lassiter had a gun, the last thing she wanted was children around. She knew that if she took them back to Gideon's cabin they'd not stay there. Besides, that would take too long.

When they got to an area she recognized, she knew that the cave where Sara was was close. When she got to it, she called down to her cousin and said she was going to lower the kids down to her. Ariel wasn't strong enough to bring Sara up, but she could use the rope to get the children down. The hole was cover, protection. They'd be safe there until help arrived. She looked up at the sky, but saw no rescuing helicopter. Did Phyllis call?

When Ariel told the children what she wanted to do, they were excited. She tied a loop in the end of the rope and Bertie put his foot in it. She put her pack on his back, then fastened the straps around the rope.

"Ready?" Ariel asked Sara. Ariel was standing on the tree that a short time before had taken Gideon's teasing to get her to walk out on. Below her was Sara, standing on one leg, leaning on what looked to be a makeshift crutch cut from a tree branch.

"I'm ready," Sara said.

Ariel had to walk back down the tree to the ground, loop the rope around her waist, then slowly lower the child to the floor below. Sara steadied him, unfastened the pack straps, then sent it back up to Ariel.

Beatrice went down faster. As she went down, Ariel waved to her, her reassembled doll sticking out of the front of her pack.

After the children were down, Ariel ran along the tree to hang over the side and look at Sara. "Water and sandwiches are in the pack. I'll be back as soon as I can. Keep them quiet if you can. There are telephones on the island and a helicopter may come for us."

"You're an angel!" Sara called up to her.

Smiling, Ariel went back to the ground. She'd been called an angel twice in one day.

The children had pointed the way to the old hot springs, but Ariel didn't follow the path. If anyone was watching, she'd be seen. She stayed close to the rocks and twice she saw what looked like newly made scuff marks. Had R. J. and Gideon gone this way?

She had gone about a mile and was wishing she'd kept a bottle of water when a hand came out of the bush and seized her ankle. If Ariel hadn't been so frightened, she would have screamed. In the next second, a hand went over her mouth and pulled her to the ground. She couldn't scream but she wasn't going down without a fight.

"Ariel! Ariel!" came an urgent voice in her ear. "If you don't stop fighting me they're going to hear us."

"David?" she gasped, then threw her arms around his neck and began kissing him.

For a moment, he kissed her back, then pulled away. "Honey, sweetheart, now isn't the time for this. There are some seriously bad things going on and we need to address them."

She didn't like his tone. She longed to tell

him about how she and Gideon had res-
cued R.J., then she alone had found the
twins and . . . but as he'd said, now wasn't
the time.

"I want to tell you how to get back to
Gideon's cabin," David said. "Then you
need to go through the woods to find some
children. Ariel, you *can* do this. You need to
put aside your fears to help these children."

Yet another man was telling her to go
away. "What do *you* plan to do?" she asked.

David rubbed his hand over his face. "So
much has happened that I can't begin to tell
you all that I need to do."

"Why is your leg bleeding and why is
there blood on your shirt?"

"I had to carry some huge kid, a teenager,
nearly a mile. He'd fallen down some rocks
and cut his head. Then there were these little kids—"

"And Larry Lassiter."

"Yeah," David said slowly, looking at her
in surprise.

"Why does Lassiter think *you* know where
Fenny's gold is?"

"Cosmic coincidence, but how do you
know about that?"

"Long story. The twins are safe and a rescue helicopter may appear at any time. Do you know where R. J. and Gideon are? And where is Lassiter?" Ariel asked.

David was looking at her as though he'd never seen her before. "I escaped him. I gave him a bogus map and when he looked in a cave, I jumped."

Ariel looked at him a moment, searching his eyes. She had known him all her life and she knew when he was hiding something. Reaching down to his leg, she pulled the fabric of his trousers apart. The gash in his leg was deep and he was losing blood.

"The last time you tore away fabric—" David said, smiling.

"That was ages ago," Ariel said dismissively. "You need a doctor. I want you to tell me where Fenny's gold really is, then I want you to stay here and hide."

"And let you go out there? Alone? Not in my lifetime," he said and started to rise. Immediately, the wound in his leg opened up and began to bleed.

"You move from here and I'll tell my mother I'm pregnant with R. J. Brompton's child."

"She'll disown you," David said, smiling.

"Then I'll go to New York and you'll never find me."

"Ariel, really, this is ridiculous. You can't find the cave and—"

She got up, looked about, then took a step forward. She was leaving on her own and she knew he couldn't follow her.

"Okay," he said. "There's a map in the front of my pack."

She pulled the pack out of the bushes and unzipped the front pocket. "Is this the pack you found in the basement, then secretly filled when we got back from the pub?"

"Yeah," he said quietly. "I just didn't want to bother you."

"Ha! You wanted to keep me from doing anything. All of you have treated me as though I can do nothing, as though I'm just excess baggage. Worthless."

"Not worthless. Not to me," David said softly, his hand on her arm.

"David Tredwell, do you think I'm stupid? You've always wanted me for how you can use me. Do you think I don't know you want a political career? Do you think I don't know that I'd make a perfect wife for a politician? Do you think I don't know that you put up with anything I do to you because I fit into your ambitious little scheme so well? You were giving your kisses to that dim-witted, big-breasted Britney while I couldn't even get you to kiss my hand."

"So all this with Brompton was to make me jealous?"

"Don't flatter yourself. I knew from the first that R. J. would treat me as a woman, not as a porcelain doll like you do."

David fell back against the bushes and laughed. "And I thought I knew what you wanted. Miss Pommy—"

"Used to intimidate me because she holds the money, but not anymore. When I get out of here I'm going to . . ." She pulled the map from the pack. "I don't know what I'm going to do, but I'm going to make some changes in my life."

"I hope you keep me in it," David said softly.

"Maybe," she said, looking at the map.

"Let me show you—"

"I can read a map." She shoved the folded paper into her bra, then looked at him. "Stay here and be quiet. Listen for a helicopter."

"Yes, ma'am," he said, smiling.

Ariel took a bottle of water from his pack, looked out between the bushes, then on impulse, leaned down and kissed him. "You don't ever leave me behind again. Understand?"

"Never again," he said. "Forever."

"You got that right," she said, then stepped up into the open.

David's map was easy to follow. She kept the water on her right, and when she saw a huge tree with half of it burned away by lightning, she put the map away. The rock looked solid, but when she tiptoed along a ledge with her arms spread out, she found a cut that overlapped itself. As she slipped through the narrow opening, she saw why Nezbit kept himself so thin. Most adults couldn't fit between the rocks, but Ariel, at just a hundred and five pounds, could.

It was so dark inside the rock, she could see nothing. As she felt her way around, her heart was beating rapidly. A hidden place like this was a den snakes would love. When her hand touched an old-fashioned lantern, she sighed in relief. Next to it were matches. She knew how to light it—thanks to years of watching *Little House on the Prairie.*

Holding the lantern aloft, she looked about the cave. It was tiny, about six feet by eight, with a stone floor and a roof that seemed to go up to infinity. Against the far wall was an old wooden fruit crate with things inside it. She put the lantern down and sat down by the crate.

Inside the crate were what looked to be the contents of a safe. Inside a plastic bag were two old, mildewed passports of Ray and Alice Erickson, age fifty-five and fifty-six, ownership papers of a forty-eight-foot sailboat, and a last will and testament. Beside the packet of papers was a jewelry box, a big thing made of mahogany, with lots of little drawers and two handles on the side.

Ariel lifted the lid, surprised it wasn't locked, but then who else could find the place besides Fenny Nezbit? And David, Ariel thought.

The jewelry chest was nearly empty, only two pairs of earrings inside, but the velvet lining showed the imprint of many other pieces of jewelry.

Legends, myths and, ultimately, a murder, all caused by the contents of a woman's jewelry chest.

Leaning back against the wall, Ariel opened the last will and testament and read it. Ray and Alice Erickson left everything to their son and daughter, to be split equally between them. There was a codicil attached

and it told everything. Two people had retired after years of running a successful jewelry store, sold everything they owned, and
bought a sailboat. They apologized to their
children for their seeming irrationality, but
they were sick of working six days a week.
They said they planned to take the best of
the jewelry with them, as they had one last
deal to make in Saudi Arabia.

"They never made it," Ariel whispered,
folding the will and putting it back in the
bag. It seemed that they'd wrecked their
new sailboat and their treasure had been
stolen and gradually sold by Fenny Nezbit.

Ariel wondered if he'd killed Mr. and Mrs.
Erickson. "No one will ever know," she said
aloud.

She put the last two pairs of earrings in
the bag with the papers and shoved it down
the back of her trousers. As she took a step
toward the opening, she heard a sound.
She leaped the next few feet to the door
and looked up. It was a rescue helicopter!

Stepping to the edge, she waved her
arms and the pilot saw her. He turned
around and another man, the copilot, used
a bullhorn to ask, "Are you injured?"

"No!" Ariel yelled and shook her head,

then she pointed to her right with both her arms. The injured people were that way.

"We have all the others," the man said through his horn. "Go to the ground and we'll pick you up."

Ariel said, "Oh yes, oh yes, oh yes" all the way down. She slipped once, then took a deep breath and went down more slowly.

The helicopter landed and she ran to it, ducking against the wind of the blades. "Are you Ariel Weatherly?" the copilot asked and she yelled, "Yes!"

She scrambled into the backseat. Part of her wanted to cry in relief and part of her felt elated. Exhilarated.

The copilot turned to her and pointed down. On the ground below them was an ambulance. R. J. was standing by a police car, a twin on each side of him, each holding one of his hands. Four big North Carolina policemen were helping two handcuffed people into the cars: Larry Lassiter and Eula Nezbit. David, Sara, and Gideon were missing, but Ariel figured they were being treated for their injuries. She leaned back against the seat and smiled as King's Isle was left in the background and they headed toward Arundel.

She was going home.

Epilogue

"To us!" R.J. said, raising his champagne glass high.

The four of them were in the pub on King's Isle, which was empty except for them. But then R.J. now owned the place so they could do what they wanted. It was over a year since they'd first arrived on King's Isle and many things had changed since then.

"To my brilliant wife," R.J. said, looking at Sara with loving eyes. "And here's to winning an Emmy."

"Thank you," Sara said, lifting her glass of orange juice. She was six weeks pregnant.

"And to mine," David said, lifting his glass to Ariel. "Who would have known you could write?"

"No one believed I could do anything," Ariel said, "including me."

"Your script was brilliant," Sara said, "and I thank you very much for it. I don't know where I'm going from here, but I enjoyed every minute of working on our movie."

David again lifted his drink to Ariel. "To my wife, a woman I thought I knew but didn't."

R. J. looked at Sara. "And to *my* wife, who never had an idea that I hired her because I loved her."

Ariel looked at R. J. "Thank you for taking my script to an agent."

"Wait a minute!" David said. "*I* was the one who read it and *I* was the one who took it to R. J."

"And I was the one who took it from him," Sara said.

"And changed it," Ariel said.

"Tweaked it," Sara answered.

Four weeks after they'd left King's Isle, Ariel found out she was pregnant with David's baby. A wedding was rushed through, but thanks to her mother's years of planning, it was not going to be a small affair. Between Southern society and R. J.'s contacts, it would be the wedding of the year. Three days before the wedding, Sara asked if Ariel would mind very much making it a double. A gown was bought, more champagne purchased, and there was a wedding that Arundel wouldn't soon forget.

For the next eight months, Ariel was hovered over by her mother and David and his mother. Bored, Ariel began to write about what happened to them on King's Isle. Somehow, the story seemed to gradually evolve into a script. She ordered a book on script writing, followed the format as best she could, and put their adventure onto paper.

She loved dramatizing how Lassiter and Fenny had quarreled, then the lawyer had shot Fenny through the head. It had been Eula who'd helped him carry the body up Phyllis's creaking stairs, hiding it in the bathtub. "Let those fancy folk from Arundel take the blame," Eula had said.

"Except the kid that wrote the paper," Lassiter had said. After he and Fenny had pulled their usual trick of having the rich tourists arrested, Lassiter had found David Tredwell's prize-winning essay and realized the boy had seen Fenny slipping into where his treasure was hidden.

For years, Fenny had dangled his treasure—"an endless horde," he'd said it was—in front of everyone, but no one had been able to find it. The night R.J. had been arrested, Fenny, drunk as always, had nearly fallen on the targets, and Lassiter, fed up, had told him that someone else knew where the treasure was. Lassiter had only half believed it, but he liked, for once, having the upper hand. When Lassiter quoted some of the essay, Fenny had gone berserk. He ran to his truck, pulled out a pistol from under the seat, and threatened to kill Lassiter. That's when the attorney realized that maybe the kid's essay was true. There was a scuffle, the gun went off, and Fenny lay dead. Lassiter would have gone to the police, but Eula raised up from where she'd been sleeping in the back of the truck. She'd heard it all. Larry Lassiter had been nervous, afraid, but Eula was as cool as ice. She was thrilled to get rid of a husband she'd hated. She came up with a plan instantly. They carried Fenny's body up Phyllis's stairs, dumped the body in the tub, and hid in the dark living room while Phyllis opened the door to her paying guests.

Eula and Lassiter ran outside and waited for the screams and chaos that would soon come. Lassiter stood at the edge of the woods and smoked one cigarette after another, but no screams came.

In the wee hours, the four city slickers carried what looked to be two bodies outside.

"They think they're clever," Eula said when the two couples separated. "But I'll get them. I'll wait two days, then I'll start worryin' about what's happened to my beloved husband." She turned to Lassiter. *"You* find the gold. Do whatever you have to, but find that gold."

But their plan had backfired, and Eula and Lassiter were taken away in handcuffs. Fenny's body had been retrieved from the freezer by the coroner. Later, R. J. had had to do a lot of talking to explain why Phyllis Vancurren's hair was on the body, even though she was innocent. She had been exonerated.

When Ariel finished the script, she was shy about showing it to David. In the end, she'd shown it first to her mother. "David and I will live in this house with you, but the regime will change," Ariel had said when she returned. She had at last come to understand how much her mother loved her.

Her mother's fear had been that if Ariel didn't marry someone from Arundel, she might leave and live somewhere else.

Not that Ariel's mother softened overnight, but she did learn that she could no longer bully her daughter into submission. As Ariel told David, "When you've found a dead body in a bathtub, it puts your mother's bad temper into perspective."

So her mother read the script first. "It's not to my taste," she said, "but I would imagine some people would like it."

That was the highest praise Ariel had ever received from her mother. The next day she showed the script to David, who loved it, and he took it to R.J. Sara saw it before R.J. could read it. She finished it that night and told R.J. that if he had to buy a studio, she wanted him to have it made into a movie and she wanted to play both Ariel and herself.

R.J. didn't have to buy anything. He read the script, then sent it to an L.A. agent and Lifetime TV bought it immediately. By the time the movie was ready to start filming, R.J. and Charley Dunkirk had bought most of King's Isle, so the shooting was done there. During the filming, Sara'd been so upset when she was lowered into the cave again that R. J. had ordered she be given oxygen.

Now, in the pub, Sara raised her glass of juice. "To brilliant beginnings."

She was referring to the way Ariel had started her script, with the story David had told her while he was in the hospital. The TV movie started with an eleven-year-old boy in a camp run by two marijuana-smoking hippies. There was no dialogue, only sixties-era music as the boy left camp and explored the island. When he saw a skinny little man with big ears slipping in and out of the rocks, David followed him. The camera showed David hiding and waiting, then when the funny-looking man left, David slipped between the rocks and saw the cave. That was before Fenny's thirty-second birthday, so the cave was empty. The scene changed to show a young David in school, trying to come up with a story about what he did that summer. He remembered the cave and the skinny man with the big ears and wrote about it. The last scene was the story being awarded a prize and his proud mother posting the essay on the Internet.

After the opening, the credits came on

and the first scene showed a spoiled, over-dressed, overly made-up Ariel haughtily demanding that her sweet, overworked cousin exchange places with her. Ariel hadn't written the script to make herself seem a snob, nor had she portrayed Sara as such a dumpling of virtue—but, as Sara said, she'd "tweaked" it. Defending herself, Sara said she'd made Ariel into a reverse Pygmalion. "You mean I went from upper class to your class?" Ariel said, making Sara laugh. Somewhere along the way she'd lost her feeling of being an outsider. She'd been welcomed with open arms in Arundel, and at last she felt she belonged somewhere.

There had been one argument, which Sara won. Right after the rescue, in a fit of giddy relief that they were safe, the cousins had laughed and cried—and told each other their stories. Ariel had told Sara about tearing apart her nightgown, then later tearing apart David's trouser leg. Sara thought they were good scenes and had added them to the script. An argument ensued, but the scene stayed.

On the night the movie aired on TV, R.J. put up a screen the size of a barn in front of the courthouse on King's Isle, then invited the whole town. When Ariel—played by Sara and seen from the collarbone up—tore open her nightgown and said, "I am a woman," the cheers could be heard to Arundel. Ariel was so embarrassed she would have slid under her chair if R.J. and David hadn't each grabbed an arm and kept her upright.

The crowd again cheered when Larry Lassiter and Eula Nezbit were hauled off in handcuffs, but when Judge Proctor was later arrested, the townspeople set off fireworks. Neither David nor R.J. knew the fireworks had been planned, so they laughed and cheered with the others.

After the Lifetime movie, R.J. announced that his own private movie studio had made a short film that he'd like to show them. Some people groaned because the barbeque was ready and a band was warming up.

Ariel and David looked at each other. Sara smiled knowingly.

What came on the huge screen was a black-and-white film that had been crafted to look like a 1930s silent movie. It even rolled a few times. With no dialogue and the movement choppy and awkward, there was

Gideon being reunited with his grandparents. When R.J. had seen the beautiful, unique house the Nezbits were living in, he'd remembered seeing something like it at an art show he'd attended in New York when he was still in college. After the ordeal on King's Isle, R.J. found the name of the architect, then contacted his parents. They said they didn't know what had become of their son. After a breakup with his girlfriend, he'd said he wanted time alone and that he didn't know where he was going or what he was going to do. That was the last they ever heard of him. R.J. figured that was when the young man had stayed on King's Isle and built that house. His name was James Gideon.

No one knew what happened to him, but through DNA testing he was found to be Gideon's father. As yet, they didn't know who his mother was.

The film showed R.J. surrounded by books, as though deep in research. Of course the truth was it had taken him one ten-minute call to an old girlfriend to find out the name of the artist whose show they'd seen together so long ago.

The next scene was Gideon with his grand-

parents. He was great in front of the camera,
alternately pantomiming great laughter, then
huge tears. When R. J. handed Gideon a big
book that said "Princeton" on it, the young
man feigned more tears, then picked R. J. up.
R. J. pantomimed loss of dignity so well that
everyone laughed. By that time, there wasn't
a person on the island who hadn't had some
dealing with R. J. in purchase negotiations, so
they knew him.

Next into the picture were the twins.
R. J.'d had a big sign put on a derelict brick
building that read COUNTY ORPHANAGE. A
woman dressed like a Victorian matron was
taking the screaming twins—who were
great hams—from Sara. She was crying,
pushing them away, then on her knees talking to them. The dialogue card said, "You
will be fine. I'm sure they will love you very
much." Sara stood up, then cried on R. J.'s
shoulder dramatically, while the twins were
pulled, screaming, toward the orphanage.
R. J. held Sara at arm's length, and the dialogue card said, "No one can love them as
much as we do. Let's buy them." When
Sara kicked him in the shin, the audience
howled with laughter. The card said, "Sorry.
Let's adopt them."

The last scene was in color, a series of snapshots of Thanksgiving and Christmas. One picture was of David and Ariel with their new baby, Miss Pommy looking on in adoration. In her mind, she'd won. Another photo showed R. J. with Bertie on his shoulders, and Sara holding Beatrice. Gideon was with his grandparents at an absurdly long table, with masses of food before them. Sara, R. J., David and Ariel, and all the others were there.

The scene changed to motion and everyone at the table looked at the camera and raised a glass in a toast. "To King's Isle," they shouted.

The roar from the residents of King's Isle was deafening. When the film ended, they got up and started dancing before the band began to play.

That was a month ago and now, R. J. and Sara, Ariel and David raised their glasses and said, "To us."

Atria Books
Proudly Presents

First Impressions

Jude Deveraux

Available in Hardcover from Atria Books

Turn the page for a preview of
First Impressions. . . .

Prologue

The moment he saw the smirk on Bill's face, Jared knew he was going to be given a job he wouldn't like. So what did a man have to do to finally be able to choose his own assignments? he thought for the thousandth time. Get shot? Naw, he'd done that three times. How about getting kidnapped? That had happened twice. Hey! How about being home so seldom that his wife leaves him for some other guy, a used car salesman who is now the father of their three kids? Nope. That had happened too. So how about getting too old for the field? Too late. At forty-nine, Jared felt that he'd reached that age about six years ago.

"Don't look at me like that," Bill said, holding his office door open for Jared to enter.

Groaning, Jared put on a pronounced limp as he hobbled toward the chair opposite Bill's overloaded desk, WILLIAM TEASDALE on a plaque in front. Sticking his leg out stiffly in front of him, he ostentatiously rubbed his knee, as though he were in great pain.

"You can cut it out," Bill said as he sat down behind his desk. "I have no sympathy for you, and even if I did, I couldn't let you out of this one." He picked up a folder, then looked across the top of it at Jared. "Most agents are glad to get out in the field. Why not you?"

Jared leaned back in his chair. "Where should I begin? With pain? I was in the hospital for three weeks after the last job. And life. I like living. And then there's—"

"Got a new girlfriend?" Bill asked, his eyes narrowed.

Jared gave a bit of a grin. "Yeah. Nice girl. I'd like to see her sometimes."

"She's a reformed what?"

"Stripper," Jared mumbled, giving Bill a sheepish grin. "So sue me. After a wife like Patsy—"

"Spare me," Bill said, and once again he

was the boss. "We need somebody to find out something, and you can do it. Remember that agent we found out had been a spy for the last fifteen years?"

"Yeah," Jared said, bitterness in his voice. He'd worked with the man about ten years ago, and had filed a report saying that something wasn't right about the guy, but he didn't know what. No one paid any attention. A few months ago, they'd found out that the agent was a spy and that he'd been feeding information to his mother country for years. "So what did you find out from him?"

"Nothing. Suicide before we could get to him."

"Please tell me that you don't want *me* to travel to wherever he was from, go undercover, and find out—"

"No," Bill said, waving his hand. "Nothing like that. The truth is that we can't figure out what his last big project was. He knew we were coming about ten minutes before we got there, so he had time to destroy a lot of evidence. But we found disks hidden under the floors, and a list of names inside a light-bulb. He had time to get rid of it all, so why didn't he destroy it?"

"But he didn't," Jared said, feeling the old wave of curiosity well up inside of him and trying hard to suppress it. Why? was the question that had caused most of the problems in his life. Even after a case was considered cold, Jared's "why" often made him continue. "What *did* he do?"

"He wadded up several pieces of paper into tiny balls and swallowed them."

"I bet somebody had fun retrieving them."

"Yeah," Bill said with a half smile. "We lost most of what went down him, but forensics managed to get a name and part of a Social Security number." He pushed a clear plastic folder across the desk, and Jared picked it up. Inside was a small piece of paper that seemed to have some writing on it, but Jared couldn't make it out.

"Eden Palmer," Bill said. "That name and a few numbers were the only things the crime lab could recover."

"Who's he?"

"Her. As far as we can figure out, she's nobody." He pulled a piece of paper from the folder in front of him. "She's forty-five, had a baby when she was eighteen, no husband then and not one since. She worked at one low-level job after another until her kid started college, then she went back to school and got a degree." He looked at the paper. "A couple of years after she graduated, Eden Palmer moved to New York, where she worked in a publishing house. When we first heard about her, she didn't know it, but an old woman she knew had died and left her a house in eastern North Carolina. The lawyer taking care of the case was looking for her, but we fixed it so he was delayed in finding her. We wanted to find out about her first." Putting the papers down, he stared at Jared.

"So how did she get connected to somebody who's been spying on the U.S. for umpteen years?"

"We have no idea." He was still looking at Jared, as though he expected him to figure out something.

"Maybe it was personal," Jared said. "Maybe the guy was in love with her. Or is she too ugly for that?"

Bill unclipped a photo from the file and pushed it across the desk.

"Not bad," Jared said, looking at the photo. It was her driver's license picture, so Jared figured she was actually three times that good looking. He studied the picture and the information. She was short, only five three, her eyesight was good, and she was an organ donor. Limp, blondish hair with a bit of curl in it surrounded blue eyes, a small nose, and a pretty mouth. She looked tired and unhappy in the photo. Probably had to wait in line for three hours, he thought. He gave the picture back to Bill. "So where do I come in?"

"We need you to find out what or who she knows."

Jared blinked a couple of times. Bill had said that only he, Jared, could do this, but this was a job for a rookie, not a senior agent. They could bring her in for questioning and find out what she knew. Probably something that she didn't know she knew. That wouldn't be too difficult. Where had she been in the last few years? Carried any packages for anyone? Jared almost smiled at the last thought, then he glanced at Bill's intense stare. What was he missing?

It hit him all at once: they wanted him to seduce the information out of her. Cozy up to a lonely spinster, then ask her what she knew. "Oh, no, you don't. I will risk my life for the agency, but I don't kiss for it."

"But James Bond—"

"Was a made-up character," Jared said, ignoring Bill's smirk. "James Bond doesn't really exist. He—" Jared ran his hand over his eyes, calmed himself, then looked at Bill. "I respectfully request that I not be given this assignment. Sir."

Leaning back against his chair, Bill folded his hands over his well-toned stomach. "Look, Jared, old friend, this case has us baffled. We don't want to haul her in here and scare her into telling us whatever she knows. If she knows anything, that is. And, as you said, maybe this was personal. This woman lived in New York for a while, so maybe she met this guy"—he glanced at the paper—"Roger Applegate—good American name, huh?—in New York. Maybe he met her, liked her, maybe they fell in love. Maybe he was planning to retire and marry her. Maybe when he knew that he'd been found out, his only thought was of protecting her name. He didn't seem to care if we investigated the criminals whose names were on the disks, but maybe he did care that we didn't involve the love of his life in something sordid. On the other hand, maybe this Ms. Palmer had no idea this man had a crush on her. He was a mousy-looking little thing who nobody noticed, so maybe Ms. Palmer was the secret object of his affection and she never knew about his great love for her."

"Or maybe she knows everything," Jared said tiredly. "And maybe you want *me* to find out one way or the other."

"You always were heavy in the brains department," Bill said, smiling.

Jared gave a sigh. In all his years in the agency, he'd tried hard to never get personally involved with the people connected to his investigations. Emotions kept you from seeing things clearly. But now, if he was understanding this, he was being asked to get to know this woman in a personal way and find out what she knew. She wasn't some underworld figure, wasn't a reformed anything. She was a— He looked at Bill. "She go to church?"

"Every Sunday."

Jared groaned. "But she did have a child out of wedlock." There was hope in his voice.

"She was seventeen and walking home from choir practice when a man leaped on her. Her parents kicked her out when she came up pregnant."

Jared looked like he was going to cry. "Lord! A persecuted heroine. Tragic happenings to an innocent," Jared said, his mouth a tight line. "Deliver me!" He glared at Bill, but Bill just grinned. Jared knew that he'd been chosen because of his age and his looks. He had dark hair, dark blue eyes, and a body kept trim by years spent in a gym. If he drank gallons of beer and ate lots of doughnuts, could he get fat in about four days? "So who left her the house?"

Bill leafed through the papers in the folder. "Alice Augusta Farrington. Born rich, but her druggie son spent everything. At least he had the courtesy to die before his mother did, so she had a few years of peace. She left the house and what was left of her fortune to our Ms. Palmer."

"How did our perfect heroine meet the rich old broad?"

"Seems the old gal took her in when Ms. Palmer was just a kid and pregnant. She, the old one that is, wanted someone to sort out all the papers in her attic. The house was built in"—he glanced down—"about 1720 by one of the ancestors of the old woman's. Ms. Palmer spent years cataloging the family papers."

"Another virtue and another talent," Jared said with a grimace. "Truly an angel. Let me guess, Ms. Palmer and her kid stayed for years, beloved by all."

"She stayed until her daughter was five years old, then left in the middle of the night." Bill looked at Jared hard. "The old woman's son was a registered sex offender. Little kids. Girls, boys, he didn't care which. We have no way of knowing, but we figure he went after Ms. Palmer's daughter, and she left her comfortable home in a hurry."

Jared looked away for a moment. He really hated people who hurt children. He looked back at Bill. "Okay, so she's not had an easy life. A lot of us haven't. But it sounds to me as though she's been enough places and seen enough that she could have met this guy Applegate. Maybe if you just *ask* her what she knows she'd tell you. Maybe—"

"Remember Tess Brewster?"

"Sure," Jared said, his jaw muscle working. "But what do you mean, remember?"

"About a month ago, we started making some discreet inquiries about Ms. Palmer. New York turned up nothing. Neither did the town where she was born. But we moved Tess into Arundel, that's where the old house is. We rented a place for Tess down the road from the one Ms. Palmer has inherited. Well, last week Tess was killed in a hit-and-run. We investigated as quietly as we could; it looks like it was a professional job."

Jared sighed. He'd liked Tess. She could drink any man under the table, and she'd been a good agent. "Do you think it's the house or the angelic Ms. Palmer?"

"We don't know, but we're sure something's there. One of the two is being watched very closely, and that's one reason we need *you.*"

"I see. *I* have managed to keep my mug out of the paper."

"Yeah, for the most part, you've been hidden from public view. Tess—"

"Was easily recognized. Her face was all over the papers for about six weeks when she testified against that mobster." Jared's head came up. "Maybe he—"

"Maybe that hoodlum she testified against killed her? He died two years ago, and we don't think he was powerful enough or beloved enough that anyone would risk killing a federal agent on his behalf. And why wait seven years? No, we think someone recognized Tess for what she was and she was killed so she wouldn't find out what Ms. Palmer knows—or what's in that house."

Jared felt that Bill knew more than he was telling, and he doubted if anyone really thought the woman was innocent. "Do you have any idea *what* this Palmer woman knows? Is it someone's name? Or is it information? Or is it something that she has? Maybe she knows what's buried in the backyard."

Bill lifted a file box from the floor onto his desk. "This is full of info about her. Everything we could find. Tess made two reports before she was murdered but found out nothing. I'll tell you what, you take that box home, read it over the weekend, then tell me what you think on Monday. If you agree to do it, fine. If you don't, then that's fine too."

Jared had worked with Bill for too many years to fall for that. If he knew Bill—and he did—a new identity was already waiting for him. Jared reached for the file box. "What's my cover?" he asked.

Bill tried to keep from smiling but failed. "We rented the house next door to her. It's just a fishing cabin that used to belong to the old woman, but she had to sell it to pay her son's debts. Between drugs and lawyers, he cost her millions. You're to be a retired policeman, out early on account of your knee, your wife of twenty-six years has just died, and you've rented this house in the middle of nowhere so you can go fishing and hunting and forget all your troubles. You need something to cry on her shoulder about. Women like that."

Jared bit his tongue to keep quiet. Bill had been married to the same woman for thirty-five years and liked to think that he knew all about women and marriage. The truth was that his wife spent nearly half the year in another state living with her never-married sister, who was rumored to be a real hellion. There was a lot of laughing speculation as to what Bill's wife got up to when she was with her sister.

"If this woman hasn't been told yet that she's inherited this house, how do you know that she won't sell it sight unseen? What makes you so sure she'll move away from the city lights to go to the wilds of rural North Carolina?"

He looked at Jared. "The truth is that we think this woman knows something and it has to do with that house. If she sells the house right away, then our theory is shot, but if she quits her job, runs out on her pregnant daughter, and jumps on the first plane to Arundel, it's possible that she's in a hurry because she knows something."

Jared took the box off Bill's desk. "So when do I leave?"

Grinning, Bill opened his desk drawer and withdrew a set of keys. "A three-quarter-ton, four-wheel drive, dark blue Chevy pickup awaits you in parking space number eighty-one. It's full of fishing gear and whatever Susie in accounting ordered for you from the L.L.Bean catalog.There's a marked map on the passenger seat and a key to the house on the ring. It's late, so you can stop in a motel tonight and read every word about Ms. Palmer before you meet her."

Jared hated that Bill knew him so well that he'd arranged all this before he'd been consulted. "What's my name to be this time?"

"We were kind to you and let you keep your first name. I hear you complained that you didn't like the last name we gave you. What was it again?"

"Elroy Coldheart," Jared said with a grimace. Kathy in the records department had let him know that she was interested if he was, but he wasn't. The next time he saw her, she'd handed him his new passport with a smile. It wasn't until later that he saw the name.

"This time you're named Jared McBride. Whatever did you do to Kathy to make her come up with the name of *McBride?*" Bill was chuckling, but he was also curious. He wanted to know everything that went on in his department.

Jared didn't answer. Lugging the big file box, he left the room smiling. He wasn't going to tell Bill anything. His only thought was to get this assignment over and done with as quickly as possible.

Chapter One

"Mom? Mom? Are you all right?" Melissa looked at her mother with concern. She'd brought in the mail and put it on the hall table, then went to get herself something to eat. She was five months pregnant, and she could eat the legs off a table. Her mother had come in from work and picked up the mail, opening a letter from what looked to be a law firm. Melissa hoped it was nothing bad. "Mom?" Her words were muffled by the peanut butter sandwich in her mouth. She'd been tempted to add grape jelly but was afraid her husband would smell the jelly on her breath. Stuart was adamant that she didn't gain too much weight during pregnancy, so at dinner Melissa ate steamed vegetables and broiled meat. It was just during the day, while he was at work at the prestigious accounting firm, that she indulged in chocolate and shrimp—together.

"Mom!" Melissa said loudly. "What in the world is wrong with you?"

Eden sat down on the little sofa by the hall table. The sofa had been a rickety piece of junk when she'd seen it in a small, out-of-the-way shop in a district that Melissa's husband didn't want them to visit. Eden had known right away it was Hepplewhite. She and Melissa had tied the sofa onto the roof of the station wagon and taken it home. It had taken Eden six weekends to repair, refinish, and upholster it. "Aren't you clever?" Stuart had said in his haughty way, as though Eden were of a lower class than he was. She'd had to grit her teeth, as she always did when she dealt with her son-in-law. Melissa loved him, but Eden had never been able to figure out why.

"Mrs. Farrington left me her house."

"Mrs. Farrington?" Melissa asked, looking at the clock. She had seventeen and a half minutes before Stuart came home. Was that enough time to make herself another sandwich?

"Go on," Eden said, knowing her daughter's mind. "I'll cover for you."

"I shouldn't. Really, I shouldn't. Dinner will be soon and—"

"It's grilled chicken breasts, steamed broccoli, roast potatoes, and sugarless Jell-O for dessert. Very good for you. Not a calorie in any of it."

Melissa opened her mouth, then scurried off to the kitchen. She was slathering peanut butter on bread when Eden walked into the room, the letter open before her. "Who's Mrs. Farrington?"

"You remember her, don't you, dear? We lived with her until you were five."

"Oh, yeah. I do remember her. Sort of. Very old. And a long time ago you mentioned a man. Was he her son?"

Eden didn't bother to suppress the shiver that ran over her body. "Yes, her son. Dreadful man. It seems that he died some time ago. Before Mrs. Farrington did."

"You didn't keep in touch with her?" Melissa was pouring chocolate syrup into her milk. It was a good thing that Stuart never opened the refrigerator or he'd see the forbidden things that Eden bought for her daughter. No, Stuart was the type who believed food should be eaten at a table and served to him by someone else, preferably his wife. He didn't go rummaging in the refrigerator looking for something to eat.

"No," Eden said tightly. "After we left I had nothing to do with her. Not that she . . ." She broke off. What happened was not something she wanted to have to explain to her daughter. I didn't want that pedophile of a son of hers to know where I was, she could have said, but didn't. "No, we didn't keep in touch."

Many times over the years she'd wondered what had happened to dear Mrs. Farrington, and Eden often felt a wave of guilt run through her when she thought about that sweet woman being left alone with her evil son. But then Eden would look at her daughter and know that she'd done the right thing in running away and never looking back. She glanced at the clock. "You now have approximately two and three-quarter minutes before the master returns, so you'd better drink that and clean out your glass."

"Mother," Melissa said primly, "Stuart isn't like that. He's a kind and loving man and I love him . . . ery uch." The last words were muffled, as her mouth was full.

"Yes, he's wonderful," Eden said, then cut herself off when she heard the sarcasm in her voice. It was tough to think how she'd tried to raise her daughter to be an independent woman, only to see her marry a control freak like Stuart. To Eden's mind, Stuart was all show. For all his talk of having a great future before him, he'd willingly moved into Eden's apartment "for a few weeks," as he'd said just before the wedding. "Until I get a place for us. A little farther uptown." Stuart had made Eden's generous offer seem as though it were worth nothing, and she'd had to resist the urge to defend herself. But that was two years ago, and now nothing Stuart said bothered her. He and Melissa were still in Eden's small apartment, still letting her cook for them and letting her take care of most of the household chores. Months ago, Eden had decided she'd had enough and was going to evict them. She'd built up her courage to the point where she didn't care if they had to live on the street for a while. It might do them some good. Teach them some lessons. But then Melissa had announced she was pregnant and that was that. Eden could still remember the smirk on Stuart's face when Melissa made the announcement. It was as though he'd known what Eden had been thinking and he'd calculated the pregnancy just so Eden couldn't throw them out. "You don't mind, do you, Mom?" Melissa had said. "It was an accident. We meant to have children, but we wanted to wait until we had a place of our own. But with Stuart on the verge of a promotion, it doesn't make sense to buy something small and dreary when in just a few weeks we'll be able to afford something grand and glorious."

Since her daughter had married, Eden often wondered if Melissa had become a marionette. "Small and dreary" and "grand and glorious" were Stuart's words, not Melissa's.

Eden took a seat on a bar stool at the kitchen island and read the letter again. "Mrs. Farrington had no other heirs, so she left me everything."

"How nice for you," Melissa said. "Any money?"

Eden kept her head down, but she felt the blood rush up the back of her neck. Anger did that to a person. There was fear in Melissa's voice, and Eden well knew what caused it: Stuart. For all that Melissa told Eden at least three times a day how much she loved her husband, the truth was that after two years of marriage she'd come to know him well. If he found out that Eden had inherited a lot of money, there would be problems.

"No money," Eden said cheerfully and tried not to hear her daughter's sigh of relief. "Just a falling-down old house. You remember it, don't you?"

"A Victorian monstrosity, wasn't it?"

Eden started to correct her daughter and say that the house had been built before George Washington's Mount Vernon, but she didn't want Melissa to tell Stuart that. He might see money in a house that old. Melissa hadn't yet learned that she didn't have to tell her husband everything that went through her mind. "More or less," Eden said, still looking at the letter. She was to go to a lawyer's office in North Carolina as soon as possible to sign the papers and take possession of the house. They're probably worried that the roof's about to cave in, she thought, but said nothing as she folded the letter and put it back in the envelope.

"What will you do with an old house like that?" Melissa asked, her eyes wide.

Eden knew that her daughter was afraid for her mother to leave. They'd rarely been apart since Melissa's birth twenty-seven years ago. "Sell it," Eden said quickly. "And use the money to buy my grandson a house in the country. With a copper beech tree in the backyard."

Smiling, Melissa relaxed, then hurriedly drank the rest of her chocolate milk when she heard the front door start to open. She washed the glass in seconds, so she was ready to turn and greet her husband when he walked into the kitchen. Stuart was tall, thin, and handsome. Melissa's eyes lit up when she saw him.

Eden gave her son-in-law a nod, then slipped out of the kitchen to go to her bedroom and close the door. For a moment she leaned against the door, closed her eyes, and remembered back to that summer when she'd been pregnant with Melissa. Eden had been just seventeen years old, just out of high school, when she'd been walking home from church choir practice one night. She'd been leaped on by a man, thrown down, and . . . She'd never been able to remember much of what happened after that. When it was over, she dragged herself up, pulled her skirt down, and staggered home. She'd wanted to call the police, but her parents had refused. They didn't want their family to be the object of gossip; they didn't want people to know what Eden had done. "But *I* didn't do anything," she'd cried. A few weeks later, when she'd started throwing up from morning sickness, her parents told her to get out of their house. Nothing Eden said could sway them. She'd packed one suitcase, taken the $300 her parents had grudgingly given her, and got on a bus going east. She ended up in North Carolina, a state she'd never been in, but it was beautiful and she loved the old houses and the flat fields.

She'd tried to get a job, but there wasn't much work to be had, and no work for a girl who was by then obviously pregnant. When she'd applied at the newspaper office in Arundel, a man had taken pity on her. He was looking at the job application she'd filled out. "You didn't misspell one word," he said, teasing her. Eden was hot, tired, hungry, and wishing she'd never been born. All she could do was look at him. Was he going to grade her application?

He looked her up and down for a moment, then said, "Let me guess about you. It's something I'm good at. Decent family, church every Sunday, good grades in school, wrestled with the high school football quarterback on the backseat of a car, and now the two of you've run away together. Or did he leave you somewhere along the way?"

Eden was too tired to play games. He'd probably eaten more for lunch than she'd had in the last two days. "Religious fanatic parents who spent my childhood telling me I was a sinner. Top of the top grades in school, but then if I went below an A plus I got the belt, buckle first. No quarterback, just a rapist on a dark night. When I came up pregnant, my parents threw me out. I now have fifteen dollars to my name, no place to live, nothing to live on. I've been looking hard at the local train tracks."

The man blinked at her a couple of times, then picked up his telephone and pushed a memory button. "Gracey? Henry here. I'm sending over a young woman. Feed her and let her have that bed in the back, will you?

She needs food and rest, then I'm going to send her out to Alice's." He paused, listening. "Yeah, I know Alice is a pain in the neck, but, trust me on this, this girl can handle her. Compared to what she's been through, Alice will seem like a dream."

Somehow, Eden managed to get out of the chair and make it to the door without fainting. Rage at the injustice of what had happened to her had kept her going, but now that someone had shown her some kindness, she feared she might collapse. The man didn't help her up or walk her to the door. Maybe he'd guessed that Eden's pride would get her there on her own. It wasn't easy to be proud when you hadn't had a bath in over a week, but she managed it.

Eden was almost run over by a pickup as she made her way across the road to Gracey's Restaurant. A tall, wiry woman, her gray hair in a bun at the back of her neck, came out to put her arm around Eden. "Honey, you're worse than Henry told me you were."

Three hours later, after Eden had eaten more than Gracey had ever seen a person eat at one sitting, Eden climbed into bed and didn't get out until the next morning. It was Sunday when Gracey drove Eden out to meet Mrs. Alice Augusta Farrington, who lived in an old house across a bridge, just outside downtown.

Eden had always loved history, and she'd loved any movie that was set in a historical context. That was good, since her parents didn't allow her to watch any movie that had been made after 1959. Their opinion was that the 1960s were the beginning of the end of Godliness in America. When Eden got out of Gracey's car and looked up at the old house, she knew that she was looking at the genuine article. This wasn't a house "built in the Colonial style." This was a Colonial house. She'd never seen Colonial Williamsburg, but she thought this house would fit in there.

"Ghastly old place, isn't it?" Gracey said. "I tell Alice that she ought to bulldoze it and build herself a nice brick ranch style."

Eden looked at Gracey to see if she was kidding. The older woman's eyes were twinkling. Eden smiled.

"Just checking," Gracey said, smiling back. "We like old houses around here."

Eden looked up at the house. Seven bays

across the front, a full porch on the ground level. There were some truly big trees on each side of the house, and she wondered if they'd been planted when the house was built.

Alice Augusta Farrington was so small that she made Eden feel big—which wasn't easy, since Eden was small herself. But Mrs. Farrington was about four-eleven and couldn't have weighed more than ninety pounds. "What she lacks in size, she makes up for in spirit," Gracey had said on the way out to the house, when she told Eden about the Farrington family. They'd built the house back in the early 1700s and had held on to it ever since. To Mrs. Farrington's mind, that made her American royalty. "DAR ha!" she'd say. "Upstarts. Go through a couple of books, find out their ancestors stowed away on a ship, and think they're worth something. Now, *my* ancestors . . ." Mrs. Farrington would then be off and running with stories about her ancestors having been aristocracy in England. "And they would be aristocracy in America if that idiot George Washington hadn't turned down being crowned king. I'd be a duchess now. What was *wrong* with that man?!"

Gracey said that no one knew if Mrs. Farrington was kidding or not, but it didn't matter, as she never expected an answer. "She likes to talk and just likes for others to listen." Eden had spent a lot of her life listening to her father pontificate about what he thought God was thinking, so she was good at listening.

When the house came into sight, Gracey told her that the outside might go unpainted for twenty years at a time, but the roof was always kept in perfect repair, because otherwise, it might leak on her precious papers. It was a local legend that every piece of paper the Farrington family had ever owned was still in that house. Receipts, recipes, diaries, letters—lots of letters—all of them were still there.

But even after what Gracey had told her, Eden wasn't prepared for her first sight of the interior. The huge, high-ceilinged center hallway was so full of furniture that a person could hardly walk. The walls were lined at least two pieces deep. A tall desk stood in front of a huge cabinet. A long table was pressed against a wall, covered in what looked to be stacks of old letters wrapped in faded pink ribbon, then smaller tables were set on top of the letters. Tables, cabinets, chairs, couches—every surface was covered with papers. Some were in boxes, some in trunks, many of them loose. Eden's eyes widened when she saw a hatbox that resembled one she'd seen in a book on antiques. Eighteenth century?

"Alice," Gracey said to the tiny Mrs. Farrington. "I found her for you."

Mrs. Farrington looked Eden up and down and obviously found her wanting. "This little thing? Too weak. And is that a child in her stomach? Am I to start running a shelter for wayward girls now?"

Gracey ignored the last question. "Henry Walters—you know, old Lester's youngest son—researched her, and she's from a good family. She's twenty-three years old and her young husband was killed in a horrible accident while defending his family. She was so overcome with grief that she ran away from home. Her family is searching for her, but she begged Henry to let her find her own place in the world, so she can make it on her own. She wants the job, and she can do it. She has a degree in American history from Vassar. When her baby is born, she will, of course, return to her loving family.

You won't be bothered with anything as burdensome as a child."

Eden's mouth was hanging open as she stared at Gracey. What incredible lies! She turned back to look at Mrs. Farrington. Should she tell her the truth and risk losing the job—whatever it was? Eden hoped she wasn't being offered the job of trying to clean this house. The dust on that furniture could be carbon-dated.

Mrs. Farrington was looking at Eden in speculation. "Family throw you out when you got pregnant?"

"Yes, ma'am," Eden said, her eyes looking into the old woman's. They were small black eyes, glistening with life and vitality. Old body; young spirit.

"How old are you really?" Mrs. Farrington asked.

Behind the older woman, Gracey was vigorously shaking her head at Eden not to tell the truth.

"Seventeen," Eden answered.

Mrs. Farrington turned so quickly that she caught Gracey shaking her head, disgusted that Eden hadn't lied. "Your whole family are liars," Mrs. Farrington said, without animosity in her voice, then she left the room, leaving Gracey and Eden alone.

Gracey wasn't offended by Mrs. Farrington's remarks. In fact, she was smiling broadly. She pushed Eden to follow Mrs. Farrington. "Go on."

"But she didn't say I was hired," Eden said. "Maybe—"

"Believe me, if you *weren't* hired, Alice Farrington would have told you. She likes you."

"Likes me?"

"She didn't say one hateful thing to you. It may be a first. Now go on, I have to go bake the pies for tomorrow."